Joy of Today

Charlotte Everhart

Nevinly Publishing

This is a work of fiction. The characters, incidents, and dialogues are products of the author's imagination and are not to be construed as real. Any resemblance to actual persons, living or dead, is entirely coincidental.

JOY OF TODAY. Copyright © 2021 by Charlotte Everhart. All rights reserved. Printed in the United States of America. No portion of this book may be used or reproduced in any manner whatsoever without written permission from the publisher or author, except as permitted by U.S. copyright law.

FIRST EDITION

Cover design by Tugboat Design.

Library of Congress Control Number: 2021923655

ISBN: 978-1-7379886-1-8 (Print)

ISBN: 978-1-7379886-0-1 (Ebook)

1. Women's Fiction 2. Family Fiction 3. Small Town/Rural Fiction 4. Contemporary Romance

This book is dedicated to my husband—my encourager, my friend, my love.
And to my mother, my very first reader and most loyal fan.

Contents

Chapter 1	1
Chapter 2	7
Chapter 3	11
Chapter 4	19
Chapter 5	27
Chapter 6	33
Chapter 7	37
Chapter 8	41
Chapter 9	43
Chapter 10	47
Chapter 11	49
Chapter 12	51
Chapter 13	59
Chapter 14	65
Chapter 15	73
Chapter 16	83
Chapter 17	87
Chapter 18	99
Chapter 19	105
Chapter 20	111

Chapter 21	121
Chapter 22	127
Chapter 23	131
Chapter 24	139
Chapter 25	145
Chapter 26	151
Chapter 27	155
Chapter 28	157
Chapter 29	161
Next In Series	173
Aknowledgements	175
About Author	177

Chapter 1

SPRING 1994

Steven Davis stretched his stiff muscles. Sleeping in the car last night might not have been the best idea. Neither had arriving in Nicolet a day and a half earlier than scheduled, but then he supposed he wasn't the first guy out there to make a dumb decision because of a woman. He might just be one of a select few to do it all for a woman he hadn't even met yet, however. Lucky for him, he'd been able to get into his apartment today, despite not having given the landlord any warning about his early arrival. If the only consequence to his impulsive decision was a sore muscle or two, he figured he was doing okay.

Tacked high in the sky, the sun shone hot and bright that afternoon, and Steven blinked rapidly as he walked out onto the small landing just outside the front door of his quarters for the summer. He sat down at the very top of the steep staircase, which led down to the driveway below, and popped the top on an ice-cold can of Coke. Drinking deeply before wiping his mouth on his forearm, he surveyed his surroundings. He could hardly believe his luck—or his view. He would live above the treetops in this little patch of paradise for the entire summer.

This lot was already set up high above the town, and while Steven was sure the main house had an amazing view, it couldn't possibly be better than what he had up here on the landing of this above-garage apartment. The quaint little town of Nicolet, Michigan, with its historic buildings and tree-lined streets, stretched out below him. As impressive as he found the vast expanse of the North Woods at his back to be, it was this view in front of him that stole his breath away. The blue, sparkling water of Lake Superior glittered all the way to the horizon, and the sugar-sand beaches extended off to the east as far as he could see.

Steven knew Sandstone Rocks National Lakeshore rested about forty-five minutes in that direction. It was first on his list of places to explore. Nicolet Harbor sat off to his left, and from his vantage point above the detached garage, he could see runners and bikers moving along the waterside path—passed occasionally by boats heading out into the open lake. The concrete, boulder-lined breakwall extended out about a quarter of a mile in the background, and it was punctuated by a candy cane lighthouse that Steven heard was still in use today. He was looking forward to watching the slow, sweeping motion of the rotating beacon from way up here on the landing.

Today, Superior was a much deeper and richer blue than the flawless sky domed up above it, and with the newly popped green foliage of the hardwoods in the foreground, it made a stunning picture.

Steven had been truly lucky to score this apartment on such short notice, and not just because of its high perch above the town. He'd been afraid he'd be stuck renting in an apartment complex which, to his mind, would have only been a slight upgrade from dorm life—a four-year experience he was more than ready to leave behind for good now that he'd finished college.

This place was not only far nicer than any apartment complex, it was far cheaper too, and since this summer's internship wasn't a very lucrative one, Steven had to watch his pennies carefully.

His grandmother had left him everything she had when she died a year ago, but after paying off his college loans, there wasn't a whole lot left over. Steven had taken a big risk in coming here, and he hoped he hadn't made a mistake. Before graduating, he received a job offer from a biomedical firm that developed prosthetics back in Lansing. His professors had recommended him to the president of the prestigious company, which was an enormous honor. It would have been a great opportunity.

The only problem was that prosthetics didn't interest Steven in the least. Besides that, he was ready for a change of scenery. He felt anonymous in Lansing with all those people, and he craved a place to call home. At the time, he wasn't sure where on God's green earth that might be, but he did know Lansing wasn't it. After growing up in a small, rural town in Lower Michigan, Steven suspected no city out there could feel right to him.

After a heart-to-heart with his department head, he was introduced to Chester Biotechnologies. It turned out Professor Lang had a close contact within the company, and he made a call. That's all it took. On paper, Chester Biotechnologies seemed like a perfect fit for Steven, and he'd been willing to give it a shot. Although disappointed not to get a job offer straight away—they wanted to test him out via a summer internship first—he was still excited.

Once the terms of the internship with Chester were settled over several extensive phone interviews, Steven began apartment hunting, and he'd stumbled upon this place. He traveled up to Nicolet from Michigan State's campus to sign the rental papers with the property owner, a kind and older gentleman by the name of Sepi Lakanen. Mr. Lakanen had insisted on meeting Steven in person before agreeing to rent out the apartment he'd advertised. Being that it was the last weekend before final exams, the timing wasn't great for Steven, but he understood Mr. Lakanen's need to vet him, so he'd hopped in the car for a quick trip to this little Lake Superior town.

He'd immediately fallen in love with the place.

Being that he was a Midwestern kid, Steven had grown up near and around the Great Lakes, but he'd never traveled far enough north to see the *Gitchee Gumee* spoken of by Henry Wadsworth Longfellow and Gordon Lightfoot, and he simply hadn't been prepared for its majestic beauty.

It had looked just like the sea that day he'd first ridden into town—a rich turquoise blue. The lingering waves, whipped up from a storm that had come through the day before, looked for all the world like the smooth ocean swells he remembered from a long-ago trip to the Bahamas he'd taken with his best friend's family. These fresh-water waves rolled in with a slow, gentle, almost hypnotic cadence before crashing against the sandy shore. Steven had driven the last five-mile stretch into town looking more at the lake than he did the road. He simply could not help himself.

Steven liked Mr. Lakanen on sight when he met him that day two weeks ago. He was a kind, grandfatherly type with a whole lot to say and a slight accent Steven had correctly assumed to be Finnish, having considered his rather unusual name.

After touring the apartment above the detached garage and speaking with Mr. Lakanen in the driveway for the better part of two hours about everything from the Russification of Finland to the stubborn tap roots of particular weeds that kept popping up in his otherwise pristine yard, the old man had made Steven an unexpected offer.

"You know, Steven," he said, "we haven't had renters for a few years now, and when we did, they were always female. It's just what my Maggie was most comfortable with," he added, shrugging. "But I know a good man when I see one, and you are that. This will be a good arrangement for you. Good for us, too, I think."

He scratched at his chin.

"Listen, I wonder if you might be interested in helping me out around here in return for a reduction in your rent."

Steven perked up at that. "What do you have in mind?" he asked, pleased that this good man seemed to regard him just as highly as Steven did him.

"I have had two heart stents placed now, and I do not know if you noticed my limp, but I just had a knee replaced this last winter. Darn thing still doesn't seem to want to work right. They are talking about going back in and cleaning things up—replacing some contraption or other. Any more of this, and I'll be bionic," he joked.

As a biomedical engineer, this kind of talk was right up Steven's alley. He wanted to ask what kind of implant he'd gotten, but Mr. Lakanen continued on, and Steven didn't want to interrupt.

"It was already difficult for me to keep up with this place before I started to fall apart. I'm sixty-nine—almost *seventy* years old now." He looked genuinely baffled. "I don't know how that can be, but it is true, as you can see." He gestured to his body, which was stooped and depleted from the passage of time, but Steven could see the evidence of the older man's youth. Mr. Lakanen was still strong, just worn now from the accumulation of added weight and years of stress on his body.

"But now, with my health being what it is . . . Steven, it is time for me to ask for a little help around here." He shook his head in self-disgust as if he'd just admitted to running over squirrels for fun. "Maggie's been after me to hire things out for some time now. It has just gotten to be too much on me. What would you say to helping me with some jobs over the summer—taking care of things like the lawn and garden, for example?"

Steven nodded with a smile and shrugged. "Sure. I can do that."

"Maggie has got bad knees herself. Poor old girl will probably be next up for surgery. She loves her flowers, but the up and down required to tend the beds is difficult for her, and it wears her out now where it never used to before. The girls have helped here and there, but they lack green thumbs."

He wiggled his own thumbs to demonstrate.

"I am telling you, Steven, all they have to do is *look* at a plant, and it shrivels up. Maggie doesn't want the girls anywhere near them. They are too busy these days anyhow."

Who were these girls? Steven wondered, but he didn't get a chance to ask before Mr. Lakanen went on.

"Anyway, those are two things I can think of on the spot, but I am sure there will be more. Maybe some heavy lifting here and there. Oh, and power washing the siding. And the staining of the deck."

Mr. Lakanen laughed good-naturedly.

"Now it is all coming back to me. But do not worry, Steven. I know you will be busy with your work, so I will have a respect for your time. It will not be too much."

"I'm sure it won't be a problem," Steven said. It might seem strange, but he would actually look forward to the work. He'd been missing those types of chores necessary for the upkeep of a home, although he hadn't realized it until now. He used to help his gran with that kind of stuff all the time growing up and during his summers home from school.

"I will take a hundred dollars per month off your rent in exchange," Mr. Lakanen said. The deep grooves in his forehead deepened as he added with a question, "If you think that is fair?"

Steven's eyebrows shot up. "Oh, that's more than fair, sir." He meant it. It probably made this place simultaneously the cheapest and nicest rental in town. The upstairs was a spacious studio apartment with hardwood floors and new kitchen appliances, not that Steven knew how to use them. His gran had been a phenomenal cook.

He'd pulled his weight in their home in other ways, like mowing the lawn in perfect stripes, weeding the flower beds, snow blowing the driveway and shoveling the walkway in the winter and, of course, taking care of all the home repairs all year long.

He didn't mind the type of work he'd done for his gran or the type of work Mr. Lakanen was talking about now. As an engineer, Steven liked working with his hands, even if it meant working in the dirt. Saving some money on rent was just a bonus. "I'm grateful for the reduced rent, so thank you for that, Mr. Lakanen."

"Sure, sure," Mr. Lakanen said, waving a hand dismissively. "And you must please call me Sepi, eh?"

Steven grinned. "Thank you, Sepi." Honestly, it would make him feel good to help this elderly man and his wife. He liked Sepi immensely, and though Steven had yet to meet his Maggie, he expected she'd be just as friendly.

The two men sealed the deal with a handshake, and as Steven got into his blue Chevy Blazer to head back down state, it was with a wide smile and a full heart. He'd made a strong connection that day with a really decent man. It wasn't until that moment that Steven realized just how very lonely he'd been over the last year. With his gran gone now, he really was completely on his own, and even though Sepi and Maggie weren't his family and never would be, they'd be close over the summer—at least in the geographical sense—as they shared the property together, but maybe a type of friendship would also develop as he spent time with them. He pictured talking with them here and there as he worked and possibly even being invited over for a relaxing tea or dinner or dessert on occasion.

There'd be the ticktock of a grandfather clock somewhere in the house as they visited with one another and little, faded doilies on the tabletops. The air in the house might even smell of freshly baked bread, like his house with Gran always had. Steven had it all pictured, cozily, in his mind.

Then, in a jarring juxtaposition, just as he'd been pulling out of the Lakanen's driveway, a white Toyota Corolla turned in on a wave of energy that startled him. With the windows of both their vehicles rolled down, the music playing in the Corolla reached his ears at a deafening volume, and Steven could actually feel the heavy bass reverberate through his body. The girl driving treated him to a megawatt smile and an enthusiastic wave as she hollered a hello that he could only just barely hear.

She'd hardly slowed her vehicle down for the turn, and it was all over and done with before he'd been able to offer her any kind of greeting of his own, but that smile had stuck with him the entire trip home. Her entire face had lit up with that smile, and even though he'd only had a millisecond to form an opinion, Steven was fairly certain she was the most beautiful female he'd ever seen.

He thought of her again now, seated up high above the detached garage holding his can of pop, and then, as if he'd conjured it up, that little Corolla appeared again. Annoyingly, his heart picked up its rhythm. What kind of guy had his heart go *pitter-pattering* over a girl he'd seen exactly once?

Not a very manly one.

Steven watched as the white car turned, slowly and methodically this time, and advanced up the driveway, quietly passing him and parking up close to the old Cape Cod-style home that belonged to Sepi and Maggie Lakanen. Unable to see into the windows of the car from the glare of the sun, Steven squinted his eyes. A minute later, the beautiful girl from two weeks ago stepped out into the bright sunshine. She wore clothes fitting for the warm day—cut off jean shorts, a green tank top, and a pair of white sandals. She reached into the backseat of the car, and as she did, he admired her shapely, athletic legs. She came out with a large platter of, what looked to be, sub sandwiches in her hands. With a swing of her hips, she closed the door and disappeared into the house.

Not more than a few moments went by before she reappeared holding her keys, Sepi limping along behind her. She opened the trunk, which was stuffed with grocery bags. Steven had already set down his nearly empty Coke can and stood to help when Sepi hollered up at him.

"Would you mind helping us, Steven, to get these groceries in?"

"Sure thing," Steven yelled back.

Once he reached the bottom of the steps, he jogged over, stopping in front of Sepi and the girl. She looked to be about his age, and she was as gorgeous as he remembered her being. Her sandy brown hair, kissed with golden highlights from the sun, fell in loose, soft waves just past her shoulders. Her skin was already tanned, even though it was still, technically, spring.

She smiled at him, not that same bright smile from before, but a softer, more timid version of it, and Steven felt an electric current zip through him, just as he had the last time.

"Steven," Sepi said, "this is Heidi. Heidi, I would like you to meet Steven."

Chapter 2

Heidi made a conscious effort to keep her mouth from hanging open as her father made the introductions. "Hi," she said at the exact moment Steven did, and when each responded with nervous laughter, she observed the amused grin that flashed across Sepi's face—though he was quick to hide it with a small cough. By the time Steven seemed to remember to extend his hand to her, Heidi had already stuffed both of hers in her shorts pockets, and the small delay it caused as she dug her right hand back out again made her cheeks burn. Having always been a colossal failure at this kind of thing, she thought she should be used to the embarrassment by now.

She wasn't.

Heidi Lakanen was destined to feel hopelessly awkward around any man she found attractive, and Steven was definitely that—and then some. Just the simple touch of their hands caused her heart to launch into overdrive. He had a solid grip, and his hand was warm and dry. As he pumped her hand, he looked her squarely in the eye. She had to remind herself to blink.

Heidi had known he'd be cute, Shelly had already told her that, and her sister was never wrong when it came to boys and their looks. But her sister hadn't mentioned his eyes. Shelly tended to overlook those smaller details.

Heidi didn't.

All kinds of things about a person could be seen by a close look into their eyes. Haughtiness, sweetness, insecurity . . . It could all be found there. Heidi gazed into Steven's cocoa brown eyes. They were warm and kind, but they also held something else—an almost sorrowful quality, sort of like the eyes of her family's old basset hound, Taro.

Heidi's smile returned at the thought. Taro was a faithful companion, and she had the sense the same could be said for Steven. She felt herself relax slightly, but when Steven grinned back, she nearly dropped her keys. It transformed him from plain old good-looking to drop-dead gorgeous.

While her father engaged him in a brief conversation about the unseasonably warm weather, Heidi studied Steven, taking care not to let on she was doing so. His hair was similar in color to hers, maybe a little more blond than brown, and he had strong, masculine features, including a prominent chin with a small, almost imperceptible cleft. She loved chin dimples on a man. His shoulders were broad, but not hulking, and he was strong and lean. He looked like a guy who took care of himself, but he was no gym rat. She couldn't stand gym rats—those guys spent more time flexing in the mirrors than they did actually working out. Maybe Steven was a runner, like herself.

"It is good you came today, Steven. This way you will have the whole weekend and be nice and settled before Monday," Sepi said.

Heidi searched for something to add. After glancing up at the apartment, which she had spent hours on Wednesday scrubbing and vacuuming, she said, "I hope you like your new place." She was glad she hadn't saved the cleaning for the last minute or it might not have been ready for him. He'd arrived earlier than she'd expected.

He cleared his throat. "Oh, yeah. It's really great. Thank you."

Silence.

Steven kicked a pebble with his shoe. Heidi worked to keep a straight face as she realized she may just have found the one man out there who was more socially awkward than she was. In a weird way, it was kind of refreshing, and she felt herself becoming a little bolder.

"Um, are you all settled in now?"

"Mostly." He paused. "I still have a few boxes to go through, but I've done all I'm going to do for today."

"That's good," she said. She searched for the next thing to say to keep this conversation going. She remembered her dad saying something about an internship, and she was on the verge of asking about it when her father broke in, having decided he'd been silent long enough. For someone like Sepi, who was never at a loss about what to say, these few minutes of sophomoric conversation had probably been torturous.

"That *is* good, Steven, because we are having a little party tonight, and you are invited."

Steven's eyes widened in surprise. "Oh, that's really, really nice of you, but I don't want to imp—"

"You will come, Steven, and that is that," Sepi stated firmly. "Now, let's get these groceries inside the house, eh? I know we have ice cream in here somewhere, and it is melting."

Heidi shared an amused look with Steven at her father's cheek before grabbing a bag out of the trunk first. Steven grabbed two with little effort.

"You can just follow me into the kitchen," she instructed, before leading the way up the porch steps and into the house. Steven paused to kick off his shoes, but Heidi stopped him. "You can leave them on. It's alright." She wanted to say something more, but try as she might, she couldn't think of anything. They made two more trips to the car and back into the house in silence before all the groceries were unloaded, and once the bags were lined up on the counter, Heidi, ignoring the rush of heat to her face, turned to Steven. "Thanks for the help."

"You're welcome. Anytime you need help, just let me know." Steven stuffed his hands in his pockets and smiled as he rocked back on his heels.

She beamed back at him, and for several seconds too long, they just stood there like that—two idiots smiling at each other. At least Steven's face was turning scarlet too. That made Heidi feel a little better. Shared embarrassment was better than feeling it all alone.

Maybe he'd want to sit with her for a few minutes and chat. She could use a break and thought she might have a little time before she would have to prep for the party. She wanted to get to know him better—see if he was as sweet as he seemed.

"Listen," Heidi began, planning to invite him for some iced tea on the back deck, "after I get these put away, would you want to sit out back and—" But her invitation was interrupted by Sepi, who popped his head in the door and asked if Steven would mind taking a few minutes to go over some of the work Steven would be doing for them.

Steven turned reluctantly away from Heidi to face her father as Sepi continued speaking. "I will show you the shed where we keep the lawn mower, and I wonder if you can help move some of this patio furniture to the back for tonight. I already moved the deck furniture up yesterday. If I had known you would be here today, I would have waited and let you do it. My Maggie told me I would pay the price for it today, but I won't tell her she was right if you won't." Sepi rubbed at his low back.

Steven promised he wouldn't say a word, and he looked back at Heidi apologetically as he moved to the doorway. "I'll see you later, I guess," he said.

"Sure, okay." She busied herself with unloading paper plates and cups from one of the grocery bags, not quite meeting his eyes. So what if he couldn't sit with her right now? She'd have plenty of time to get to know Steven tonight.

That reminded her.

She looked up. "The party starts at five."

Steven spun around. "Oh, right. What's the occasion?" He still looked unsure about joining them all in a social setting so soon after meeting them. Heidi couldn't blame him. It would be a boisterous crew tonight.

Before she could answer, Sepi spoke from the doorway. "It is my birthday." He grinned and shook his head. "Not my idea at all, although I always love a good party. You will soon learn, Steven. The women in this house are not to be crossed. And that is free advice, eh?"

Heidi laughed, and Steven grinned at her appreciatively. When he did, she felt it on a visceral level. Finding her reaction to him slightly disconcerting, she tried to sort through it as she put the groceries away. Sure, she was always pretty awkward with men, but not many men had ever affected her like this. She'd only had one serious boyfriend, and that had been back in high school. The relationship hadn't quite lasted six months, and it had been exhausting to make it go on even that long. If all boys were as needy as that guy had been, she wasn't sure she had the time or inclination to make a serious relationship work anyway, not that anyone had come knocking on her door in a while.

No, that wasn't quite true. Men came knocking, just not for her. It didn't matter anyway. Heidi was happier dating casually, although she wasn't sure she could classify what she did as dating at all. Usually she just joined Shelly and whichever boyfriend she happened to have at the time, along with one of his friends, and almost always, she felt like a total loser.

Heidi gave her head a quick shake. Time to reset her thinking. Her life was full enough. She didn't need a man right now. She might not need one ever, although she wasn't opposed to settling down with some nice guy in the future—the distant future. For now, she had plenty to keep her busy, and her close relationship with her family kept her from feeling the least bit lonely. Yes. Her life really was full, sometimes to the point of being hectic as it was today.

Party planning or not, Heidi felt she was racing against time on a daily basis. Things were a little better now that school was out and her volunteer work had concluded. Over the years, between school, work, and familial responsibilities, there really hadn't been a whole lot of time left over for a boyfriend anyway. Her parents needed more and more assistance with things, and that extra work usually fell to Heidi, since she was the oldest. She really was happy to help, but she worried about what would happen when she left for medical school. That was to say, if she got in at all.

Heidi didn't think she was flattering herself when she described her role in the family as that of the glue. It was simply the truth. Her parents, who definitely met the definition of elderly now, had always been old, possibly from the very beginning of time. And her sister, Shelly, had always been and would always be the baby. She was the fun-loving whirlwind of a daughter, while Heidi was the practical, dependable one.

These dynamics had always worked in the past. But with their parents' advancing age and Heidi (hopefully) leaving town indefinitely in a few short months, things would have to change. She'd been dropping hints to her parents that maybe it was time for them to sell this place and move into a condo. Either they weren't taking the hint or it wasn't computing. But whether they simplified their lives or not, Shelly would need to take over some aspects of Heidi's role when she was gone, and Heidi needed to use this summer to get her sister used to the changes that would possibly be coming, and not just with respect to their parents. It would be a big adjustment for them as sisters too.

Chapter 3

Shelly sat on the fourth hole with her feet up on the dash of the golf cart, sunning herself. This was the life. She was getting paid to drive around outside in the fresh air and sunshine, and she was making great tips. She always did during men's league. Women's league . . . now that was another story. The ladies weren't nearly as generous with her, and the reason why was no great mystery. Their husbands loved her, so they had to hate her. A few weeks ago, Shelly overheard Mrs. Thames refer to her as "that little hussy" when she'd been changing into her work uniform at the back of the women's locker room. The other women had eaten it up.

Never one to take anything on the chin, Shelly had marched over to the group of women, stretching her mouth into the widest smile she could muster. "Good morning, ladies!" she said. All but Mrs. Thames glanced down at the floor, having enough grace to look sheepish that Shelly had overheard them.

Mrs. Thames stared her down smugly. "What are *you* smiling at?"

Shelly had placed a hand over her heart. "Oh, I'm so sorry. I thought about giving you a nasty look, but then I realized . . . you've already got one."

Mrs. Thames' expression was priceless, and her scowl caused deep grooves to appear around her mouth. Shelly wondered if all that heavy makeup on the older woman's face might just crack and flake right off onto the blue indoor/outdoor carpet. The thought made her laugh out loud. "I'd be careful if I were you," Shelly warned as she used the scrunchie on her wrist to secure her hair in a ponytail. "Those nasty looks'll just give you more wrinkles."

Shelly had the pleasure of seeing Mrs. Thames turn almost purple at having been bested, and by a hussy no less, and she winked at the entire group before turning on her heel. She felt her ponytail bounce as she left the locker room with an exaggerated spring in her step. Shelly knew she'd get an earful from the manager later, but putting those women in their place had felt so good, she'd do it again in a heartbeat.

When Shelly relayed the story at home later that night, Heidi and Maggie had been horrified into speechlessness, but Sepi had chuckled. "You sure put that nickel millionaire in her place, Shelly girl. Franny Thames is almost as bad as her husband. Truth be told, it would do them both good to be brought down a peg or two in life. The wife will think twice before taking you on again, I expect."

Maggie found her voice. "Sepi, don't encourage her. Whatever happened to turning the other cheek?"

Sepi grinned at his wife. "The Bible says there is a time for everything."

"I don't think the Lord meant there was a time to be vicious," she scolded. She turned to Shelly. "I think what you did was a mistake. You could have simply walked out past those women with your head held high. Who cares what they think anyway? You sank down to their level."

"I don't know, I was pretty comfortable there, so maybe it's my level too."

"Oh, Shelly," Maggie murmured.

Sepi's eyes sparkled.

"Sorry to upset you, Mom, but I'm not even a teensy bit sorry about standing up for myself. That woman is awful to me every time I see her. She's a total bully."

Shelly echoed that sentiment later that same evening with Heidi when her sister brought it up again. They were stretched out on Shelly's bed, chatting before turning in, as was their habit when they were both at home in the evening. When they'd been younger, they used to drift off to sleep mid conversation, and their parents would find them together in one or the other of their bedrooms come morning.

"I've never had any trouble with her," Heidi admitted. "I wonder why?"

Shelly shrugged and picked at a thread that had come loose on one of the pink embroidered flowers on her quilt.

"I feel like she's hassled you from the first day you started there."

"I know. And I couldn't stand her from the moment I met her. She was a complete bitch. I figured out why in a hurry, though, as soon as I found out who her husband was. He's been flirting with me in front of her. I wish I'd known she was his wife."

Heidi's lips twitched. "*He* flirted?"

"What? You think I brought this on myself?"

Breaking into an all out grin, Heidi answered, "Shelly, I know you! You flirted right back. Am I right?"

Shelly smirked. "Maybe."

Heidi laughed and fell back onto her pillow. "Maybe? Don't *maybe* me. I can picture it now. You batting your lashes and sticking your chest out right in front of the man's poor wife."

"She's definitely not poor," Shelly grumbled.

"Oh, she's poor alright. Remember that magnet we used to have on the fridge till it broke?"

Shelly remembered and sighed. "Some people are so poor, all they have is money," she recited.

"Yep, and *that's* Mrs. Thames. I feel sorry for her, and so should you. She has to go home every day to that man. The country club is full of people like that, not that they're all like Mr. and Mrs. Thames. Some are really nice. You can just tell they aren't happy."

This was the first summer the two sisters had worked at the River Run Country Club. It was the area's most exclusive golf course. Heidi had been hired first, followed by Shelly a week later. Sometimes they worked the same shift, but often they worked opposite each other.

Shelly laid down next to Heidi. "Well, I meant what I said earlier. I don't regret how I handled it with Mrs. Thames."

"She *was* awfully mean, I'll give you that," Heidi conceded. "And fine, you're not sorry. But you should at least tone it down with the men out there. Their wives just feel threatened by you, that's all. All the plastic surgery in the world won't make them young and beautiful again."

"If they do feel threatened, that's their problem," Shelly had insisted. "It's just a little harmless flirting. Plus, the tips are too good to give up." She often made double the tips that Heidi did, even though the women tipped Heidi much better than they did Shelly, not that that was saying much. Their dad had been spot on with the whole *nickel millionaire* thing. The women out there really did tip her with nickels sometimes while Heidi occasionally got a whole dollar. Lucky her.

"Hmm," Heidi said with a smile. "Flirting with men for tips. I guess you really are a hussy."

Shelly's jaw dropped. "Oh! That's nice!" She turned and pulled the pillow out from under Heidi and smacked her over the head with it, prompting a full-blown pillow fight.

Shelly grinned now as she remembered it. She'd felt like a kid again. Their dad had to holler up to them from the base of the stairs to keep it down.

Hearing men's voices and the hum of approaching golf carts brought Shelly back to the present, and she opened her eyes. She hopped up and walked to the back of her modified golf cart where the coolers were and struck a pose. Heidi had been wrong. She never stuck out her chest. Her boobs weren't much of an asset to her. Her butt and her legs, on the other hand, those were always openly admired, and she'd learned long ago to play to her strengths.

When her boss, Dot, ordered Shelly her uniform, Shelly had her order a size two—one size down from her normal size so the shorts would be tight. Then she had her friend, Lucy, who was handy with a needle and thread, hem them for her. Now, instead of hitting almost to her knees, like Heidi's did, her shorts stopped several inches north of there. Although Heidi had insisted to Shelly that she was violating the dress code, Dot still hadn't said anything about it, and judging from the way the men on the board ogled her legs, she didn't think it would be an issue.

Shelly didn't have to wait long for the golfers to round the corner and come into view. The first cart that appeared was one of the club's. The second was a privately owned cart she was all-too familiar with. Her smile wavered slightly at the sight of that red cart, but she recovered quickly when the men spotted her and cheered. She flashed them a wide smile.

Coming to a stop behind her in the club cart, one of her favorites, Bert something-or-other, said, "It's always a good day on the course when you stumble on the beer cart and a Lakanen girl."

"You can say that again," his partner agreed.

"So, what'll it be today, boys?" she asked.

"Oh, I'll take a Pabst, and Sammy here wants a Bud Light."

"Coming right up." Shelly moved to open the cooler at the back of the cart. "Any snacks?"

"Nah. But thanks, honey."

Shelly was grabbing their drinks from the cooler when she felt a hand pat her on the butt and linger there, cupping her. Bert let out a startled sound before exclaiming, "What are you thinking? Get your paws off her, Johnny!"

The hand moved just before Shelly did a slow turn to face John Thames. This, unfortunately, was not the first time Mr. Thames had touched her like this. Just a few days ago, he'd goosed her, pretty hard actually—enough to leave a small bruise. Shelly had been standing alone in the doorway of the wait station and had been so startled by that painful pinch that she'd completely frozen and hadn't reacted at all. Mr. Thames simply walked calmly past her towards the men's room with a small smile. All she could do was stare after him.

This time, Shelly's first inclination had been to spin around and slap him hard across the face. But she checked herself. John Thames was one of her best tippers, and he had enough clout around here to get her fired. She supposed that was probably true of his wife, as well, but Shelly happened to know Dot couldn't stand that woman either. In fact, Franny Thames was only tolerated because of who she was married to. Her husband was a personal injury lawyer in town, and he was loaded. Sepi called him an ambulance chaser. They'd grown up in the same neighborhood, but Shelly was pretty sure they hadn't been friends.

Instead of smacking the smug smile off his face, Shelly forced a smile of her own and said, "Mr. Thames. Hi there! What can I do for you?"

He raised his eyebrows suggestively. "What a question. I've got some ideas."

She faltered a second before responding playfully, "I'll just bet you do."

"C'mon now, Johnny. Order your beer and leave the girl alone. She's not interested in a lecherous old fart like you," Bert said good-naturedly, but when Mr. Thames wasn't looking, he met Shelly's gaze and mouthed, "Sorry."

She winked back at him and finished up the transaction, pocketing just over fifteen dollars in tips from the four men, although ten of those dollars came from Mr. Thames.

"Now, you come find us over on six. I'm sure we'll be ready for more," Mr. Thames said. He looked her up and down. "I know I will be."

"Um, yeah, I'll try." Shelly made a big show of checking her watch. She knew exactly what time it was, but if she had to look at Mr. Thames another second she might just gag, ten dollars or not. "I'm only here another half hour."

"Where you running off to, sweetheart?"

Shelly cringed on the inside. "It's my dad's birthday tonight."

Johnny chuckled. "Is that right? Sepi Lakanen's having another birthday, is he? Isn't that guy older than sin? I suppose you'd better live it up with him now while you still can. I hear his heart's not so good."

Shelly went rigid, and Bert shook his head in disgust. "Johnny, what the hell's the matter with you?"

"Just stating the obvious is all," Mr. Thames replied with a smirk.

"Well, you're being an ass. Sorry Miss Lakanen," Bert said. "Next time I'll remember to bring a muzzle for him."

Shelly forced a smile. "Have a good one, boys. I'll try to make it to the sixth tee before I leave."

Mr. Thames leered at her. "You do that."

Having moved all the patio furniture out of storage and to the back of the house, Steven was now busy spraying it off to get it cleaned up and ready for the party tonight. A party he was, apparently, going to be attending. Sepi told him the entire membership of the local Finnish club—whose official name Steven persisted in being unable to pronounce even after several attempts, but which was unofficially referred to as *Da Crew*—would be coming over for the backyard birthday barbecue. Sepi warned Steven he was about to get a real Finnish education in *Sisu*. What *Sisu* was, Steven still wasn't completely sure, but after twenty minutes of explanation by Sepi as they'd hauled furniture together, Steven had deduced that it had something to do with tenacity and resilience.

If that was the case, then Steven could see that Sepi had *Sisu* in spades. Despite having admitted he could no longer do this type of heavy lifting, Sepi was determined to work alongside him. Understanding his landlord still needed to feel like a strong, capable man, Steven worked it out so that the lighter pieces were the ones to find their way into Sepi's hands, and he was fairly certain he'd accomplished it without the older man knowing it was deliberate.

After moving the last pieces to the backyard, Sepi sheepishly informed Steven that he needed a short birthday nap before the party, and Steven encouraged him to go inside and rest. It was at least eighty degrees today, and Sepi looked wilted by the time they'd finished hauling chairs.

Steven's clothes were sticking to him as well, and as he cleaned the furniture with water from the hose, the back spray cooled and refreshed him.

He thought of Heidi.

If he'd thought that smile was special, and he had, her eyes were out of this world. He'd never seen eyes that color before—a deep amber. When he'd seen her that first day, as quick as it had been, she'd given off the impression of being a sort of wild, free spirit with her windows down and music cranked up too loud. Today, she seemed a little more reserved. A bit more on the shy, introspective side—like him. Steven had always admired people who had multifaceted personalities. He felt he himself was horribly stuck as a one-dimensional, much-too-serious, boring, introvert. Oh, he wasn't shy, and he knew how to be social, but it didn't come as easily for him as it did other people, and it didn't recharge his battery the way a solitary run would.

Curiously, he'd always been drawn to extroverts, those free-spirited types who seemed able to adapt to almost any situation and never took life too seriously. His closest friends had all met that description—past girlfriends too. He seemed to be happiest when he was surrounded by people like that—with one notable exception. The person he'd been the closest to in his whole life, the one he'd loved the most, had been much the same as him.

Steven's grandmother had been one of the most soft-spoken people he'd ever known and with the gentlest, loveliest of spirits too. She'd raised him and given him a home and a family when his own parents decided he was too much trouble. They'd left him with her one day, his father's mother, when he was just two years old, and they'd never looked back.

Steven could honestly say he'd been better off with Gran, and he'd never felt any need whatsoever to try to find his wayward, drug-addled parents. As a kid, yeah, okay—maybe he'd wondered about them. What kid wouldn't be curious about his parents? But now, as far as he was concerned, they were gone forever. He hardly thought about them anymore. He'd had a wonderful childhood, and though he and Gran hadn't had much by way of material things, he'd been rich beyond measure.

Steven wondered what Heidi's story was. It seemed as though she might live here with her grandparents as well. The two of them might just have a few things in common. Her soft smile and quiet demeanor reminded him of his gran, and he was eager to get to know her better tonight. Glancing at his diver's watch, Steven saw he had two hours before the party. He hoped that would be enough time for this resin and wicker patio furniture to dry. He finished spraying the last piece and put the hose down in order to move the tables and chairs into positions that would make sense for a party.

"Well now, aren't you a dear to clean everything off!" a kind, feminine voice exclaimed from behind him. Steven turned to see a silver-haired, petite lady standing in the grass, holding a hanging floral basket and metal shepherd's hook. "I had planned to ask Heidi to do that. Won't she be happy she no longer has to add that to her list? I've been sending that girl out on errands all day. She's picking me up some coolers and bags of ice as we speak." She glowed at him.

"Oh, it was no trouble, ma'am," Steven assured her.

"I assume you're Steven, the wonderful tenant I've heard so much about. Sepi and I are so happy you'll be staying with us for the summer. I'm Maggie."

They didn't shake hands since Steven's were wet and Maggie's were full, but they smiled at one another, and Steven told her it was nice to meet her before offering to help her with her plant and hook.

"Oh, thank you," Maggie said, handing him the items. "I thought this might look nice right over there on the edge of the patio where the path begins."

"That will look nice," Steven agreed, though he wondered if anyone would notice it. The Lakanen yard was a veritable garden nursery. He was no expert in flowers, but he recognized a few of them—crocuses, daffodils, and tulips—all springtime bloomers. He expected she had something blossoming all throughout the spring and summer. He set the basket on the pavers as he positioned the hook and stepped it down into the soil. "I like the plant."

"Isn't it pretty? It's a bleeding heart."

"I don't know much about plants and flowers, even though I'm your new gardener," he said sheepishly.

"Don't you worry, I'll teach you. All I really need you to do is help me weed the beds and prune, anyway."

"Well, I am an expert at weeding. I used to help my grandmother with her garden. And if you show me what to prune, I'm sure I can do that well enough."

"Aren't you sweet! I'm sure your grandmother thought so too," Maggie proclaimed with a smile and nod of her head. When he'd placed the plant on the hook and made a few adjustments so it was all nice and straight, Maggie thanked him and suggested, "Steven, why don't you get cleaned up. I'll organize this furniture the way I want it for tonight, and you can get a little rest in. Trust me, you'll need it."

He looked at her quizzically. "Why's that?"

"Because Sepi's friends make him seem shy by comparison." She leaned in closer. "They're *Finns*," she said pointedly, as if this explained everything.

Chapter 4

"You're late," Shelly said, opening the door to the car she shared with her sister.

"I know, sorry. Mom's had me going all day."

"Oh, good," her sister said with obvious relief. "Is everything ready, then? Because I really don't want to have to do anything. It's been a hard day, and I'm exhausted." Shelly buckled her seatbelt and pulled down the visor to check her hair in the tiny mirror.

Heidi rolled her eyes. "Spare me. You've been riding around on a cart in the sunshine all day. I'm the one who should be exhausted. I ran all over town on errands this morning and prepared food in a hot kitchen all afternoon."

Shelly acted like she didn't hear her. "Ugh, my hair looks like I've been tumbled through the dryer on high heat." Using the brush they kept in their shared glove compartment, Shelly began to work out the tangles.

"It's seen better days," Heidi agreed.

Shelly stopped brushing and looked at her sister in mock indignation. "Gee, thanks."

Heidi delayed her answer to her sister's initial question until she'd pulled out from the golf course and onto the busy highway. "Everything's ready except for the grilling, which Dad will have to do. Mom's always refused to learn, and I don't think our first attempt should be on a night when we need to feed fifty hungry people."

Shelly laughed. "Probably not," she agreed. "You know we're going to be the youngest ones there, and by two decades at least."

"Yeah, but Da Crew has more energy than the two of us combined, so there's that."

"There is that," Shelly echoed, lightly tapping her fingers outside of the open window against the side of her car door. "Will we limit the beer this time?"

"That's the plan," Heidi said with an emphatic nod of her head. She was thoughtful for a moment. "We've done a little bit of a role reversal, haven't we? Now *we're* the chaperones." She took her eyes off the road briefly and flashed her sister an amused smile. Shelly grinned back.

The last time their parents had entertained their friends, some of them had gotten a little too rowdy, and rowdy old folks, the sisters had quickly learned, were surprisingly difficult to tame. Her dad had suggested they go easy on the beer tonight, even though it was a Finn favorite, by shifting to the other Finn favorite mid evening—coffee. Heidi thought it was a great idea.

She hoped Da Crew would behave themselves in front of Steven. It was important to her that he approve of them. She wanted him to approve of her too, and she'd spent a little longer than she'd intended going through her stuffed closet to try to find the perfect dress for the party. It seemed paradoxical to her no-nonsense personality that she was as fond of clothing as she was, but she could easily shop the legs off of Shelly, and that was saying something.

For a few seconds, the only sound inside the car came from the radio and Shelly's continued light tapping on the door. They listened to a few lines of Soul Asylum's "Runaway Train" before Shelly broke in with another question. "What are you thinking right now?"

Heidi didn't miss a beat in replying. There weren't many secrets between them. "I'm just thinking about the new tenant. He'll be there tonight."

Shelly perked up. "He's here already?"

"He came a day early. Dad thinks he must have gotten here last night because he pulled into the driveway this morning just after I drove you to work. By the time I finished the grocery shopping, he was already mostly moved in."

"Isn't he hot?" Shelly asked with a bright smile.

"Yeah. He's cute." Heidi worked to keep her voice casual. It was important not to let Shelly know just *how* cute Heidi found him to be.

"Cute? Are you kidding?"

"What?" Heidi asked, confused.

"Puppies are cute, Heidi. Middle school boys are cute."

"Okay, fine. He's hot then."

"I told you." Shelly sighed. "I can't wait to meet him. What's his name again? Steve?"

"He goes by Steven. He's really, really nice."

Shelly leaned towards her, looking at her intently. "Wait, so you talked to him?"

"Yeah, but not for long."

Shelly studied her. "You mean, not for long *enough*," she finally said.

Heidi didn't argue. It would be pointless anyway. Her sister could read her like a book, although Heidi was getting better and better at concealing certain things between her pages. Now Shelly, *she* was an open book. She hid nothing from Heidi.

"So you're interested," Shelly pressed.

Heidi began to sweat, and she dialed up the AC. *Keep it light*, she said to herself. To Shelly she answered, "No. I mean, it's summer, and I wouldn't mind a fun little romance in my life. But you know me."

"I *know* you," Shelly agreed, "but I don't *understand* you. Aren't you even a tiny bit interested in settling down with someone? We're the age mom was when she and dad got married. You never date anyone seriously."

Heidi chuckled. "And you do?"

"I date *all* the time," Shelly protested.

"I know. That's my point. You're a serial dater. You just dumped that poor Jason guy, and you didn't even date him long enough for me to learn his last name."

"That's because I knew I could never be serious about Jason."

"You've never been serious about anyone."

Shelly sighed in exasperation. "Well, maybe now I'm looking to be. I'm ready. But, Heidi, you have to at least go out with guys before you can get serious about somebody. You don't even date a little bit anymore."

It was Heidi's turn to sigh. *And why do you think that is?* "How many times have we talked about this?"

"I know, I know," Shelly said, conceding the point. "But I still don't get it. I mean, I know you have all your little goals and plans, which is great. But plenty of people go to medical school *and* date. Some doctors are actually *married*, and some even have kids," she teased before growing serious again. "You can walk and chew gum, you know. Plus, and I'm just throwing this out there, you don't know for sure that you'll even get in anywhere. As you've already seen, it's tough."

Heidi shot her a fiery look. This was a sore spot. She'd applied to five medical schools, and four had sent her outright rejection letters back in February and March. All of her hopes now hinged on being accepted into the Mayo Clinic Alix School of Medicine, where she was currently wait-listed. The window of acceptance from the waiting list was from March to the end of June. It was down to the wire, and Heidi was trying desperately not to fret. It wasn't working, and she obsessively checked the mailbox and answering machine each day.

"Oh, I'll get in. Somewhere. If not Mayo, I'll reapply to other schools this fall. I'll apply all over the place if I have to. And nice vote of confidence, by the way," she added, looking at her sister with a scowl.

Shelly shrugged. "You know I believe in you. Whatever you end up doing, you'll be fantastic at it. You've never been bad at anything. I just think you need to be realistic. Your first mistake was only applying to the top schools in the country. You're too selective by far." She shot Heidi a glance. "And not just with schools," she said meaningfully before continuing on. "And even if you lower your standards and apply to some medical schools for *normal* high achievers, it still might not happen. I just don't want you to be crushed if it doesn't. You've had this laser-sharp focus on becoming a doctor since forever, but look at Joel Ainsley—he never did get into med school, and he was a freaking genius."

"I'll get in," Heidi repeated. "I know I will. Look at my MCAT score—ninety-eighth percentile. And all my volunteer work, and my grades. My essay rocks, I've got fantastic references—"

Heidi stopped talking when Shelly sighed heavily. She needed to be careful.

"You've known what you wanted to be in life from that day I broke my arm on the slide at school," Shelly said.

And it was true. Heidi had been powerless to help her sister that day. She'd never experienced such fear in her life—before or since—and she could still remember how it had felt. She could picture it vividly. Shelly screaming, her arm a bloody mess. Her face contorted in pain. The fear in the eyes of the rest of the kids and even the adults who'd come to help. From that moment, Heidi had decided she wanted to be on the other side of that kind of situation—helping others, knowing what to do, being in control, just like the doctors who helped Shelly were.

Her sister continued, "I just don't know how you can be so sure. I mean, look at me. I'm going to graduate next semester with a degree in something that was earned completely by accident. What am I going to do with a Spanish major and an early childhood development minor—in the Upper Peninsula! It's not like we have a booming population of Spanish-speaking toddlers up here."

Shelly sighed and tapped her fingers again. "I could choke my advisor. He's completely useless. 'Just take classes that interest you,'" she said, imitating the deep, monotone voice of Professor Hum-Drum. That wasn't his real name, of course, but that's what Shelly had been calling him for the last four years. Heidi didn't even know his true name.

"I'm twenty-two years old and don't have any idea what I'm going to do with my life, Heidi, and here you are with yours all planned out. You graduated on time. I'm still in school earning a degree I can't use. It was *my* broken arm. Why didn't *I* glom on to the idea of medicine?"

Heidi could have laughed out loud. Shelly fainted at the sight of blood. She was no more suited to medicine than Heidi would be to working in childcare—in Spanish or any other language. Yes, she had her life all planned out, but it seemed a very real possibility that it may not happen according to her timing, if it happened at all. She'd graduated right on time, spring of 1994, while Shelly needed an extra semester to get her credit hours in.

Her sister still had several months to remain a child, more or less. But Heidi was staring adulthood and real life in the face, and if she was being completely honest, it was terrifying. If Mayo didn't accept her, she'd be stuck in limbo for a year while she waited out yet another long, drawn-out application process. And what if she didn't make it into any of *those* schools? She didn't want to think about it. Instead, she focused on her sister.

"You'll figure it all out, Shell-Shell. And nothing says you have to stay here. There really aren't a lot of jobs to choose from in Nicolet anyway. You should explore other places. Go somewhere where it's not winter half the year."

Shelly shook her head vehemently. "I'll never leave. You know that. I don't feel the slightest pull to move away, and I honestly don't know how you can even consider it. This is our home. Why don't you go to nursing school here? That's still medicine."

"You've already asked this question, and my answer is still the same. I don't want to be a nurse."

Shelly threw up her hands. "I just don't get you. You're being stubborn and selfish."

"Here we go again." What else could she say? Variations of this same argument seemed to be happening more and more whenever they talked about Heidi's plans, and with each new conversation, her sister lashed out even more. *Selfish* was a new one, though. Shelly didn't mean it; Heidi knew that. She also knew Shelly was just hurt and maybe even a little jealous, but it was still annoying.

Her sister didn't get it. She didn't understand how Heidi could consider leaving this place, and Heidi knew exactly why it confounded her so much. The town of Nicolet, named after one of the many French explorers who'd come through the area, really was heaven on earth. Added to that, the two sisters had never been apart for more than a day or two in their entire lives.

"I'm sorry," Shelly's contrite voice broke through Heidi's thoughts.

Heidi answered automatically. "It's okay."

Shelly sighed. "No, it's not. I keep doing this—getting mad, I mean. I just . . . I don't want to lose you. That's the biggest part of it. It doesn't help that this single-minded ambition of yours only highlights the fact that I don't really have any of my own. At least not anything that *you'd* consider ambitious."

Here we go some more, Heidi thought. Only her sister could turn an apology into another fight. Wisely, she bit her tongue and remained silent, allowing Shelly to steer the conversation wherever she wanted to.

"It's like I've said before. I'm not sure it matters what my career is. I'd be perfectly happy as a secretary somewhere or working in retail. I'd even be happy just driving the beverage cart for a while after college, although I'd have to do something else in the winter. Maybe work at the ski hill or something. Whatever I do, it won't really matter anyway because once I'm married and have kids, I'm hoping I won't have to work, so I can stay home with them, and I already know you think that's terrible. Like I'm selling out."

She waited for Heidi to say something. But Heidi wasn't going to take the bait. There was no way this would end well if she responded.

The truth was, Heidi *did* think it was pretty terrible, but she'd never said so and she never would. She'd grown up hearing Shelly talk about how she wanted to be a marine biologist or just a plain marine, or a cosmetologist or, for a week in the seventh grade, an ostrich babysitter. Her sister was easily distracted, which made it hard for her to pick a goal and work towards it, but it was also true that she sold herself short. She was smart and fun and had so much to offer the world. How could she settle for a post collegiate career in golf cart beer distribution, for goodness' sake?

As for being a stay-at-home mom, Shelly wanted to follow in their mother's footsteps. She always had, and that Heidi did respect.

Mostly.

Being that it was the nineties now, women should have some sort of career ambitions, even if they did take a break for a time to raise their kids. That was Heidi's closely held opinion anyway.

Establishing a career should come first. Babies second, if at all. But Shelly seemed to feel completely the opposite. No surprise there.

When they were little, Shelly had been over-the-moon in love with her Cabbage Patch baby, Adele. Heidi's baby, Adrian, wouldn't have even made it out of the box if it weren't for Shelly. She would have remained enclosed behind the plastic, tied securely to the cardboard backing along with her magic bottle, always within reach but never in her mouth.

Poor little wrinkle-faced Adrian would have been hopelessly neglected, stuffed away in a closet somewhere, but Shelly had swooped in and adopted her as her own, and from that day on, if the Cabbage Patch twins weren't in her arms, they were either "napping" or being strolled around the neighborhood by their six-year-old mother. Heidi could still picture her, purse slung over her shoulder and wearing their mother's pink high heels—three sizes too big—with bright red lipstick caked on her lips and around her mouth.

Heidi didn't have huge aspirations for motherhood herself, and she wasn't sure why. That mothering gene was either delayed in its expression or missing altogether. In spite of that, she could appreciate Shelly's desire to have the kind of family they themselves had—two kids, two loving parents, one tidy family unit. Their dad went to work, and their mother stayed home with them. It had more than worked for all four of them, and for Heidi, having her mother available and so present and active in her life had been one of the most beautiful and precious gifts she had ever been given.

The countless after school chats with her mom over cookies and milk were some of her fondest memories and probably always would be. Often, friends of hers and Shelly's, whose own houses were empty after school, would come over for a little after-school snack and some light mothering. They'd all loved it, and a few of the girls still talked about what it had meant to them.

So, while Heidi considered herself a feminist, she didn't have any problems with a woman wanting to stay at home and raise her children for a few years. Not that *she* would ever do something like that herself. In today's world, a woman should be able to make her own way in life if necessary, and that meant at least having a marketable skill to fall back on. A person just never knew what life might throw at them. But it didn't appear that her sister would have a fallback skill, and that was a worry for Heidi.

But if Shelly lacked ambition or goals with respect to her career plans, she knew who she was and made no apologies. She was a confident, good-timing, live-for-today, glass-half-full type of person and always had been. She drew people to her in a way Heidi would never be able to do. But sometimes, like now, when she was upset, her sister could also be a real pain.

"Don't put words in my mouth, okay? I don't think you're a sellout."

Shelly grabbed her hand and squeezed, resting her head back on the seat and closing her eyes. After a few beats of silence, she spoke. "Okay, and I'm sorry. I know I'm being bitchy. I just . . . I had kind of a bad day, or a bad end to the day."

"What happened?" Shelly didn't usually have bad days. She was the annoying kind of person who turned all those stinking lemons into lemonade where Heidi was more likely to stick her lemon in her mouth and suck on it until she choked.

"John Thames happened."

Heidi's eyes grew wide. "Uh-oh. Tell me."

"He was just a jerk, that's all."

"Because of what you said to his wife?"

Shelly opened her eyes and tipped her head to the side. "Huh. I hadn't even considered that, but . . . no, I don't think that was the reason."

"Well, out with it. What happened?"

"Oh, you know him. He's just arrogant, that's all."

"Why are you trying to downplay this? Obviously, he upset you. I want to know what he did."

"Fine. He put his hand on my ass, which I suppose is better than the pinch I got the other day, which still hurts"—she reached down and rubbed her right cheek with a small wince—"and then he said something mean about Dad."

Heidi felt her protective instincts kick into high gear. "What? He pinched you? When? Why didn't you tell me about that?"

Shelly shrugged.

"Shelly, this is a big deal. That's twice he's groped you. He doesn't get to touch you like that! Did you tell him to get his hands off you?"

"Bert did."

Heidi nodded in approval. "Good. I love that guy. Listen, if he touches you again, *you* have to say something. If not to him, then to Dot." Heidi paused. "Actually, maybe you should tell Dot, regardless."

Shelly turned her head to look out her window. "Maybe I will."

"I'm not kidding, Shelly. You can't let this go on. Do you want me to say something?"

"No! I said I will, Heidi. Geesh! I don't need you to swoop in and rescue me."

"Okay, good. Thank you." Heidi glanced at Shelly again. "What did he say about Dad?"

Shelly shook her head and blew out another sigh. "Oh, you know. Just that he's old."

"Well, Mr. Thames is nearly Dad's age, so that's dumb."

Shelly glanced at her with a question in her eyes. "How do you know how old he is?"

"Mom told me he was just a year or two behind Dad in school, and that Mr. Thames was always picking fights with him because he was a jealous prick." She glanced at Shelly with an amused smile. "Of course, she didn't use that word. Anyway, he was a great athlete, but Dad was better. Mr. Thames was always trying to one-up him on the football field, and I guess he was desperate to break Dad's track records, but he never could. Apparently, they had some kind of professional issue too—at the bank. Mom wouldn't say what. And then—you'll never believe this—years ago before we were born, she said he, you know . . . came on to her."

Shelly lurched forward in her chair. "What? Are you kidding me?"

Heidi shook her head.

"Does Dad know?"

"Of course Dad knows! They were at some high-rolling party in town, and after it happened, she got Dad, and they left."

"What, that's it? They just left? Dad didn't do anything about it?"

"I did ask, but you know Mom. She wouldn't say."

"Don't you love how she gives you just enough details to drive you absolutely insane? Why can't she ever tell the entire story? And why am I just finding out about this now?"

Heidi shrugged. "I don't know. I guess I forgot until now."

"You forgot." Shelly shook her head. "Incredible. You're almost as bad as Mom."

"Hmm. Mom's the best, so I'll take that as a compliment."

"You make me crazy sometimes."

Heidi looked at her and grinned. "Right back atcha, sister."

Chapter 5

After rounding the corner of the house and taking in the setup for the backyard party, Steven had to blink his eyes a few times. Not only were there tables and tables full of food dishes and platters covered in plastic wrap, but two grills were already heating up and four oversized coolers were lined up next to a small table loaded down with a couple of punch bowls and stacks of blue, plastic cups. Twinkle lights had been strung loosely from the bottom of the deck over to the tidy shed, and small tiki torches had been placed and lit along a path from the patio to another small building at the back edge of the yard. A *Happy Birthday* banner hung from the deck's railing, and bunches of balloons were tied to the backs of several chairs. Music streamed out from a set of outdoor speakers mounted above the door of the little white shed.

Steven shook his head. Someone had majorly transformed this already beautiful yard, with its impressive gardens and incredible view of the town and water below, into a festive and lively party space in only a few hours' time. Steven was hugely impressed.

"When we throw a party, we go all out," a familiar voice said from behind him.

He smiled and turned to face Heidi. "You did an amazing job. This looks great." *And you look amazing too.*

She wore a yellow, halter-style sundress that hugged her curves in all the right places. It was all Steven could do to keep his gaze above her shoulders. She'd braided her hair back off her face, and he noticed with some appreciation her delicate neck and jawline. Soft wisps of hair had escaped the braid, and they framed her face in loose curls that moved gently in the breeze. With her flushed cheeks and pink lips, she looked exquisite and extremely kissable, and Steven suddenly felt a heat under his collar that had nothing to do with the warmth of the day.

She waved a hand to dismiss his compliment. "Oh, I didn't do anything."

Steven figured she was merely being modest.

"Is that for my dad?" she asked, nodding at the wrapped gift he held in his hands.

"Um, it is, yes," Steven said, hoping his surprise didn't show. So Sepi was her father and not her grandfather. "Where should I put it?"

"I'll take it." Reaching for it, she gave it a gentle shake. "What is it?"

"Um, it's a rain gauge." Suddenly, Steven felt very foolish, and he spoke quickly, "When we talked a few weeks ago, Sepi mentioned that he'd always been meaning to get one. He said he likes to keep track of stuff like that—rain, snowfall, and . . . stuff." He shrugged.

"That's a great idea," she said, resting a reassuring hand on his arm. "Really! My dad loves gadgets. Let's put it over there." She pointed to an empty table near the shed and held Steven's hand, walking him over to it. He was momentarily startled by her touch, but he followed without hesitation.

After setting the wrapped box down, she turned to him, still holding his hand, and as much as he hated to break the contact, he wiggled out of her grasp. His hand had begun to sweat, and the last thing he wanted was to leave her with the impression that he was an awkward, sweaty-handed loser.

"Sorry," she said, flashing him a grin that revealed she was anything but. "I'm a touchy-feely type, and I forget not everybody is."

Steven wanted to be swallowed up by a sink hole. He was fairly certain even his ears were blushing. "No, no, it's fine."

Her amber eyes sparkled with amusement. "While I'm at it, I should probably apologize for nearly running into you that day in the driveway a few weeks ago, but I was in a big hurry. I always am." She laughed. "But it's fantastic to meet you, Steven." She treated him to that megawatt smile again. "I'm—"

"Honey!" Maggie hollered down from the deck. "The Kainulainens are here, but I'm just getting the pasties out of the oven, so could you head to the front and greet them? Bring them 'round back. We'll all be out in just a minute."

"Okay!" she called back. Looking at Steven, she rolled her eyes. "Sorry, I'll be right back. Don't wander off too far. I'm not done with you yet." She winked and graced him with an unquestionably flirtatious grin that had Steven wondering if he was in Nicolet at all. Maybe he'd stumbled upon paradise, instead.

As he watched her walk away around the house to the front yard, he admired her figure and the gentle, seductive sway of her hips—he just couldn't help himself—and he thought about their exchange. She'd had such an easy, carefree way about her just now. Actually, *vivacious* was the word that came to mind. She'd been so shy earlier.

Added to that, she'd behaved as though they hadn't seen each other at all that day, and he'd gotten the sense she had been introducing herself all over again. Strange. He supposed they hadn't really had much opportunity to talk that afternoon, so maybe she'd thought to start over. They kept getting interrupted. He looked forward to the rest of the evening, where there would certainly be ample opportunity to spend some time with her.

Steven, realizing he was thirsty and looking for a way to pass the minutes, grabbed a beer out of a cooler. After popping the top and taking a gigantic swig, he looked down at the label. This was good stuff. *Karhu.* He'd never heard of it before. He stood a moment with a hand on the back of a red-cushioned chair and faced the town below. This might just be the best property in the entire area, set up so high like this. The view could never get old, and he took it all in again for a few moments.

Steven wanted to live here. It was more than just a beautiful place. It felt *right* somehow in a way that he couldn't explain, and he felt a hope rise up inside of him that his internship at Chester Biotechnologies would lead to something permanent. He was good at what he did, so it wasn't out of the question.

The company did a lot of work in the development of spinal implements—things like cables, cages and screws. They designed and manufactured total joint implants as well. These were the specialty areas of biomedical engineering that Steven had always favored, so for him, this company was almost too good to be true. Eventually, his goal was to work in the O.R. with surgeons—teaching them how to use the devices he created.

He blinked. Twice. And then he smiled.

The dream job in the dream location with the dream girl suddenly felt perfectly within his reach.

No more than five minutes passed from the time Steven sat down with his beer than he heard Heidi calling for help from the same screen door off the deck that Maggie had used earlier.

She stuck her head out and her face registered surprise. Sheepishly, he smiled back at her. He'd assumed he was a guest tonight, but maybe they expected him to work at this party. Or maybe he wasn't supposed to be drinking yet.

The sweet smile Heidi flashed him eased his worries even before she spoke. "Steven, hi! Could I bother you for just a minute? I need to get these pasties down there, and this warming tray is too heavy for me to carry."

Steven popped up, setting his bottle down on a table, and jogged to the steps, taking them two at a time. He entered the kitchen off the deck and stopped short. Heidi's hair now hung loose around her shoulders, and she was wearing a different dress. This one was one of those long ones girls sometimes wore that went all the way down to the ground and made a guy crazy as he tried to guess at what was underneath. It had tiny straps, leaving the flawless, glowing skin of her shoulders and arms bare. The dress looked light and flowy—perfect for a warm evening. But why had she changed? And how had she changed so quickly?

"Thank you so much. Here," she said, handing him a deep metal food warmer containing dozens of pastries the size of his hand. The smell wafting up from it made his mouth water. "Oh, and here's the lid," she said, placing it over the dish with a small *clang* before directing him to place it down on the table nearest to the deck, where there was an outlet.

Maggie was moving here and there and everywhere in the kitchen, putting the final touches on a few dishes, and Sepi was grabbing boxes of hamburger patties out of the freezer.

"I will head down with you, Steven. Maybe you can help me get these burgers going," Sepi said.

"Sure thing, and listen, happy birthday to you, before I forget." Steven adjusted the warmer in his hands. The dish was getting heavier in his arms, and it was a relief when he was finally able to set it down on the table at the bottom of the stairs.

Sepi thanked him effusively for coming and for the birthday wishes, and he was still talking several minutes later as he checked the coals in the grills and began to open the packages of burgers. "The thing about birthdays, when you get to be my age, is that they start to feel a little more special. You just don't know if you will get to have another one. So tonight, I will enjoy myself and my family, and my *friends*, eh?" He poked Steven gently in the chest with the clean tongs. "I am glad you are here, Steven."

Steven nodded, inordinately pleased. Sepi considered him a friend.

"Now, do you mind, Steven, if you help me with these burgers?"

"No, no, of course not," Steven assured him, and together the two men spent the next twenty minutes grilling and greeting the friends who trickled into the yard at a steady and somewhat alarming rate. They came from above them via the house or from around the side yard, and Steven had to marvel at just how popular Sepi appeared to be. Steven doubted he himself would have this many people at his funeral, let alone a birthday party.

That was a sobering thought.

Grilling, sipping beer, and conversing with Sepi and his friends left Steven feeling sated even before digging into any of the food. There were burgers, subs, calico beans, chips, salads, fruit bowls, all kinds of finger foods, and those delicious-looking pastries he'd brought down earlier, which he remembered Heidi had called *pasties*. Sepi's friends were absolutely scandalized to discover that Steven had never heard of them before that night, but apart from his trip to the Bahamas with his best friend, Ben, Steven hadn't traveled much, and pasties seemed to be a regional thing here in the U.P. He already knew what he'd be eating for dinner that night.

"Just remember, Steven," one of Sepi's friends said with a grin, "a *pasty* with a short *a* is for eating. A *pasty* with a long *a* is for something else entirely." He waggled his bushy eyebrows suggestively.

Steven's mouth opened, but no words came out. He had no time to react before the man turned to a small group of men behind them and proudly repeated his little witticism. Steven listened to their laughter and turned to look at Sepi with raised eyebrows.

"It's a good thing they are pronounced differently," Sepi agreed in mock solemnity. "Wouldn't want to confuse the two, eh?" He winked at Steven.

"I saw a girl wearing pasties once. Kept waiting for them to fall off," one man called out. "But don't tell my wife," he finished to loud guffaws and pats on the back. Steven eyed him up with an amused grin. The man looked to be older than sin but spry as a slice of ginger.

Still chuckling to himself, Steven left to grab two clean platters from the kitchen, putting the ginger-slice of a man in charge of his grill for a moment. He excused his way through a group of octogenarians congregating at the base of the stairs who were discussing Metamucil supplements, and he ran up the steps, only to stop dead in his tracks yet again when he stepped into the house. One Maggie and two Heidis occupied the space in the kitchen—the Heidi in the short, yellow dress, and the Heidi in the long, floral one.

"Oh my—!" Steven grabbed on to the door frame as his brain slowly plodded its way into figuring out that there could really only be one Heidi in this kitchen. "Twins?" he managed to ask.

The three women stopped what they were doing in comedic unison, all turning to stare at him. He must have looked pretty pathetic, standing there in his confusion, and the twin in the tight, yellow dress began to laugh, her eyes brimming with tears of mirth. The other twin gave her sister a small shove and smiled in sympathetic understanding while Maggie shook her head ruefully.

"Steven, I'm so sorry. Did we forget to tell you our girls are twins?"

Steven managed one quick nod.

"Oh my goodness! How did that happen?" Maggie didn't wait for a reply, continuing, "So, who haven't you met? Or have you met them both without knowing?"

Steven looked from one girl to the other uncertainly. He felt extremely foolish, but he explained nonetheless, "Well, I've talked to them both, but I've really only formally met Heidi." He paused, looking between the two identical beauties. "I just don't know which one she is," he admitted with a chuckle, seeing the hilarity of the situation.

"I'm Heidi," the girl in the long dress replied. She smiled self-consciously.

"And I'm Shelly," the girl in yellow added. She still smiled widely in amusement. "We really only just met tonight, although I did see you *first*." She shot an indecipherable look at her sister. Heidi sent her own message back with her eyes, and although no words were used at all, Steven could see the two sisters had clearly just had a conversation.

This was beginning to make sense now. Shelly was the fast, crazy driver of two weeks ago, and Heidi was the slow, careful driver of today. Steven was in a bit of a predicament. He was attracted to twin sisters.

Both of them.

Equally.

Even though he'd hardly spent any time with either of these women, he felt a little tug in his chest whenever he did interact with them. The tug was there just thinking about them, truth be told. He'd thought about Shelly's smile for two whole weeks downstate as he prepared for the move, and he'd so looked forward to seeing her again that he'd driven up a full day early, which was so pathetic he would never mention it to anyone. Ever.

And then, today, he'd spent all afternoon thinking about Heidi after helping her with the groceries. Earlier this evening, when he'd been talking with Shelly, he'd felt that little tug again, and then again a few minutes later with her sister when he'd helped with the pasties. It didn't seem to matter which sister he was interacting with. His response to each of them was the same. Shouldn't he have known on some level that they were two different people? Obviously, if they were one and the same person, it would be no issue. But they weren't.

This wasn't going to work.

Steven felt completely deflated. He'd allowed himself to do some daydreaming when he'd gone up to his apartment that afternoon—yet another thing he'd never reveal to a living soul. It was embarrassing just to think about it, especially now. He was the adult male version of the teenage girl who doodled her crush's name all over her school folders. He hadn't doodled anything, but he had pictured himself being a part of this family, even settling down in a neighborhood close by with "Heidi" and coming over with their fictitious kids for dinners at his amazing in-laws' house.

When had he become so . . . middle aged?

While the rest of his buddies were busy playing the field and picking up chicks in bars, Steven had himself married with children after a few short interactions with a couple of twin sisters and their geriatric parents.

All Steven could say in his defense was that he was lonely. There was no shame in admitting it. He truly was all alone in the world, and it was a kind of empty feeling he wouldn't wish on anyone. But he was in a position to change that now, and he was ready to. He was ready to settle down, and there was no shame in that either. Steven was nearly twenty-three years old, and whatever meager oats he'd sewn, wild or otherwise, he was completely over it now.

Now he longed for roots.

Chapter 6

Poor Steven. If Heidi had wondered about him being comfortable at this party before, now she was really worried. Even though it rankled a bit to see Shelly flirting with him so openly, she was glad her sister was there to draw him out and engage him in conversation. She was good at that kind of thing. And while Steven had loosened up and was talking and laughing and smiling more and more, Heidi watched his eyes. She'd noticed a small sparkle in those basset eyes earlier in the evening when he'd come inside the house, but it was gone now. Something about finding out she and Shelly were twins had thrown him, and it made her a little insecure. Those vibes she'd felt from him earlier ... he might have thought she was Shelly.

She should have known.

Even if Heidi was interested in dating Steven—which, of course, she wasn't—if this played out the way it usually did, he'd want Shelly. Everyone did. After twenty-two years of existing in her sister's shadow when it came to men, Heidi was used to it by now. The moment Steven showed a preference for Shelly, and she assumed he would, she'd sit watching from the sidelines. Just like always.

The three of them were sitting at their own small table up on the deck. Shelly had her back to the party down below, but Heidi had positioned herself so she could see the guests. Wanting to be available to help in case anyone needed something, she popped up every so often to throw away an abandoned plate that threatened to blow away or to check on the food. Her parents were rosy-cheeked and in their element with their friends, and Heidi wanted them to continue to relax and have a good time.

She didn't want them to have to lift a finger at this party now that all the preparations were over and done. But because she was so focused on trying to anticipate the needs of every guest before her parents noticed, she felt like she was missing out on the fun.

Hopping up again to restock the cups on the drink table, Heidi sighed. Sometimes she wished she could be oblivious to this stuff, like her sister was. It was hard not to feel resentful. After seeing to the task, she was walking back up the steps when she heard Shelly say, "There's so much for you to see and do here, especially since you like to be outside. I wish Heidi and I were around this weekend to show you all our favorite places."

"Are you going somewhere?" Steven asked.

"Just work," Heidi said, answering for Shelly as she plopped back down in her chair.

"We work at River Run Country Club," Shelly explained. She turned to Heidi. "Which reminds me—I call dibs on the cart this weekend."

"And leave me inside to wait tables with Dot for two days straight? Yeah, that's not happening."

Shelly gave Heidi a playful smile and a gentle kick under the table. "It was worth a try," she said to Steven with a little shrug. "That's one thing you should know about my sister, Steven. She's quiet, but she's bossy." She grinned at Heidi.

"I'm older, so it's my right," Heidi informed Steven with mock superiority. She returned Shelly's kick.

"I was only four minutes late to the party that day in the hospital. *Four* minutes secured my future as the perpetual baby of this family, Steven."

"Don't let her fool you," Heidi rejoined. "She loves being the baby. Our parents can never say no to her. I haven't decided if they're just too weak-willed or if she's some kind of genius at getting her way. Sometimes she even gets to me. Just ask me at the end of this weekend who spent more time on the beverage cart."

Shelly shook her head. "I see what you're doing. You're trying to manipulate me into letting *you* take the cart. It's not going to work."

"We'll see," Heidi said with a small smile.

Steven followed their exchange with a fascination and puzzlement that was endearing. "Are you fighting right now or teasing?" he asked.

"Oh, we never fight," Shelly said with a straight face.

"We bicker," Heidi corrected.

"What's the difference?"

Shelly cocked her head to one side before replying. "Bickering is more fun."

At eight o'clock, the party kicked up a notch. This time of the year, it didn't get dark until almost ten, so even Nicolet's old folks stayed out late during the summer. Heidi, half-listening to Shelly as she laughed and flirted with Steven, looked around the spacious backyard at the group gathered for her father's special day.

She'd grown up with Da Crew. They were all so different: white-collar workers and blue-collar workers, men and women, old and . . . not-so-old. But what they all had in common was their love of Finnish American culture. Most had ancestors who had come over in the 1800s or early 1900s, but there were a few, like her father, who had actually lived in Finland.

To be fair, her father had no memory of his homeland. He'd immigrated to the United States with his parents when he was only two years old back in 1926. The Finnish culture was carefully preserved in his household, however, and was passed down to him. Both Finnish and Swedish had been spoken in his home growing up, and Sepi was still fluent in both languages. It was to his everlasting regret that he hadn't pushed his daughters to learn the languages of his motherland, but Heidi had picked up enough over the years to recognize many words and even occasionally understand the overall gist of conversations.

Even now, as Heidi listened carefully, she could hear a few conversations happening in each of those Scandinavian languages. It was one reason her father loved this group so much. It helped him hold on to that important piece of his heritage. There were other reasons, of course, but the bottom line was this group loved each other's company. Officially, the club met once a month, but its members gathered together much more often than that to socialize with one another as they were doing now. They were good and true friends, even if they did have occasional spats from time to time about politics.

Speaking of which, Heidi could see that Luke Aho and Fred Koski were at it again. Surprisingly, instead of their usual arguments about the role of unions or whether Nicolet was most influenced by the French or the Finns, this time they were gesticulating wildly and arguing about which was the better beer: Karhu or Lapin Kulta of all things. And the Waaras had had too much to drink, which was no surprise at all. They were dancing to the music under the lights near the shed, but their dancing had taken on more of a lurching quality, and Heidi worried one or the other of them might fall. Mrs. Waara had already broken one hip a few years back. Somehow, without their knowledge, they needed to be cut off. The elderly weren't supposed to drink like fish, were they? But this group could drink the entire Nicolet State University hockey team under the table.

Heidi got up to find her dad. He wasn't where she'd last seen him. He'd know just how to handle the situation, but before she could step away from the table, Steven put his hand over the top of hers, interrupting Shelly. "Where are you going?" he asked.

The feel of his warm hand on her skin gave Heidi goosebumps. She shouldn't feel such a thrill over something so innocent as the touching of their hands, but she couldn't help it, and her cheeks flushed hot. She could feel Shelly's interested gaze resting on her, which only made it worse. Mentally, she shook it off. She was being ridiculous.

"I need to somehow cut off a couple of my parents' friends on the sly. I was just going to find my dad."

"Can I help?" he asked.

"That's nice. Thank you, but my dad will know what to do." Heidi turned around, taking in the scene below for a moment before looking back at her sister.

Chapter 7

Shelly followed Heidi's gaze. "It's the Waaras again," she said with a shake of her head. "You know, Heidi, I was thinking it's past time we sang and cut the cake anyway. We've got all that coffee in the carafes inside. They're ready to go. Cake and coffee might take the focus off the beer," she suggested.

Shelly looked around at the guests again. Most were standing around visiting and drinking, but some were playing horseshoes and bocce ball, and a few were heading down the deck stairs with beach towels draped around their necks.

"What are they doing?" Steven asked, scrutinizing the group with the towels. The three of them watched the small group head up the gravel path that led to the small outer building on the edge of the property.

"They're taking a sauna," Shelly answered.

Steven squinched his brow together. "A sauna? Now? At a birthday party?"

The girls nodded their heads together.

"And, by the way, you're saying it wrong," Shelly informed him. "It rhymes with *cow*. *Sow-na*."

"Huh," Steven said, still puzzled. "You know, I thought a *sauna*—" He looked at Shelly for her approval over his pronunciation. She gave it with a nod and satisfied smile. He was so darn cute! Shelly loved his cupid's bow mouth. She could watch those lips move all day . . . and all night. Steven continued, "I thought a sauna was something you took after a workout at an athletic club. I didn't know you guys had one out here on your property."

"Tons of people have them, most right inside their houses. We like ours out here so we can roll in the snowbanks on our way back to the house in the winter. Have you ever taken one?" Shelly asked him.

Steven's jaw dropped. "You roll in the snow with your bathing suits on?"

"Who said anything about bathing suits?" she answered with a wink and was delighted to see Steven's face redden.

Heidi jumped to his rescue, repeating Shelly's question. "Have you ever taken a sauna, Steven?"

Steven cleared his throat before answering. "Once or twice. I didn't really like it, to be honest."

Shelly felt her mouth fall open, and Heidi hid a smile behind her hand.

"That's just not possible," Shelly said emphatically. "You must be doing it wrong."

Steven looked at Heidi and cocked his head. "How many ways of sitting in a hot wooden box can there be?" He smiled at her, and Shelly felt a surge of jealousy she worked hard to push back.

Heidi removed her hand, revealing an amused grin. "You'd be surprised."

"Anyway," Shelly broke in. "I think the cake will solve the problem. Nobody likes beer and cake together. Steven, can you help me get everything and bring it down? Heidi, you can find Mom and Dad and let them know we're shifting gears."

Heidi stood reluctantly, eyeing up Shelly in that way she did when she wanted her to know that *she* knew exactly what was going on. She saw right through Shelly's careful orchestration of who got to be with Steven, and she'd give her an earful later. Shelly didn't mind. This was old hat for them by now, and she reminded herself there was a reason things always played out like this. Heidi might not know it, but it was for her own good. It just so happened that Shelly usually benefited as a result. One of these times, it would pay off for Heidi in a big way. Shelly knew it would.

⚘

As they entered the house from the deck, Shelly turned to Steven and remarked, "You seem to be having fun, Steven."

"You know, I really am."

"You sound surprised."

"Well, I didn't really know what to expect, so—"

"I was really excited when Heidi told me you'd be coming tonight," Shelly interrupted, flashing him one of her dazzling smiles.

Steven tilted his head to one side. "Oh, well . . . good."

"It'll be fun to have you around this summer. I'll be sure to show you a good time." She grinned playfully.

"Okay, uh, thanks."

Heidi was wrong about Steven, Shelly decided. He wasn't really shy. He was just one of those people who took a while to warm up. She knew his type. They liked to observe, get the lay of the land, before they let their hair down. She couldn't wait to see Steven with his hair down.

"Here, can you take this cake out to the table near the gifts?" She handed him the box containing the large sheet cake. "I'll take these two carafes, and then we can come back for the rest." Shelly set one carafe on the kitchen table and opened the screen door for him. "So, what do you think of Nicolet?"

Steven waited for her to come through behind him before answering. "It's awesome. I had no idea it was so pretty up here. It's even nicer than western Michigan, I have to admit."

"Do you think your internship will turn into anything more?"

"I hope it does. I can picture myself living here."

"You know a good thing when you see it, then. That speaks highly of you. I'll never leave this place. I love it too much. I'm not like Heidi, who can't wait to blow out of here."

Steven stopped on the stairs and turned to look at her, carefully balancing the cake. "She does?"

"Oh, yeah. Don't get me started on that, though."

They dropped off the cake and two coffee carafes before turning back to the house to get the rest. In the end, it took three trips. Shelly didn't mind. It gave her more time to chat Steven up. She found out he liked to run and that his guilty pleasure was pizza. He hadn't had any serious girlfriends in over a year, and since he'd met his last girlfriend in a bar, he'd sworn off bars forever. That actually suited Shelly just fine. The bar scene really didn't do it for her anymore either, although she did love to dance. Maybe she'd go back now and again, if only for the dancing.

When the time came to sing to a smiling Sepi while he held on to Maggie's hand like a young schoolboy, Shelly stood next to Steven, close, but not touching. She could feel the warmth of his body heat radiating off of him and onto her bare skin. The impulse to lean into him, to touch him, was strong, and Shelly might have given into it if she hadn't had a sudden prickling sensation.

She looked down at her arms and saw goosebumps there. It still had to be above eighty degrees outside, so her reaction wasn't because she was cold. A wave of emotion rolled over her, and then she knew. It was Heidi. Something was wrong.

Her sister stood across from her, close to their parents. Heidi's eyes shone bright as they wrapped up the birthday song that, impressively, had been sung in three-part harmony, and although Heidi smiled, Shelly could see that it wobbled, as if it had been ordered to stay put and was now rebelling. Before Sepi blew out his candles, she shifted away from Steven.

Chapter 8

Sensing a change come over Shelly, Steven glanced at her. Her relaxed posture had tensed beside him, and she seemed to have been alerted to something. He followed her gaze to where it rested on Heidi, and he looked back and forth between the two sisters. They were staring intently at one another. Again, just like earlier in the kitchen, he got the sense that they were communicating. That idea only firmed itself in his mind a few seconds later when he saw Heidi give a small, nearly imperceptible nod and turn to walk up the stairs of the deck and into the house. When he looked back at Shelly, she was smiling again, clapping for her father once he'd blown out the last candle.

Together, he and Shelly moved in to man the cake table. At the table beside them, several of the ladies worked together, pouring coffee from the carafes into Styrofoam cups while Shelly sliced the cake and Steven served up the ice cream.

"What's Heidi doing?" he asked casually as he scooped some ice cream onto the plate Shelly held out for him. Heidi still hadn't come back down. He'd been watching for her.

"She's just inside taking care of a few things," Shelly said brightly, handing the plate off to Mr. Waara along with a fork, napkin, and a smile. She readied the next plate for Steven.

Steven, normally not one to pry, dug a little deeper. "It just looked like she was a little upset earlier, and she hasn't been back down yet."

Shelly stopped what she was doing and peered up at him. "You could tell that?"

"Well, yeah," Steven answered, somewhat uncomfortably. He was definitely prying.

"It's just—Heidi's pretty good at hiding her emotions, so I'm surprised you noticed that."

Steven couldn't help himself. "What was wrong?"

Shelly tilted her head a moment before speaking. "Heidi sort of looks so far into the future that she trips over her own feet sometimes," she said simply, as if this might explain everything.

"Oh."

She readied the plates in silence for another few seconds before speaking again. "Look, I don't want to say too much. Heidi can speak for herself, so I'll just say that she gets a little emotional on our parents' birthdays lately, especially Dad's, and Heidi doesn't do emotion well. I mean, she goes out of her way to keep from feeling things too much. Even hugs can make her uncomfortable, unless they're from us. Her family," she clarified.

"We had a scare with Dad a little over a year ago—his heart—and Heidi specifically prayed for at least one more birthday to celebrate with him. She's very spiritual like that. Anyway, she got what she asked for, and now we're celebrating another one. She was like this last year too. So grateful, but really emotional."

Shelly stopped talking briefly to take a specific order from the woman they'd called Mrs. Waara. She wanted a tiny piece of cake and no ice cream. She was on a low-carb diet. Steven fought a smile and wondered if she knew how many liquid carbs she'd just consumed in the form of Finnish beer.

"Anyway," Shelly said, addressing him again. "I've already said more than I meant to—nothing new there." She laughed. "But the bottom line is that birthdays, they mark time. And our parents, they aren't so young anymore, as I'm sure you've already noticed."

She looked at him expectantly then, as if she were daring him to agree with her. When he stayed silent, she nodded with a sort of approval and continued, "We were a total surprise. My mom wasn't supposed to be able to have kids, and then there she was at forty-eight years old, feeling sick every morning. It took her weeks to put it all together and take a pregnancy test. My dad was nearly fifty when we were born."

"I wondered," Steven said simply.

"What did you wonder?" she challenged, a slight edge to her voice.

"What your story was," Steven said simply. "We all have a story."

Shelly was quiet. "Sorry. I've grown up hearing kids laugh at how old our parents are. I'm a little protective."

"That's okay. I get it."

"What's your story, Steven?" she asked, peering at him intently.

Plopping a scoop of ice cream on the plate she held out to him, he answered, "I'll tell you sometime."

Shelly continued to look at him another minute, something unreadable in her eyes, and then she leaned in and planted a quick kiss on his cheek. Steven was so startled that he dropped the ice cream scooper on the table with a thud. Shelly, completely unaffected by comparison, held out another plate and waited for him to scoop out another serving. When he met her amber eyes, they sparkled.

Chapter 9

After he and Shelly finished serving up the dessert, Steven excused himself to wash the sticky ice cream off his hands. Once that chore was completed, he looked around the empty kitchen. He didn't know this house, and he had no idea where Heidi might be. This was a house with three levels. He imagined her bedroom was upstairs since he didn't think it would be downstairs in the walk-out basement. On the one hand, he wasn't exactly comfortable poking around the Lakanen house. On the other, he felt a pull to find her, to see if she was alright. He made his decision, which he thought Gran would have called *gallant*.

"Hello?" he called out.

When there was no response, he tried again, this time a little louder.

"Hello?" Heidi's muffled voice echoed back.

It had come from down the hallway off the kitchen, and Steven moved in that direction. He spoke in a normal speaking voice as he entered the hallway. "Heidi?" Suddenly, he felt self-conscious. He didn't really know Heidi, or anyone else in this family for that matter. He only *felt* like he did. He didn't have any business intruding like this. Too late now. "It's me, uh, Steven. I'm just . . . checking on you."

A door ahead of him off to the left opened a crack, and Heidi peeked out. He could only see a small portion of her face, but he thought she might have been crying.

"Do you like dogs?" she asked.

Steven raised his eyebrows. "Yeah. I like dogs."

"I'm in here with Taro, our old boy. You can come in."

Steven approached the doorway, and Heidi swung it open with one hand as she held the collar of the most pathetic-looking animal Steven had ever seen with the other. The tricolored basset hound had long, droopy ears and mournful, droopy, brown eyes. Everything about him was just . . . well, droopy. But looking back and forth between Heidi and Taro the hound, Steven would have been hard-pressed to say who looked more depressed.

Now that she was in full view, it was obvious that Heidi had indeed been crying, as was evidenced by her splotchy face and red nose. Based on what

Shelly had said about Heidi and emotions, Steven was surprised she'd invited him in here to see her like this.

"Are you okay?" he asked gently.

Heidi closed the door behind him before letting go of Taro's collar and speaking.

"I'm okay. I just get like this sometimes. Especially lately."

They were both quiet for several beats. Steven took in the large cherry desk and matching bookshelves in what was clearly the study. At least a dozen pictures of Sepi with his wife and daughters hung on the wall in front of the desk. This was a very close family. Steven had already known that, but if he had somehow missed that fact, these pictures would have told the story well enough.

"I was raised by my grandmother," Steven said as he walked towards the grouping of photos. "She's all I had in the world."

Heidi cleared her throat. "Is she . . . still alive?"

"No."

"I'm sorry."

"Thank you. She was relatively young, just seventy-two, when she passed."

"Close to my dad's age," Heidi lamented. "What happened?"

"A stroke. It happened in the night while she slept. I was still away at school. It was close to the start of summer break. I would have been home with her three days later."

"I'm sorry. Were you close?"

"Very. She was on the quiet side, but she'd get feisty with me. We had some really great times. She was the best person I've ever known."

Something about you reminds me of her. Maybe he'd tell her that one day.

"I'm sorry, Steven," she said a third time.

Steven nodded. "So listen, I just wanted to find you and see if you were okay. I remember her last few birthdays. They felt kind of bittersweet."

"How do you mean?" she asked cautiously, feeling him out.

"Just . . . conflicting emotions. I remember feeling so grateful to be celebrating another year with her, but I knew there weren't an endless number of birthdays left to celebrate."

Heidi nodded. "So you're saying you know how I feel tonight."

"I think I might have some idea."

"My dad has this thing he says. He got it from his mom, and I guess she used to say it all the time. *There's only the joy of today and the hope for tomorrow.*"

Steven thought for a second, scratching his chin. "I like it."

"I like it too. I think about those words almost every day lately, and I really am trying to just live in the day, like Shelly does, but I can't seem to get it right."

"It's a balance."

"I don't do it very well."

Steven rested an arm on the back of the oversized office chair. "Shelly mentioned something about medical school?"

"Wow, she's covered a lot of ground with you tonight," Heidi joked.

"She's an excellent conversationalist," he said, nodding, and watched in dismay as Heidi's face fell.

Breaking eye contact, she leaned forward and gave the decorative globe on the desk a slow spin on its axis. After a few rotations, she glanced up at Steven once more. "I'm not. A good conversationalist, I mean. I'm more like our mom.

Shelly's like Dad. She's the type of person who can sit down on a flight to Florida and talk the entire way to a complete stranger, and by the end of the flight, have their phone number and address. This actually happened."

Steven laughed. "I don't doubt it. I can picture it. But quiet is good too. My Gran was quiet. Peaceful. I liked being with her."

Heidi beamed.

"Are you excited about medical school?"

Heidi's smile turned rueful, and she shook her head. "I'm terrified I'll get in, and I'm terrified I won't."

"That makes sense." He'd spoken in all seriousness, but Heidi must have thought he was joking, because she chuckled.

"Stop. No it doesn't! How could it?"

"Because you have a lot to give up and a lot to gain all at the same time. That's bound to be stressful."

Her posture sagged. "Oh, Steven. It is. It's so stressful. And being a twin sister makes it even harder."

"I'm sure it does. You two seem very, very close."

"We couldn't be more different from each other. We're like dusk and dawn, and yet we're closer than I could ever explain using words."

Steven thought about the two wordless communications he'd witnessed tonight as he reached down to pet Taro, who had just laid down at his feet with a loud, satisfied grunt. He wasn't usually this forward, but there was something he wanted to know. He glanced up at her. "Do you and Shelly ever talk to each other without words?"

A surprised smile transformed Heidi's face. "We do, sometimes."

Steven nodded. He'd been right. "What's that like?"

"Um . . . well, usually it's pretty ordinary. Like when you just look at someone and you can read their expression. We pick up on each other's moods right away without having to ask and without any hints. But then other times . . ."

He stood and took a small step toward her. "Other times, what?"

Shaking her head, she answered, "I'm not sure I can explain it to you very well." She paused, considering her words. "It's like this. If something bad happens, or if one of us is really upset or in trouble, we can, I don't know, almost *hear* it, even if we're far apart. It's not really hearing though, it's more like a feeling, but with a message to it. Or maybe it's more of a sixth sense than anything else. I don't know," she finished, shrugging her shoulders helplessly.

"That's . . . really, really cool. So, when has that happened, or would you rather not talk about it? Maybe it's private." He winced. He was doing a lot of snooping in her business today.

"I don't mind telling you about it, but I wouldn't tell just anyone."

The tug in his chest intensified at the suggestion that he might be special.

"I guess the easiest time to explain was when Shelly broke her arm at school in the second grade. I was inside with the teacher taking a test I missed for being out sick, and Shelly was outside on the playground, which was on the other side of the school from the room I was in. I still remember, I was answering a question about the comparative and superlative forms for *tall*, you know, *tall, taller, tallest*, when I just *knew* Shelly was hurt. I knew something terrible had happened, and she needed me.

"I started crying and telling my teacher that Shelly was hurt, and that I had to find her. She, of course, thought I was crazy and tried to calm me down and get me to refocus on the test. So, I ended up running out of the classroom all the way out to the playground with poor Mrs. Carstens, who was *not* a small woman at all, chasing after me. I found Shelly next to the slide with recess monitors and kids all around her. She had this scary-looking compound fracture, I'll never forget it, and she was screaming and calling for me."

"Wow, that's . . . crazy."

"Do you know what's even crazier? Only our family knows this, but I *felt* it."

"How do you mean?" Steven asked. A small shiver ran through him.

"I felt her fracture in my own arm. I'm sure it wasn't nearly as painful, but my arm actually hurt. No lie."

This was getting really, really cool.

"You had pain in the same arm?"

"Well, no. In my opposite arm, actually. Shelly and I are what you call *mirror twins*."

"Is that even a thing?" Steven asked, head cocked to one side.

Heidi nodded.

"I've never heard of that. I've never heard of any of this."

"Mirror twins are like mirror images of each other—opposites. I'm right-handed, and Shelly's a leftie. She has a small dimple in her left cheek. Mine's on my right." She smiled and pointed to it.

Steven had to put aside an outrageous impulse to kiss it. He'd already had lips-to-skin contact with one twin tonight. He was playing with fire, and boy did he know it.

Heidi continued, "Like I said, even our personalities are opposite." She shrugged again.

Steven was beyond intrigued, and he had tons of questions he wanted to ask. Maybe he would, eventually. For now, he listened.

"Anyway, back to the communicating-without-words thing. There have been other times, and it's happened to each of us. We can't explain it. We've looked it up, and our parents used to ask our pediatrician about it, but all the literature says there's no such thing as ESP between twins."

"I guess you two know otherwise."

"I guess we do."

And then, fittingly, a knock came at the door, and Steven watched as Shelly's concerned face appeared in the small space between the door and the jamb.

The look of concern quickly turned to one of surprise, and she pushed the door open all the way. "Oh, Steven! I didn't know you were in here." Shelly folded her arms and stood in the doorway, and Steven quickly realized he should probably give the two sisters a minute. He turned to leave the small study.

"Thank you, Steven," Heidi called after him.

He twisted back around. "Oh, I didn't really do anything."

"No, you did." She looked down at her hands. "I feel better."

Steven smiled. "I'm glad to help." And he was. This evening—for many reasons—would go down in the history books as one of his favorites of all time. He didn't want it to end. He didn't really want this conversation to be over either. In fact, there was one more thing he wanted to say to Heidi, and he turned fully around before he spoke. "Heidi?"

She tilted her beautiful face up and met his eyes. "Yes?"

"You're an excellent conversationalist too."

Chapter 10

Shelly couldn't always—or even usually—reason out her emotional responses to the things that set her off, so she wouldn't try to figure herself out right then. All she knew was that she was upset to find Steven and Heidi together in her father's study. She couldn't have kept the annoyance out of her voice even if she felt like trying, which she didn't. She rounded on her sister after closing the door. "Why were the two of you holed up in here together?"

Heidi spoke with that exaggerated calmness that always made Shelly a little nuts. "He came into the house looking for me, that's all."

"You guys were in here a long time," Shelly accused.

"Well, I was upset."

Shelly mocked her. "Yeah, you look really torn up."

Heidi shot her an exasperated look. "Knock it off! You *know* I was upset. You felt it. But I'm not now." She shrugged. "He made me feel better."

Shelly wasn't sure how she could know she was being ridiculous and yet dig in her heels despite that knowledge. It wasn't a quality she was proud of, but she wasn't sure she could change it. "*Right*, he made you feel better. Did he kiss you?"

"What? Shelly, come on. Of course not."

Shelly took a deep breath and looked at her sister for a quiet moment. Finally she said, "I need to know if you're interested in him, because I am."

Heidi squatted down next to Taro and mumbled something at the floor, something like, *Of course you are*, but Shelly couldn't be sure and she didn't want to open up that can of worms right now anyway. Instead of asking Heidi to repeat herself, she waited her out.

"No. I'm not interested in him," she finally answered.

Shelly pushed further. "So you're fine with me moving in on him." She spoke this as a statement, not a question.

Heidi pinched her lips together and looked up, but she didn't meet Shelly's eyes. "Yep."

"You're sure." Again, another statement.

Heidi threw up her hands. "Shelly, I said yes. What more do you want from me?"

The truth, Shelly thought to herself. More and more, Heidi was shutting her out. They'd always been so close—thick as thieves their dad would always say. It didn't feel that way anymore. Something had shifted. Something subtle, and Shelly didn't even know when it had begun. She definitely didn't know how to go about fixing it.

But if she wanted Heidi to open up to her again, an attitude adjustment on Shelly's part would probably be a good start. She'd been a little crankier with her sister than usual. She'd fix that tomorrow. For now, tonight, her twin's words were enough. Heidi might be interested in Steven, but not enough to fight for him. That was all Shelly needed to know. She'd sort the rest out later.

Chapter 11

By the time Heidi made it back outside after doing a little kitchen cleanup in order to allow her red eyes and swollen lips some time to recover, the party had found its second wind. With the cake and ice cream out of the way, dancing and games had resumed, and guests meandered to and from the sauna with regularity. A large group of her parents' friends had pulled chairs into a circle and were talking and laughing as they sipped their coffees. The members of Da Crew were definitely riding their sugar and caffeine highs with as much enthusiasm as kids on Space Mountain, and it didn't take long for Heidi to see that Steven had caught the energy. In fact, he seemed to be the center of attention. A few short hours ago, Heidi would have assumed he would be far too shy to engage like this. Clearly, she'd have been wrong. He must be one of those people who just took some time to warm up. Warmed up or not, she wondered what he thought of her twin.

Shelly was taking any and every opportunity to flirt outrageously with Steven, and there was lots of touching going on—a hand resting on his arm here and squeezing his knee there. Her sister was a natural born flirt, and she didn't discriminate. Young or old, hot or homely, it didn't matter a whit. Shelly joked and smiled and giggled playfully, no matter where she was or who she was with, drawing laughs and generally lifting the spirits of those around her.

Although there wasn't usually quite this much touching.

Shelly flirting with Steven was a foregone conclusion, and although her sister's playful nature was the thing Heidi loved most about her, she'd be lying if she said she wasn't annoyed by it tonight. Even so, she did her best to smile and laugh along with the others.

Heidi's smile did falter once, though nobody noticed, as she watched Shelly use her thumb to wipe a bit of frosting from the corner of Steven's mouth. The color that rushed to Steven's cheeks nearly matched the color of the bleeding hearts in the hanging basket behind him, and Heidi felt her own face heat in what must have been a sympathy blush. Who knew that was even a thing? If it *was* a thing, she was the only one who felt it. Everyone else was delighted.

"Now that you've cleaned him up, better plant one on him, honey," Anika Stevens advised with a sly smile, drawing laughter from the rest of the group.

"Aw, don't waste your time on that one, Shelly!" Jake Maki hollered from across the lawn. It seemed Shelly and Steven had caught the attention of people outside their circle as well. Even though Heidi hadn't ever really wished to be the center of attention herself, sometimes she wondered what it must feel like.

Mr. Maki continued his warning, "You know Yoopers and Trolls don't mix."

"I happen to *love* Trolls," Shelly called back with a laugh.

Steven raised his eyebrows at the members of their group. "How did I become a Troll in this scenario?"

Da Crew was happy to fill him in. Trolls lived under bridges, and everyone knew that a Troll, with a capital *T*, was someone who lived below the Mackinac Bridge—in Lower Michigan. And once a Troll, always a Troll. It didn't matter if a person had lived in the U.P. for decades. If they weren't born in the Upper Peninsula, they would never gain *Yooper* status, and if they had been born below the bridge, they would always and forever remain a Troll.

Steven could accept this. He joked it was at least better than being a cheesehead from Wisconsin. "I'm a little disappointed that I can't ever be a Yooper," he said honestly. "But I guess I can live with that. Still, I'll eat your pasties, drink your beer, find that crazy *Sisu* you guys keep talking about. I'll even pretend you're right about how to pronounce *sauna*," he said, pronouncing it incorrectly on purpose.

They all groaned. Heidi grinned.

And then he paused with a finger held in the air until they'd quieted down. He had everyone's attention. Heidi looked at her sister, and they shared a smile. Steven was fitting right in.

He chuckled. "But I will never, *never* sit naked in that sauna with any of you Finnish exhibitionists."

That proclamation was greeted with uproarious laughter and guffaws that lasted several minutes, but perhaps nobody laughed so hard and so long as Heidi. She even snorted a little, which only fueled her laughter further. A few of the guys gave Steven good-natured pounds on the back as they passed him on their way to get more coffee. She watched them walk to the carafes, still shaking their heads and smiling as they poured.

Turning back to look at Steven, Heidi's own smile faded. Shelly had linked her arm through his and was whispering something to him. Heidi quickly averted her gaze. She didn't want to see Shelly touching Steven. No, she admitted to herself. What she wanted was to feel Steven touching *her*.

Chapter 12

Steven didn't see the girls for the rest of that weekend, and he was so disappointed he could almost taste it. Even though they'd told him they'd be working all weekend, he thought he might spot them at least once or twice, if only in passing.

There was no denying the attraction he felt for them both. His experience with each of them at the party made that quite clear. It was also clear he might never be able to decide who he liked better, or who he was more interested in.

His conversation with Heidi had revealed that even if she didn't like to show emotion, she absolutely felt it on a soul-deep level. He felt he'd connected with her in that place. And Shelly... Shelly was outrageous and fun and made him feel alive in a way he didn't normally feel on his own. Her enthusiasm for life was contagious.

There was no doubt about it. If he didn't keep these two beautiful twin sisters firmly in the *friend* category, it would be disastrous. Steven knew that. But still, he wanted to spend time with them. That would be alright, wouldn't it? Friends spent time together. He would just have to tread carefully, have some self-control. He could do that—no problem. So what if they were beautiful and fun and smart... and beautiful? He could still keep things strictly platonic.

Yes, he could do that.

Steven helped Sepi and Maggie finish cleaning up the back of the house the morning after the party before starting on the lawn. After helping Maggie get the warming tray and coolers washed up and put away, he worked side by side with Sepi stacking chairs and removing twinkle lights.

According to Sepi, the golf club had requested all hands on deck to help staff two separate tournaments over the weekend—one on Saturday and one on Sunday.

"Why do they host a tournament on the Lord's day?" Sepi shook his head in disgust. "Now my girls will have to miss church." He grabbed a lawn chair to stack.

Steven stood on a short ladder, working to free a section of twinkle lights. "That's too bad," he sympathized.

"Do you go to church, Steven?"

"I used to, sometimes, with my grandmother. I haven't been in a while, though."

"You will come with us, if you like, to our church. It is the Lutheran church, of course. The red brick one, just down the road." He laughed and added, "You would be right at home. You already know half the congregation from last night, eh?"

Steven chuckled. He loved when Sepi stuck an *eh* at the end of sentences. He'd heard a lot of *eh*s last night at the party. It must be a Finnish thing—a *Yooperism*. "They were a fun bunch," he answered.

He imagined sitting through a church service with Da Crew in the surrounding pews. He could hear it now. Every prayer would end with a loud *amen, eh?* He assumed it would be a different sort of church experience than he'd grown up with—less monotonous and more lively. And even if it wasn't, having one or both of the Lakanen twins sitting beside him would definitely liven it up. He actually looked forward to it, but not tomorrow.

"I appreciate it, Sepi, but I already reserved a spot on the Sandstone Rocks boat tour in Bayshore for tomorrow morning. I was thinking I'd make a day of it and do a little hiking to some waterfalls and beaches while I'm there."

Sepi stopped what he was doing. "Oh, you will *love* it over there, Steven. That area is a beautiful part of the Lord's creation. I would go there with you, but I must be at church. My Maggie signed me up to usher. She loves to volunteer me for things."

Steven noted Sepi didn't seem in the least bit put out, but that came as no surprise.

Sepi went on, "You worship in the outdoors tomorrow, and then you will come with us to the Lord's house next week."

It seemed that was final. Steven didn't argue, but then he didn't care to. Instead, he grinned as he turned back to his work. Sepi was one of a kind.

The boat tour had taken Steven all along the Sandstone Rocks shoreline, which was comprised of majestic beaches, sand dunes, and sandstone cliffs. The boat's captain told them that the natural works of art on the face of the sandstone were created by minerals—namely copper, lime, and iron—when they seeped out of the cracks in the rocks and trickled downward.

As awe-inspiring as the shoreline was, the interior of the Sandstone Rocks National Lakeshore was perhaps even more picturesque with the miles and miles of wooded trails, which at times paralleled the lakeshore and at others wound along rivers, inland lakes, and waterfalls. He hadn't seen nearly all he'd hoped to see, but Steven finally called it quits after at least ten miles of hiking. He turned around at a place called Chapel Falls and, aware of the irony, he vowed to let Sepi know he'd made it to church after all. He even said an awkward little prayer. He might not mention to the older man just how out of practice he was.

By the time Steven pulled back into the Lakanen's driveway, it was well past ten o'clock in the evening. His blood hummed through his veins at the sight of that little, white Corolla parked out front, and he thought about its two identical, yet starkly different, drivers. Steven had thought about them, off and on, all day. Spending a full day alone seeing the sights meant that he'd had a lot of time in his own head to think.

Too much time.

He ping-ponged between thoughts of the internship that would begin tomorrow and thoughts of the twins. Both caused his stomach to do little flips. Even though he was nervous about the internship, at least he knew what to expect for the most part. With the girls, he truly had no idea what might happen.

Despite yesterday's determination to stick like glue to the platonic, he'd somehow managed to erode that plan far enough down to where he actually found himself flirting with the idea of dating one or the other of them down the line. He'd allowed himself to fantasize about what that would be like. *So much for self-control*, he thought to himself at one point. He couldn't even control his thoughts.

But honestly, who knew what the future held? Maybe in time friendship with one of them *could* turn into something more. Certainly, nothing could happen right away. Steven wasn't dumb, and although he knew nothing about identical twins, he knew enough to know that dating one sister could get messy in a hurry if the other sister wasn't okay with it, and as things stood right now, he had the sense that both sisters might return his interest—Shelly, at least.

Back in her father's study, Heidi had talked about living too much in the future. Steven needed to be careful not to set his sights too far in advance himself. He needed to focus on the present, on his internship—working hard every day to achieve his goals in the professional sense. That was the most important thing.

As Steven slowly climbed the steps to his apartment, his legs felt like jelly and his stomach growled. He hadn't eaten anything since his snack of packaged peanut butter crackers and a banana that he'd carried with him in his pack. That had been sometime around one o'clock that afternoon. The small, red cooler sitting outside of the door to his apartment was a welcome sight. A smile played on his lips as he carried it inside and set it down on the counter in his modest kitchen. Two pasties, a slice of cake, and a bottle of Lapin Kulta were tucked inside, along with a note.

Dear Steven,

Welcome home. We know you must have enjoyed the sights today and you must also be very hungry. Best of luck on your first day of work from us all. Please come for dinner tomorrow at six to tell us all about it.

Your friends,

The Lakanens

And friends were what they became to Steven over the next few weeks, all four of them. He got to know Sepi as he worked alongside him on various chores, he had long conversations with Maggie as they spent time in the gardens together, and he reveled about town with the twins as they showed him around and introduced him to their friends. He even spent his evenings with them. Steven ate more dinners at the Lakanen house than he did in his own kitchen. Afraid of wearing out his welcome, he tried to refuse a few times, but they insisted, and the invitations kept coming. Whether the girls were at work or not, he continued to accept them.

Friendship with the Lakanens filled and fulfilled his life outside of work. As for the internship, Steven couldn't imagine a better match. He wanted a job with Chester so badly he even dreamed about it at night sometimes. Somehow, he just knew. He was meant to build a life for himself here in this place, and one way or another, Chester and the Lakanens would be a part of it.

Although Steven continued to remind himself that the twins were out of bounds for anything romantic, he was aware of the undercurrents that moved, unmistakably, beneath each and every interaction with them, especially with Shelly who was as subtle with her flirtations as the loud fog horn that sounded from Nicolet Lighthouse every time a haze rolled in off the lake. With her, he had to play dumb a lot—pretending to miss the significance of her deliberate inuendo and suggestive body language. Steven wondered how long he could maintain that façade of ignorance. Shelly was growing bolder by the day.

Just yesterday they'd gone to the beach, the three of them, and Shelly asked Steven to rub suntan lotion on her back and shoulders. She could easily have asked Heidi to do it, but one look at Shelly as she eyed him up with that signature smile of hers, and it was obvious they both knew exactly what she was doing.

Heidi had known too.

As he took the lotion from Shelly's outstretched hand, Heidi rolled her eyes and flopped over onto her stomach, burying her face in her towel. Steven felt a momentary sheepishness at that, but he just couldn't help himself. He'd enjoyed every minute of rubbing that lotion in.

At first, Steven hadn't been completely sure whether Heidi had any feelings towards him or not. She wasn't obvious, like her sister, but he definitely felt vibes from time to time. It was just hard to weed out if they were real or imagined. But after catching her staring at him countless times over the weeks and blushing before looking away, he grew more confident that she just might.

Friends. We're only friends. He said these words to himself more times than he could count.

The three of them certainly did *friend* things together. In addition to the frequent hang-outs at their house for dinners, drinks, bonfires, and games of bocce ball, they did other things like going out for dinner at a local place called 906 Pizza, which, hands down, had the best pizza Steven had ever tasted. They went to the beach together loads of times, and the twins had laughed and laughed as Steven worked up the courage to go all the way into the lake that first day. It couldn't really be called swimming, what he'd done. It was more of a running out into the frigid water, dunking for a half second, and running back in to shore again while his balls beat a hasty retreat up into his body. Nobody had prepared him for just how cold Lake Superior would be. It was actually painful.

Fun times were spent with the girls individually, as well. With Shelly, Steven had made a day of cliff jumping off Sable Rocks. It was one of the coolest places Steven had ever experienced. The massive expanse of volcanic rock, black as soot, seemed more like something you'd find in Hawaii, not this small, Upper Peninsula town. People went there to jump and dive off the high cliffs into the water some twenty feet below. At first, Steven had wondered if it was safe. The water didn't look deep enough by half. Lake Superior was so clean and so clear, he could see straight down to the rocky bottom. But try as he might to touch with his toes after each jump, he never could.

Shelly had drawn a crowd almost immediately, and Steven could see she relished the attention. While some people were there simply to watch her expert dives and flips, he imagined others were there to see if her pink bikini would stay in place. It did.

Steven was profoundly disappointed.

Another evening, he and Shelly borrowed Sepi's and Maggie's cruiser bikes and rode leisurely around the harbor, stopping for ice cream and looking out over the lake from a park bench. She'd entertained him with funny stories of her childhood until well after sundown. The best story, by far, the one that had him laughing so hard he got a stitch in his side, was when Shelly described the buzz cut she'd given Heidi at four years old.

Shelly had used Sepi's electric razor and left her sister with a mostly shaved head, punctuated periodically with a few random tuffs of hair. Inordinately pleased with herself, Shelly had considered it a work of art until she looked in the mirror and realized they were no longer identical. After a few tears—by both sisters—Shelly remedied the situation by having Heidi buzz her hair off in the same pattern. By the time Maggie found them, standing there like two little chicks in a nest of baby-fine hair, there was nothing left to do but shave the rest of their heads completely.

"My poor mom. She cried so hard that day! And she had to put up with the sympathetic stares of all the people in town who assumed Heidi and I were cancer patients. For months!" Shelly had laughed right along with Steven. "I'll show you pictures when we get home," she'd promised.

Later that night all four Lakanens joined him in the living room as he'd shuffled through the old photos, and Steven had broken down into hysterical laughter all over again. This time, the whole family joined in.

Shelly was a guaranteed good time. She was flirty and energetic, and whatever they did together, Steven had a blast. Heidi was different. Still fun, just... tamer. They discussed medicine and engineering and were never at a loss for things to talk about as they made their way along miles and miles of trails she was introducing him to. He told her all about his ongoing internship at Chester Biotechnologies because he could tell his work there interested her. She always wanted details about the latest projects he was working on, and he loved that she had a firm grasp of science so she could follow right along. He looked forward to their runs as much for the conversation as for the exercise. Maybe more.

One morning, after Steven and Heidi finished stretching and set out on the North Ridge Trail at a slow, warm-up pace, he broke through the long, peaceful silence they'd shared. It wasn't even six o'clock yet, but it was already light outside. The birds all seemed to wake up at once, and the quiet that had existed in the woods just a few moments before was replaced with a veritable symphony of bird calls. Steven added his voice to the mix.

"How come your sister never comes on these runs with us?" he asked.

Steven counted six footfalls before Heidi answered. "Shelly thinks running is boring. She'd rather do other things for exercise, like kayaking or surfing or climbing rock faces. She likes to hike trails, but she hates running them. I've tried to get her out here with me a million times. It's just not her thing." She paused and turned her head to look at him. "Why?"

"Just curious."

Heidi continued to look at him. She appeared on the verge of asking something more when she suddenly tripped, bumping into him. Steven reached out with both hands to grab and steady her, accomplishing more of an embrace than anything else.

"Whoa, you okay there?" He spoke into her hair. She smelled faintly of coconut and early morning sunshine.

Heidi giggled. "Sorry, I'm fine." She pulled back from him, and Steven reluctantly let her go. She'd fit against him perfectly. "It's a standing joke in my family."

"What is?"

"I do it when I bike too. And when I drive, for that matter. I can't look in a direction without veering off that way."

Steven grinned. "That's a bit of a hazard," he said.

She smiled back, and they started out again. "It really is. It's a hazard running too, apparently. I promise, I'll look forward from now on." Heidi shot him one last amused look before focusing on the trail in front of them. It was a nice, wide trail with plenty of room for them to run side by side. The trail they'd explored yesterday had required them to run in single file. It was harder to talk that way. Steven liked this trail infinitely better. He felt chatty today.

He filled his lungs with the fresh morning air, feeling them expand before blowing it all back out again on a contented sigh. "Sometimes, Heidi, I feel like I need to pinch myself. It's incredible to me that some people don't even know this place exists."

Heidi laughed and picked up the pace. "We like to keep it that way. It's part of the Upper Peninsula charm. We don't want crowds of people coming up here."

"I've said it before, I know, but I want to stay."

"What's the latest at Chester?"

"Hmm, nothing new, really. I'm still loving it. Today I get to scrub in on a lumbar fusion at the hospital with our lead engineer."

"Oh, that's right! You mentioned that. I'm still jealous. Do you know anything about the case yet?"

"Yeah. It's a young mom. She's twenty-eight, and she's already had one attempt at a fusion using autograft bone to fix bilateral pars fractures and a spondy. Unfortunately for her, that fusion failed, so now they're going in with allograft."

"A spondylolisthesis?" Heidi clarified.

Steven shot her a look of surprise. "That's right. It's cool you know that."

Heidi smiled like a cat that got the cream before asking about the difference between allograft and autograft. She was so darn sweet. And smart! To be able to share his work with her like this, where she understood what he was talking about, it fed something in him. Met a need he couldn't explain.

"Autograft is where the patient donates her own tissue, or bone in this case, usually from the iliac crest, for placement in the spine, joint, or wherever. Allograft is donor bone from someone else."

"Which one . . . is better?" Heidi asked, short of breath.

Steven slowed their pace. He was feeling a little winded too. "Good question. Autograft usually outperforms allograft in younger people, but in this mom's case, it failed. She wants another shot at it, so they're going with allograft."

"Where does Chester fit into this? I didn't know they worked with donor . . . stuff."

"We cut to size, sterilize, and preserve grafts." Steven laughed at himself. "Listen to me. *We*. I'm jumping the gun."

"Well, it could be *we* very soon, right?" she reasoned.

"I can only hope. It's going really well so far, so I guess we'll see." He turned to her and smiled, and she graced him with one of her own.

They ran together in silence for several minutes before Heidi spoke. "Today's the last day of June."

Steven turned his head to look at her sympathetically. "I know."

"Steven, what if it doesn't happen?"

"It will. You'll make it happen. If not this time around, then the next."

"Ugh! I can't even think about that right now. My confidence is shattered."

"I'm sorry, Heidi. Hang in there." He wished he could do or say something more to encourage her, but he knew if Heidi didn't hear today from Mayo, it meant she wouldn't be called up from the wait list. It wasn't looking good for her. Still, he found himself saying, "It could still happen, right? The day's only getting started."

"I'm not holding my breath."

He understood. Her odds were next to nothing at this point. "I'm sorry. I'm sure it's not a good feeling."

"No," Heidi agreed. "But this run is already helping. I woke up with my stomach all in knots, and they're gone now."

"I'm glad. It works for me that way too."

"I guess the silver lining is that Shelly will stop being so grumpy with me. She'll be thrilled about this."

Steven furrowed his brow. "Are you sure about that?"

"Yeah. Why?"

"Well, I think she's pretty torn, to tell you the truth."

Heidi turned her head fully to look at him. "Meaning?"

Steven put his arms out as if to catch her. "Watch it there, girl. Keep your eyes on the road," Steven joked as she nearly bumped into him again. He wouldn't have minded. They both chuckled before he continued, "I just mean that she wants you to get in for *your* sake, and she *doesn't* want you to get in for her own sake."

"Have you two talked about this?"

"It's come up," Steven answered simply. When he and Shelly had been warming up on the hot, black rocks after several jumps off the cliff at Sable Rocks the other day, she had mentioned it. They'd been lying on their stomachs, facing each other, and she'd shocked him when she looked up at him and said, completely out of the blue, "I'm not a very good sister, Steven."

He had tried to reassure her that she was a fine sister, but she'd been adamant. "What kind of person wants her sister to fail at her lifelong dream?" she asked with a sad smile.

Steven had contemplated that for several seconds before replying. This was the most serious she had ever been with him, and he wanted his words to be just right. "The kind who loves her sister so much she can't imagine life without her."

"She's pulling away from me. I can feel it, but I don't know why."

Steven had thought on that a minute before responding. "Do you think it's a defense mechanism? Like maybe she knows how hard it will be to be apart, so she's pulling away now to protect herself?"

"Maybe," Shelly had said doubtfully. "If she is, I don't get it. That won't help at all." She had sighed and remained silent for a few minutes, and the next time she spoke, it was to suggest they head back home.

Heidi's voice broke into Steven's thoughts. She spoke cautiously. "I didn't know you two talked about stuff like that."

"We don't, usually."

"Oh."

Steven thought she sounded relieved.

Chapter 13

Shelly had lain awake most of the night, wrestling with her thoughts. Heidi hadn't received a call from Mayo yesterday, which meant her sister wouldn't be going there in the fall. Feelings of relief and regret warred against each other into the wee hours until Shelly gave up on sleep altogether. She dragged herself out of bed and moved to the lounger in front of her large picture window. Wrapped in a blanket, she sat and looked out over the dark expanse of water. It looked as bleak out there as she felt on the inside.

Her poor sister. How had Shelly hoped for this? How could she have hoped for Heidi's dreams to crash and burn? She was a horrible, terrible sister—selfish in the worst way. That realization had only grown over the course of the day yesterday, and Shelly replayed all that had happened as she stared out the window into the darkness.

⚚

She and Heidi had worked at River Run together all day, although Shelly was scheduled on the cart and Heidi worked the clubhouse. Maggie had promised to call if there was any news, and each time Shelly returned to restock the cart, she got butterflies in her stomach before shooting her sister a questioning look from across the room. Each time, Heidi gave a quick shake of her head before looking away and continuing her work. As the day wore on, Shelly felt more and more hopeful that the call wouldn't come and Heidi would stay put with her where she belonged, but that hope changed to something else as she picked up on Heidi's increasing despair. Heidi began to wilt and droop like a week-old floral bouquet. That last time she'd checked in with her sister, the pain on her face when she thought no one was looking was enough to make Shelly want to burst into tears herself.

In the end, those tears came, and at the worst possible time too. Because of her concerns for Heidi, Shelly was off her game. As a result, with an hour left to go of her shift, she made a small mistake. A foursome of Mr. and Mrs. Thames and another couple, who Shelly discovered was Mrs. Thames's sister and her sister's husband, pulled up to the twelfth tee where she'd parked the beverage cart. The women, Mrs. Thames and her sister, approached her, whispering to one another and looking at her in a way that let her know she was the topic of conversation. They wore matching smirks, and each eyed her up and down before ordering their four drinks.

Even though they'd made her feel about an inch tall, Shelly greeted them with an outward confidence and exaggerated sweetness, as was her way when she had to deal with Mrs. Thames. But then she'd slipped up making change for the awful woman, shorting her significantly.

"What's this?" Mrs. Thames had said, looking at the seven dollars Shelly had placed in her hand.

"What do you mean?"

"What I mean is, where's the rest of my money? I gave you a fifty. Can't you count?"

"Maybe she thought the rest was her tip." The sister giggled, and behind her, the brother-in-law snorted. Mr. Thames leered at her with a smile that appeared simultaneously amused and turned on. It made Shelly feel filthy, and she tried to shake off the feeling as she double checked her till. She'd thought Mrs. Thames had given her a twenty, not a fifty.

"I'm sorry about that," Shelly muttered, seeing her mistake. She counted out the correct change and handed it over to Mrs. Thames.

The older woman took it all and counted it out slowly before shooting a glare at Shelly and tucking it away in her pocket. She gave nothing back as a tip. Instead she said, "I'm not surprised you can't do basic math. Bimbos are really only good for one thing."

Mr. Thames and his brother-in-law threw their heads back and laughed, and that's all it took. Shelly was powerless to stop the flood of tears that filled her eyes, and though she didn't sob, a single tear escaped onto her lashes. Regrettably, Mrs. Thames had the satisfaction of seeing it before Shelly quickly wiped it away.

"Oh, my!" she exclaimed loudly. "Have I hurt your feelings?" And then, leaning closer to Shelly, she whispered, "Where's your smile now?" She reached into her pocket and threw a dollar bill at Shelly. It fell to the ground at her feet. "There. If nothing else, you can use it as a tissue. Go on. Pick it up," Mrs. Thames said with a smirk.

The sister raised a hand to her mouth and giggled again. "Franny, you are so bad!"

Mrs. Thames looked absolutely delighted with herself, and for once, Shelly had nothing to say. No biting comebacks or one-liners popped into her head. Instead, she looked at the sisters, each one in turn, and then at the men. Their faces revealed a sick sort of pleasure they were taking at her expense.

Wordlessly, Shelly turned and got back behind the wheel. She wouldn't give them the satisfaction of picking up that dollar bill. But it didn't matter. They'd still been entertained. Even over the hum of her cart, she could hear their laughter as she drove on to the next tee.

Shelly avoided the Thameses for the rest of her shift, not caring that they might complain about being left high and dry for the remainder of their round. She even brought the cart back a little earlier than she might have otherwise done, so she was unloaded and ready to go at exactly five o'clock.

Heidi had needed a little more time to close out a table, so Shelly figured she'd hang out in the kitchen with the new cook, Lenny. He was a little rough around the edges—Shelly had heard he'd just gotten out of jail—but she liked him. He might have a tough exterior, but inside he was a total softy. A few days after he'd started in the kitchen, she'd hit a sweet little chippy out on the cart path near hole five, killing it. There was nothing she could do for it, and she stood there looking over it helplessly as a small amount of blood trickled out of its tiny mouth.

It was the first time Shelly had ever killed anything, and she was devastated. There was no way she could drive her route all day, passing that poor little chipmunk over and over again. Seeing that blood. She'd managed to hold back her tears until she entered the kitchen through the back door at the exact time that Heidi came through the front doors to pick up an order. All it took was a look from her sister, and Shelly had lost it. She threw herself into Heidi's arms, and the kitchen staff froze as she began to sob.

Their silence didn't last. A few of them laughed as they listened to her tell Heidi what had happened through her tears, but Lenny shut that down with one threatening look. Then, without anyone realizing what he was doing, he left the kitchen out the back door without saying a word. Shelly had a feeling she knew where he was going, and she'd been right. A few minutes later he returned and, patting her on the back, told her he'd taken care of it. What kind of ex convict would scoop up a dead rodent for her? A sweet one, that was who.

Since then, Shelly was convinced: jail or not, Lenny was a good guy. She hadn't quite persuaded Heidi of that yet, but Heidi was far too quick to judge people. She'd see in time that Lenny was just a great big tattooed teddy bear.

As an ongoing thank you, Shelly now kept him hydrated with Arnold Palmers whenever they worked together, so before heading back to the kitchen, she made him one behind the bar. Smiling, she sprayed the lemonade gun. He drank these babies like they were going out of style while he cooked. How he wasn't running to the bathroom every other minute was a mystery.

Shelly checked the glass windows of the kitchen doors first to make sure nobody was coming out with a tray, and holding the drink, she pushed through. The heat and noises of the kitchen assaulted her senses. It was all sizzles, smells, clanging, and shouting. There was no way she could do that kind of work. It was too sweaty and stressful and chaotic. Plus, and probably more importantly, she really wasn't much of a cook, although she did have plans to learn . . . someday. Maybe she'd have Heidi teach her this fall.

Lenny had been barking orders at Jack and Ryan, two cousins who were going into their senior year at Nicolet High.

"Get those steaks going. The potatoes are nearly done, so keep an eye. I'm taking my break before things pick up for the dinner rush." He turned and his face lit up at the sight of Shelly. When he saw what she held, he grinned so widely she observed the dark gap where a right top molar should have been. "Is that for me?"

"You know it," she said and handed it to him.

"Aw, girl, you're the best!" Lenny drank deeply from the glass, ignoring the straw. "Hits the spot every time. I was just coming out for one of these."

"Well, there you go. Now you don't have to take that break," she joked with a smile.

"Oh, I'm taking it," he said before gulping down some more. He eyed her up over the rim of the glass.

"I can sit with you."

He wiped his mouth on the back of his hand. "You wrapping it up already?"

"Yeah. I'm done. We worked the early shift."

"Heidi done, too, then?"

"Almost."

Lenny whistled. "Good. That girl's been in a mood."

"I know. Sorry. She didn't get in to medical school, so she's just a little upset right now, but she'll be—"

Her sister's sharp voice interrupted from behind her. "Shelly!"

Shelly jumped and whipped around. "Oh, Heidi!"

"Why are you talking about me?" Heidi's gaze flicked over to Lenny and then back to Shelly. "To him!"

Shelly looked back at Lenny helplessly. He shrugged and gave her a look that told her she was on her own before walking away, glass in hand. Shelly grabbed Heidi's arm and moved them to a corner at the back of the kitchen. "Listen, he asked what was wrong with you today—I guess he could tell—so I told him. I'm sorry."

Heidi shook her head and pinched the bridge of her nose before speaking. "You know, Shelly, telling that loser my personal business isn't even the worst part. What's worse is that it's barely five o'clock, and you've already decided I didn't get in. Mayo's on Central Time, remember? I still have an hour. Why are you so quick to want me to fail?"

Shelly flinched. "Fail? What are you even saying? I don't want you to fail."

Heidi merely stared at her. She looked so tired. "Whatever. Let's go."

"Heidi, come on. Don't be mad," Shelly pleaded. She hated it when Heidi was mad at her. It didn't happen all that often, which was good for Shelly because everything in her life went pear-shaped when she was on the outs with her twin sister. She needed Heidi to understand what she felt, but the problem was that Shelly wasn't even sure she could put into words what that was. Her thoughts and emotions were all over the place. All she knew for sure was that she felt sick about Mayo not calling. She really, really did, and she needed her sister to know that.

But it wasn't to be. They drove home in almost complete silence. Shelly tried to talk, but Heidi wasn't interested. Fine, Shelly decided. If Heidi wanted to take it out on her, if that would make her feel better, she could handle it.

Once they were home, Heidi continued to ignore her completely. The call never came, and as much as Shelly wanted to be there for Heidi, she knew her sister needed space.

Even so, she held out a small hope that Heidi might come to her room to talk. She stayed up until midnight waiting, and before turning in for the night, she got up and checked to see if Heidi's light was still on. Normally, she left her door open at night, but she'd closed it, and no light was visible from the crack between the door and the floor. It was the first night in a long time where they didn't rehash the day together, and Shelly had gone to bed unsettled.

That had been yesterday. Today was a new day, and with the eastern horizon waking up and the light working to chase away the dark, Shelly wondered what today would bring. She had the sense that anything was possible. When the sun finally appeared, the sky exploded in color. Oranges, yellows, pinks, and reds reflected off the still water so perfectly it was almost impossible to tell where the sky ended and the lake began.

Her mood had been as black as the night sky, but now with the dawn, Shelly felt the stirrings of something else. Something better and brighter. Everything really was going to be okay. Heidi would be fine once she licked her wounds, and she'd come up with a new dream. Shelly's stomach did a flip-flop when she considered the possibility that the new dream might just include Steven.

Shelly had done her level best to let Steven know she was interested from the very beginning, and if he'd been like all the other guys she'd dated, she'd have him well and truly hooked by now. But Steven wasn't like all the others, and lately, Shelly had the sense that he might have the hots for Heidi. She wasn't sure how she felt about that. If he did, Shelly had to admit—it spoke well of him.

She smiled. Until now, no one had ever been good enough for Heidi. It was just a little too bad that the one who'd finally made the cut had to be Steven because he was everything Shelly had always pictured for herself when she was finally ready to settle down.

If Heidi stayed, and Steven stayed, they very well could end up together. And while that really wasn't what she hoped for, the silver lining of that scenario would be the likelihood that Heidi would stick around long term because Steven wasn't the kind of guy you broke things off with. He was the kind of guy you married.

But for now, Steven was a wild card. As much as Shelly hated it, she'd just have to wait and see how things would play out with him. Having sweat the impending loss of her sister for months, she could handle a small question mark where Steven was concerned. It would work itself out in its own time anyway. All that mattered was that Heidi was staying in Nicolet, and Shelly finally felt like she could breathe again.

Chapter 14

Heidi opened her eyes and blinked several times before turning over to look at the clock on her nightstand. It was only a quarter to six, but soft morning sunshine was already filtering in through her translucent window curtain.

It was the first day of July. The window for wait-list acceptance at Mayo had closed with a painful thud last night. She hadn't gotten into the program. Truth be told, Heidi had held out hope all day yesterday until the moment she'd gone to bed. Now, however, she needed to face facts. She wouldn't be going to medical school in the fall.

Instead, she'd have to find a steady job and begin, again, the arduous task of applying to other schools, perhaps even reapplying to the ones that had rejected her for this year. The thought of it made her feel a despair so deep she could feel it settled, heavily, at the bottom of her stomach. There was another emotion lingering there, as well. Humiliation.

Now everyone would know. They had probably already known she wasn't good enough. Who had she thought she was? She was just a small-town girl living in a place that sometimes wasn't even included on maps of the United States. It wasn't uncommon for national news networks to put up maps of North America where the U.P. was shown as a part of Canada.

Heidi laughed to herself. "Sure, I'll just blame geography for not getting in," she said, speaking to the walls of her room.

"Okay, now I know you're losing it."

Heidi sat up with a start to see Shelly swinging open her door. Her sister never woke up before eight o'clock in the morning, if she could help it, yet here she was, fully dressed and holding a tray with coffees and donuts from their favorite bakery. "What's all this?" Heidi asked.

"I thought you might need a little cheering up today." Her sister smiled brightly, just like always. It should come as no surprise. Shelly had gotten exactly what she wanted, just like always.

Heidi's nostrils flared and her heart pounded as her twin fully entered her bedroom, uninvited, and set the tray down on her bed. She wanted to wipe that stupid smile off Shelly's face. Today was the day Heidi's dreams had crashed and burned, and here Shelly stood, first thing in the morning, with celebratory coffee and donuts.

"Get out," Heidi said in a low voice, staring down at her hands. Shelly had just moved to join her on the bed, and Heidi looked up in time to see Shelly's eyes widen in surprise as her mouth fell open.

"Get out!" she repeated, louder this time.

"What? Heidi! What in the world's the matter with you?"

What was the matter with *her*? "You want me to think you got these dumb donuts to make me feel better, but that's just a ruse. You'd sit here with me as I choked them down, pretending to be all sad and sorry for me, but you'd be celebrating, and we both know it. Well, I won't give you the satisfaction."

The sisters stared at one another for a long, drawn out moment, but when Shelly's chin began to tremble, Heidi looked away. She refused to feel bad about this, and she wouldn't apologize. She was determined, and she would not waver.

Shelly spoke with a tight voice. "Heidi, I'm sorry. I can see why it would look that way to you. I haven't been very supportive. I know I haven't. But I do feel bad that you—"

"The only reason you can say that now is because you've gotten your way—again. If I'd gotten in, you wouldn't be here with donuts. You'd be giving me attitude, calling me selfish or whatever new insult popped into your head."

"That's not true," Shelly sputtered, but one look into her eyes told the story well enough. Unfortunately, it was true, and they both knew it.

Heidi spoke with an almost eerie calm. "Please, if you love me at all, get out. I can't do this with you right now."

Shelly blinked rapidly over increasingly shiny eyes. "Okay. But before I go, I need you to know that you're the *most* important person to me, the person I love *most* in the universe. I couldn't sleep last night because I was heartbroken for you. I'm sad for you, Heidi, I really am. But you're right. It's true, I can't help but be happy that you're staying here, and I think—"

Without warning, a tightly coiled anger inside of Heidi sprang free, and she jumped out from under the covers like a jack-in-the-box. Jabbing a finger in her sister's face, she shouted, "Are you not listening to me? I asked you to *leave*! Get out of my room! I really don't think it's too much to ask. I don't want to hear how happy you are right now, okay? I'm *not* happy, and just this once, I want this to be about *me*. How *I* feel. Not you. So, get out and give me some space!"

Shelly shook visibly as she stood, and Heidi understood why. Whatever dynamics had existed between them, this was brand spanking new.

"Heidi! This is crazy! You—" Shelly's voice broke. Her eyes were wet and red, and she'd begun to splotch all over. Her poor sister was an even uglier crier than Heidi was, not that she was at all sympathetic at the moment. She just needed some time. Was it too much to ask for a teeny bit of space to grieve?

Shelly looked pleadingly at Heidi once more, but Heidi could see the moment her sister finally understood that Heidi meant what she said. Leaving the tray on the bed, Shelly turned and rushed out of the room. A few seconds later, Heidi followed and closed her bedroom door once again. She wanted to slam it shut, something she'd literally never done, not one single time. Even during those angsty teenage years, she'd kept herself in check most of the time, emotionally. Shelly was the one who erupted like a volcano every other week during high school.

Heidi stared at the closed door and bit down on her knuckles. She'd thought maybe she would feel better after giving Shelly what she'd had coming to her for years, but she didn't. She felt worse. But she would not cry. Instead, she stood quietly there at the door and listened to the hushed tones of her parents' voices talking to Shelly, who was, of course, howling. No doubt their parents were comforting her, which was just . . . classic.

Heidi should probably feel deeply ashamed of how she'd just treated her sister, but at the moment, she refused to feel anything. That was the only way to keep her emotions in check. She needed to stay numb. She needed to stuff away her feelings. She needed to eat donuts.

And did she ever. Two peanut donuts, two apple fritters, and two coffees later, Heidi sat in her bed and looked down at her bloated stomach. Great. Now she felt fat, on top of everything else. She was a fat, mean, reject.

Over the noise of crunching peanuts, she'd heard the shower turn on in the bathroom across the hall. She'd forgotten that Shelly had to work today, and Heidi was relieved to know that she didn't have to go in herself. She was off, which meant she could lie in bed like a beached whale all day if she wanted to.

Glancing quickly at the clock, she realized she'd missed her run with Steven that morning. Probably just as well. A belly filled with coffee, donuts, and rejection—not to mention guilt—would have made her too sluggish to run anyway. They'd planned to run up Mt. Joliet together that morning, which was tough enough as a hike. As a run, it was downright brutal, and she wouldn't have been in the right mindset to make it all the way to the top. As every serious runner knew, only half of running was physical. The other half was mental. It would have been yet another failure. Later, she'd leave a message apologizing to Steven and explaining that she just hadn't felt up to it. He'd understand.

By quarter to ten, Shelly had left for work. Normally, Heidi would have dropped her sister off so she could keep the car for the day, but sitting for any length of time alone in a car with Shelly was out of the question for now, and she didn't want to go anywhere or do anything anyway.

By noon, Heidi was completely stir crazy. Sitting around and doing nothing sounded great in theory. In practice, it blew. After showering and getting dressed, she felt a little better . . . a little more human. Her parents invited her to have lunch with them out on the deck, but since she was still full from her earlier bout of gluttony, she sat with them and sipped an iced tea instead.

She looked around as she gently rocked in her wicker chair. Deck life was amazing, especially deck life at her house. The view, the gardens, the sounds and feel of the breeze—all of it helped to ground her. Center her. It must have shown on her face, because Sepi remarked, "You've got the color back in your cheeks there, Heidi-ho. I'm glad to see it, eh? Are you going to be alright then?" Sepi asked.

"I'll be okay."

"You need to make peace with your sister," Maggie pointed out.

Heidi sighed, still rocking. "I know. I will."

"Good girl." Maggie smiled, but it looked like it took effort. Her mother was tired.

"Are you okay, Mom?"

"Of course! Why do you ask?"

"I just wondered if maybe you're coming down with something. You look a little tired out."

"Oh, I'm just fine. Just have a little headache from my allergies is all."

Heidi missed the look her parents exchanged as she sipped tea through her straw.

∼

The high point of Heidi's day came a few hours later. She was just returning from her second walk with Taro—anything to combat the listlessness she felt—when Steven pulled into the driveway. Wearing a light blue dress shirt and silver tie, he looked professional, grown up, and more handsome than ever. Heidi's breath caught as he stopped alongside her, window rolled down. Even her depressed heart could appreciate the appearance of a hot man in the driveway, and it kicked into a faster rhythm.

"Hi," he said with a kind smile. "Glad to see you out moving and getting some fresh air."

"Hey!" She hoped he couldn't pick up on the breathless quality of her voice. "I decided I couldn't lie in bed all day in a heap of tears, even though I wanted to," she admitted with a sheepish smile.

"I kind of had you pictured like that, to be honest. This is a nice surprise."

She checked her watch. "It's only three. You're off early."

"I know. When you didn't show up at my door this morning, I figured you might not be up for a run because of . . . everything. I went back inside and got ready for work instead. I went in early so I could get out early because I thought we could hang out, maybe." He hesitated. "If you're free, that is."

Heidi's cheeks went pink with pleasure, and she shrugged with a smile. "I'm free."

Steven grinned. "Great. Let me get out of these work clothes, and we can decide what to do."

Heidi nodded, and Steven began to move the car forward. "Wait!" she called after him. It occurred to her that they might still salvage that run up Mt. Joliet. She jogged to his window, pulling Taro along behind her, and suggested it. He lit up at the idea.

"Let's do it! I'll get my running gear on. Meet you back out here in ten?"

"Make it five."

∼

For Heidi, this unexpected opportunity was like a widening patch of clear, blue sky after a week of rain. She couldn't get changed quickly enough, and even though she rushed, Steven was already outside of his apartment waiting for her when she arrived. Was he as eager as she was to spend time together? Probably not, she told herself. He was probably just excited to tackle Mt. Joliet.

Ever since she'd first mentioned it to him last week, he'd been antsy to run to the peak. Half of the appeal was the challenge it would pose. From base to peak, there was almost a 600 foot gain in elevation. Running to the top would take a little over an hour if they kept a good pace.

"So, how are you?" Steven asked once they were on their way. He stole a quick glance at her before looking back at the road.

"Not great, but not too horrible either, I guess."

"I'm sorry you didn't hear from Mayo. I called last night and talked to Sepi. He said you were taking it pretty hard."

"Yeah. I was a little bummed."

He looked at her with raised eyebrows.

"Okay, okay. I was full-on devastated."

"You don't look devastated now," Steven observed.

"I'm still not great, but I definitely feel better than I did earlier."

"So, what's your next plan?"

"Long term? Medical school. That won't ever change."

"And for the short term?"

She shook her head and looked at him. "You know what? I have no idea, which is a first for me. I guess I'll get a job somewhere, and I'll apply to some other schools while I work and save money."

"Sounds like the dream's still alive."

Heidi liked how that sounded. "Yes. The dream's still very much alive."

As usual, they took a few minutes to stretch at the trailhead and warmed up at a slow jog. While they ran, Steven filled her in on the back surgery he'd scrubbed in on that morning. Heidi was absolutely fascinated as she listened to him describe it. She asked for a play-by-play, and he delivered, explaining it with so much detail Heidi could nearly picture it all in her head.

Listening to Steven talk about his work, it really did seem that he'd found the perfect match with this internship. He'd landed exactly where he'd hoped he would, and she was truly happy for him. Now he just needed a job offer.

If Heidi were a betting person, she'd put money on him being offered the job at Chester before summer was out. The chance to stay here would make him over-the-moon happy, and she had to admit the idea filled her with a sense of excitement too.

Before it became too difficult to maintain conversation as the slope steepened, she marveled again at the beauty of this place she'd been fortunate enough to call home all these years, and they talked about all the things they loved best about it. Ranking at the top of both of their lists were the miles of running trails, although the lake was a close second. It was ironic that Steven dreamed of staying here while she dreamed of leaving.

In the end, Steven made it up to the top of Mt. Joliet without stopping. Heidi had to stop once to catch her breath, which surprised her. It was true that she always had more stamina in the morning, but she struggled a lot more than usual today. Steven had offered to wait for her, but she encouraged him to keep going. It would have been cruel to ask him to break his momentum. Only another runner understood the fierce competition that could exist inside of a person to compete with themselves—to prove, if only to themselves, that they were strong and capable. She wouldn't take that from Steven.

The final climb required using both hands and feet to crawl up the rock face, and by the time Heidi made it within reach of the very top, she was panting heavily and her calf muscles were on fire. She was definitely not on her game at all today.

"Here."

Heidi looked up to see Steven crouched above her and holding out his hand. She grabbed hold, and he hoisted her the remaining distance to the top.

"Thanks," she said breathlessly. He was breathing normally, and if it weren't for the sweat near the collar of his shirt, no one would have been able to guess he'd just raced to the top of Mt. Joliet. "Have you been up here long?"

"Just a few minutes," he lied. "You were right. This place is amazing."

"It's one of my favorite spots."

"I can see why," he said, looking all around them. "I'm going to have to do this run again. I love everything about it. The trails at the base, the climb, the view from the top . . ." He looked at her then and appeared to want to say something more. Heidi waited, but instead, he cleared his throat and averted his gaze.

She squinted up at him, shading her eyes with her hand. It was especially bright up here with the sun's rays bouncing off the light-colored rock. "What is it? What were you going to say?" she asked.

He shook his head. "Nothing. I was just reminding myself of . . . something."

What? What were you reminding yourself of? She didn't ask, although she really wanted to know. It definitely had something to do with her. Instead, she said, "Let me know when you plan on coming back, and I'll come with you. I should be able to get to the top next time, especially if we go in the morning. I'm embarrassed I had to stop today."

"Don't be. You're in great shape."

Heidi smiled with pleasure and they remained quiet for a time, taking in the view. She loved that they could be together and not talk at all. Neither of them felt the need to rush to fill the silences.

Heidi thought again of how easy it was to be with Steven. He hadn't brought up Mayo again, and she found she didn't need to talk about it. At least for the time being, that awful heaviness in her chest had lifted, and she felt that everything just might work out in the end. *Trust the good Lord's plan*, her dad always said. Maybe that wouldn't be as hard to do as she'd thought. Or maybe everything was still crap, and she was just being given a moment of peace as a gift.

She'd take it.

Tilting her face up, Heidi closed her eyes and allowed herself to simply *be*. The breeze blew gently through her ponytail and the sun warmed her face. Heidi thought maybe she should just stay up at the top of Mt. Joliet forever, but then her stomach made a loud rumble and Steven laughed.

She opened her eyes and was met with Steven's handsome, grinning face. "Well," she said, returning his smile, "I guess that's our cue. I obviously don't want to miss dinner. Mom's making pulled pork sandwiches tonight. We always have a ton left over. Do you want to eat with us?"

Steven hesitated. "I feel like I'm always mooching off your family when it comes to food. Plus, I wouldn't want to spring anything on your mom. I feel like she's been a little tired lately."

"I've noticed that, too, now that you mention it. I'll have to ask her about it. I've been a little wrapped up in myself lately. But tired or not, my mom is one of those people who loves to cook. There's not much that can keep her out of the kitchen. Plus, she adores you. My parents would have you over for dinner every night if they could."

Steven's smile turned quizzical, and he slanted his head. "What do you mean, 'if they could?'"

"Just that they don't want to crowd you too much. My dad told my mom they need to be careful not to monopolize your time since you're young and have a social life that doesn't include two old people."

Steven laughed. "At this point, your family makes up my entire social circle. And believe me, I'm not complaining."

Heidi's cheeks warmed even further. "I'm glad." She held his gaze until the intensity of the moment caused her to look away. She didn't know what she was doing with Steven. Was this friendship or something more? What did she want it to be?

She thought about that question almost the entire way down the mountain. Once they slid down the rock face, they did a slow jog back to the parking area, and they covered most of that ground in companionable silence, giving her lots of time to think. What she came up with was this: It was time to reimagine the coming year. She could take the opportunity to explore those areas of her life she'd neglected in her single-minded pursuit to become a doctor—and that included her love life. She'd still chase the dream, but she was ready to open herself up to a little romance, and that meant it was also time to come clean with Shelly about her real feelings for Steven.

Of course, before that could happen, they'd have to clear the air with one another. It shouldn't be a big deal, but Heidi dreaded it anyway. They'd had plenty of fights before, but usually it was Heidi doing the forgiving. She wasn't used to being the one in the wrong.

Once the two of them made peace, she'd tell Shelly how she felt about Steven, and then, after that, maybe she could talk to Steven about her feelings. The thought of it made her stomach do somersaults. What if he didn't feel *that way* about her? She didn't want to make things weird between them.

As for coming clean with Shelly, it would really be more of a formality than anything else. She likely already knew Heidi's true feelings but had been content to play along so she could get what she wanted, but this time Heidi needed to assert herself. She had a take-charge personality, but when it came to competing with her twin over a boy, she'd sort of always rolled over and played dead, letting Shelly call all the shots. This would definitely be a first, and Shelly might be surprised and maybe even a little miffed, but she'd come around. Especially since she would be eager to get things back to normal between them. Heidi figured she might as well use that to her advantage.

The truth was, she wanted to see where this thing with Steven might go. She'd been fighting against it, but she knew deep down she was looking for more than friendship with him, and now she had the time to test the waters. Still, a question nagged at her. What if he was like everybody else, and he chose Shelly? Heidi didn't think she could take another rejection right now. It would sink her.

Chapter 15

Steven glanced surreptitiously at Heidi for the umpteenth time as he drove the twisty, windy country road back to Nicolet from Mt. Joliet. She was his friend, he reminded himself.

Friend. He and Heidi were just *friends.*

And, really, he should be grateful. It hit him today that, so far, Heidi had proven herself to be one of the best friends he'd ever had—hands down. They shared similar interests. She was a good listener and a great conversationalist, in spite of how she viewed herself in that regard. She was quiet, but interesting. Smart too. A real go-getter, and so, so sweet.

As fun and lively and . . . well, *hot* as Shelly was, lately it was Heidi Steven found himself thinking about in the quiet hours of the night. But Shelly was the one putting out all the signals. Heidi . . . well, Heidi he still wasn't completely sure about. Her signals were mixed, at best. And it didn't matter anyway.

They were just friends.

But . . .

And there it was, the equivocation he should have known would come. Who was he kidding? He liked Heidi. A lot. And what if she liked him too? Now that she wasn't going off to medical school that year, or—as Steven couldn't help but hope—ever, maybe she'd be open to something more with him. If Steven got a permanent job at Chester, well, then who knew what could happen between them?

He sighed. He was doing it again.

"What's wrong?" Heidi looked concerned.

Steven started. "What do you mean?"

"You sighed," she pointed out.

He thought fast. "Sorry. I was just thinking about work. Hoping I can stay on and all that." This much was truthful, at least.

"They'd be lucky to have you," Heidi said loyally.

"Thanks." He smiled at her, wishing he could reach down and hold the hand that rested on top of her tanned, glorious legs. The Lakanen twins had been gifted with the best legs he'd ever seen on a woman. He could stare at those legs all day. Instead, he brought his gaze back where it needed to be—on the road.

Steven knew he couldn't be the first man in the world to walk this tightrope with identical twin sisters. Maybe someone had written about it. It'd be really great if there was a manual floating around out there somewhere that he could read to get a few tips, as well as to reassure himself that everything he was experiencing was normal. Because the truth was, he was still attracted to both, and that just felt . . . wrong.

He was *more* attracted to Heidi based on how they clicked on an intellectual level, but somehow he knew he and Shelly could also fit. There was so much more to her than all that outward confidence and attention-seeking seductiveness. He saw underneath all that. She reminded him of one of those Russian nesting dolls. Those colorfully painted wooden ones that opened up to smaller and smaller dolls until you reached the center. She had more layers than an onion, and he hoped someday she'd find somebody who would understand the rare treasure they had in her and take the time to peel all those layers back. A part of him had wondered, from time to time, if he was that guy.

His thoughts about the girls confounded him, and he was an engineer. He was supposed to be at least marginally intelligent, but he didn't feel smart when it came to the Lakanen twins. To be honest, he felt a bit like a lady killer, a mack daddy, and he didn't like it. He couldn't stand guys like that. He was a one-woman-at-a-time kind of man. And while it was true that it was mostly Heidi he thought about these days, Shelly was there in the periphery of his mind too, and it'd be a lie if he said she wasn't.

It didn't help that Shelly always came on so strong. She seemed intent on letting him know she was his for the taking, but the way he felt about Heidi, he was going to have to shut her down, and maybe sooner than later.

It would be a whole lot easier to let her down gently by saying he wasn't looking for a relationship and needed to remain friends with them both. But how could he tell Shelly he wasn't interested because he wanted to date her sister? Something like that would have to be executed very carefully. It was important to get it just right, to get it *perfect*, because he could not drive a wedge between twin sisters, and he cared about these particular twins too much to cause any kind of trouble between them. Briefly, Steven wondered if he could talk to Sepi about this. He wasn't sure.

For the moment, he consoled himself with the knowledge that Shelly was what Gran would have called a *gadabout*. She definitely wore rose-colored glasses, and layers or no layers, she was just about as fun-loving as a person could get. Someone like that couldn't feel too badly for too long about anything—not because she was shallow, but simply because she was a glass-half-full kind of person. Most likely, she'd move on in a week. Two at the most.

Even if it was possible he'd created a bit of a mess, Steven couldn't feel sorry about it. He believed in signs, and Heidi sticking around now instead of taking off to Minnesota felt like a sign to him, and he couldn't ignore it.

He glanced at her again and found her studying him. She blushed and graced him with her soft smile, biting down on her lower lip before looking away. Steven felt that now-familiar tug in his chest. That look, that was all the encouragement he needed from her.

Soon. He'd make a move soon.

The Lakanen house smelled divine, and Steven's mouth watered the moment he walked through the door behind Heidi.

"Are you sure they won't mind us coming to the table like this?" he asked uncertainly, stealing a quick sniff of his armpits without Heidi noticing and feeling relieved that at least he didn't stink. Gran had always insisted that he be washed up for dinner as a boy, and the rule hadn't changed as he'd grown into a man.

Heidi laughed. "Don't worry. We aren't formal over here. So long as we have our shirts on, we're fine."

Steven knew she must be referring to the "No Shirt, No Service" policy enforced by restaurants and stores, but he couldn't help the image of a shirtless Heidi sitting across from him at the dinner table. That would be a dinner he'd never forget—a feasting of the eyes. Steven slammed those eyes shut in an effort to erase the image. It was fitting they were having pork tonight because he'd just determined himself to be a total pig.

"It's too quiet in here," Heidi said, looking around from side to side as they entered the kitchen. "Where is everyone?" She turned to Steven in puzzlement.

Steven shrugged. The table was set, and even the milks were poured. That was one of the many idiosyncrasies he'd noticed about Sepi Lakanen. Because his mother had had brittle bones, he insisted his girls drink an eight ounce glass of milk every night at dinner. He liked to quote the dairy commercials to them when they complained. He'd hold up an index finger and say, "Milk. It does a body good." Giving Heidi a quick once-over, Steven had to agree.

He took a deep breath. Pork indeed. He might as well start snorting.

"Hello?" Heidi called out. "Mom?"

Steven heard Maggie's distant voice answer through the sliding glass door. "Out here!"

"Oh, they're on the deck," Heidi told him over her shoulder, leading the way to the screen door.

She pulled the slider halfway and stopped. "What—?"

Steven peered over her shoulder and saw Sepi, Maggie, and Shelly on the back deck with plastic champagne glasses in hand and a congratulations banner rolled out behind them, hanging from the railing.

"What's going on?" Heidi asked her family before glancing back at Steven in bafflement.

"Come on out here, daughter, and we will tell you," Sepi directed with a beaming smile. He looked behind her and noted Steven's presence. "You too, Steven. Sit tight everyone. I'll pour another glass."

"What in the world are we celebrating?" Heidi asked again, turning to Maggie. "Mom?"

Maggie smiled with tears in her eyes and shook her head silently while Sepi poured and handed glasses to Heidi and Steven.

Steven thought he knew—feared he knew—exactly what was going on, but Heidi appeared to be completely in the dark. Maybe he was wrong. He was ashamed to admit he hoped he *was* wrong.

Maggie placed one hand over her heart. "Shelly asked to be the one to tell you. We called her at work, and she came home. We all wanted to be here."

Heidi's eyes were wide. She looked almost scared when she asked, "Tell me what?"

Steven looked at Shelly, who took two steps forward so that she was standing directly in front of her sister. Steven was positioned on one side of the twins, and their parents, arm in arm, were on the other.

With her free hand, Shelly reached out and touched Heidi's face in a small caress before she opened her mouth to speak. No words came out. Instead, a single tear tracked its way down her left cheek while she swallowed several times.

When she finally spoke, her voice was strained with emotion. "You have always wanted good things for me, Heidi, even if it meant you got the short end yourself. Remember switching with me in sixth grade band? You took that awful tuba I got assigned to and gave me your violin. And when we turned twelve? Our bikes? I still cringe when I think about that. How could I have thrown such a fit over a color? But you switched with me then too. And Ricky Massier in the ninth grade. Remember him? Because I do. I remember it all.

"It's been like this from the time we were little. Don't think I haven't noticed. You're the selfless sister, and I—" Shelly's voice broke, and she swallowed again, twice, before continuing, "I've been the selfish one."

Heidi looked ready to argue, but Shelly shook her head again. "No, it's the truth, and we both know it. I don't want things to be that way anymore. I want good things for you, Heidi, even if those things aren't necessarily good for *me*." Shelly paused and took Heidi by the hand, giving their joined hands a small swing.

"Today Mom took a call from Mayo's medical school." Heidi's eyes, which had been resting on their hands, shot up to take in her sister's face. "They had a last-minute withdrawal from the program, and they want you to fill the spot."

Heidi shook her head slowly.

"You got in, Heidi. You got into medical school, and I wanted—" Shelly seemed to choke on her words.

Heidi, whose mouth hung open in disbelief, continued to shake her head. "What is this?"

"Your dream came true." Shelly broke her grasp on Heidi's hand to wipe away another tear. "And I wanted to be the first to congratulate you." Shelly handed her glass to Steven and put both hands on Heidi's shoulders. She looked her sister straight in the eye. "Sincerely," she said before she pulled her sister into a tight hug. "I'm really happy for you. Please believe that."

Heidi returned the embrace with one arm since she still held her glass of champagne.

"Are you serious right now?" she asked over her sister's shoulder.

Shelly didn't respond.

"Shelly, I will absolutely kill you if you're not serious right now," Heidi threatened.

Laughing, Shelly pulled back. "I'm serious. Ask Mom."

Heidi looked to Maggie. "Mom?"

Maggie appeared ready to burst with pride. "It's true, honey. I took the call myself." She squealed. "Congratulations! Your father and I are so proud."

"So proud," Sepi echoed, and the two of them drew their daughter in for hugs from them as well.

Standing very still and very rigid, Steven continued to hold both his glass and Shelly's as the family in front of him hugged and celebrated the news. He felt like an interloper, and a wretched one at that, because he could not, no matter how much he might try, make himself feel completely happy about this unlikely turn of events.

His reaction disappointed him.

This was all Heidi had ever wanted. He should be one hundred percent happy for her, but he couldn't be. This was the kiss of death for a relationship that had very nearly been and now would never be. How could he mourn the loss of something he'd never had? But he did. It was a shot to the heart. He'd already made plans for the two of them.

When Heidi turned to him, Steven quickly flashed her a smile, but it must not have been quick enough. Who knew what she'd seen in his unguarded expression? He hoped not everything, but when her smile faded and she met his eyes, he could see she understood at least some of what he'd been thinking.

They stood that way, gazing at each other in silence. Sepi and Maggie seemed to know they needed a moment, because they excused themselves and went inside the house with the explanation that they would need a few minutes to put dinner on. Even Shelly, with an almost comical expression of dawning realization as she looked back and forth between the two of them, mumbled something about helping out with dinner before taking her glass out of Steven's hand and leaving them on the deck alone.

Heidi was the first to break the silence. She gestured to Steven's glass. "You haven't had your champagne."

Steven looked down at his full glass and then at hers. "We forgot the toast, I guess," he said, keeping his voice light. He worked to pull up the corners of his mouth.

Heidi returned his smile with a similar effort. She seemed stunned. "I can't believe this! It doesn't seem real. Maybe . . . maybe it's not real. I mean, you're right, we didn't even toast."

Steven swallowed hard. His face ached from the effort of forcing this prolonged smile. It felt fake, more like a grimace. He only hoped it didn't look like one. "It's real, I promise. Listen, congratulations, Heidi. I know how much you wanted this. You've worked so hard to get here. Been so driven. You deserve it."

"Thanks. I just—I can't believe it. I feel like any moment somebody's going to call and say, 'Oops, we made a mistake. Just kidding. You're still a loser.'"

Steven shook his head. "You could never be a loser. Everything about you shines."

Heidi tipped her head to one side, her warm, amber eyes looking intently into his. "That's . . . so nice. Thank you, Steven."

He looked down at his feet for a moment before forcing his gaze back to hers. "Well, it's the truth. I've never met anyone like you, and I doubt I ever will again."

Heidi was silent as she stared at him, and his heart thrummed in his chest. This might be the closest he ever got to telling her how he felt about her, but he saw it had been enough. She'd heard the unspoken words—he could see it in her widened eyes—and he waited for what she might say in return.

But then Heidi broke eye contact, and the moment passed. "Listen, let me just go in quick and tell my mom to add a plate to the table. She probably already—"

Steven interrupted her with a small shake of his head and tried to keep the disappointment from his voice when he said, "That's okay. Tonight you should eat as a family. I'll come for dinner another time."

Heidi took a step towards him. "But—"

"Really." He held up his left hand. "I would feel like I was intruding, even if you all swore up and down I wasn't."

She protested again.

Steven held his ground and worked to maintain a smile. "It's okay, honestly. I've got some leftovers from 906 Pizza in the fridge that need to get eaten. You know how I love pizza. I'll be fine. I'll just kick up my feet and relax tonight. I'm tired from that run anyway, so it'll feel good."

"Well, okay," Heidi conceded. "If you're sure."

"I'm sure. But thanks for the invite. And again, congratulations."

"Thanks, Steven." Heidi smiled back uncertainly.

Giving the Lakanens time as a family had absolutely been the right thing to do, but eating cold pizza in front of the television wasn't Steven's idea of a great evening. *Tombstone* was playing, and for a while it held his interest, but once his last slice of pizza was gone, his mind began to wander, and he clicked off the TV with the remote before setting it down next to his empty plate on the coffee table.

Eating dinner alone was something Steven hoped he wouldn't have to do too often in the future. He craved the rich connection of a family gathering together around the kitchen table for the final meal of the day. Sharing stories, making jokes, even talking politics. The Lakanens had given him a taste of what that was like, and now that he'd experienced it, he knew he could never be truly happy without it.

Steven gave a hefty sigh and ran a hand through his hair—he needed a shower. He got up to do just that when he heard a faint knock at the door. A peek behind the curtain revealed Shelly standing there on the landing. He groaned softly but opened the door anyway.

"Hey," she said. "You done with dinner?"

He forced a smile. "Yep. How was the pulled pork?"

She shrugged. "Fine." She looked over his shoulder into the apartment. "Can I come in?"

Steven hesitated, but only briefly, and Shelly didn't seem to notice. "Sure," he said, opening the door further and inviting her in. Once he closed it behind her, he followed her into the apartment. She stopped at the kitchen counter and rested her hands there as she surveyed the small space.

"It's nice up here, isn't it?"

"It's great," Steven agreed. He studied her for a moment. She didn't look sad, but he knew she must be. He was about to ask her, but she beat him to the question.

She spoke tentatively. "How are you?"

"I'm well, thanks," he answered with an exaggerated politeness that might have made them both laugh at any other time. Now, however, they studied each other with an air of solemnity that had rarely, if ever, existed between them. "How are *you*?" he asked her.

She shook her head. "No, Steven. How are you really?"

He examined her face further, and he could see what she was really asking. Did he play dumb on this or come clean? It seemed pointless to pretend he wasn't feeling what they both knew he was. Deciding to be honest without giving everything away, Steven said, "I guess you probably understand better than anyone else what I'm feeling, not that it even compares to what you must feel yourself. This must be hard."

Shelly nodded and glanced down at her hands. Her fingernails were painted a bold red, and she tapped them lightly on the Formica countertop. "It is. I thought it might be like that for you, but I wasn't sure if you and Heidi had . . ." She trailed off, leaving the unspoken words to linger there, charged, in the space between them. She caught his gaze and held it.

Steven heard her loud and clear and set her straight. "Nothing's happened, if that's what you mean."

"Oh." Her relief was obvious as she sagged against the counter and smiled.

He was quick to add, "But it's true that I wondered if something might."

Her smile did a slow fade. "Oh," she repeated, straightening her posture once more. Sometimes, she was an open book, this woman. One look at her face and he could almost *see* what she was thinking. Even right now, it was obvious. She was deciding how best to pry without seeming to pry. Steven, in spite of himself, grinned as he watched her trace circles on the countertop with her red fingertips. Finally, she settled on what to say. "*Hoped*, you mean."

Steven raised his eyebrows in question, the small smile still playing on his lips.

"You didn't *wonder* if something might happen. You *hoped* it would," she clarified.

Steven cocked his head to one side before admitting it. "Yeah, okay. Hoped."

Shelly pressed her lips together. "You know, Steven, I'm not used to being . . . overlooked."

Steven cursed at himself silently. This is what he'd been hoping to avoid. He'd known better, and he was annoyed with himself now to find himself in this position. "Shelly . . ."

"Oh, I'm not trying to make you feel bad or anything," Shelly explained, speaking quickly. "I'm just being honest. Men tend not to choose Heidi. I've always wondered why. They always choose me instead." She shrugged. "That's just how it's always been. And you know what, I'm always glad when they do."

Steven's annoyance quickly redirected itself at Shelly. He didn't like what this conversation was revealing about her—a hubris he hadn't realized she was capable of. The edge in his voice was barely concealed when he asked, "Yeah? And why's that?"

"Because if they can cast Heidi aside like that, it means they aren't good enough for her anyway. I've always figured it's win-win. I get to have a little fun, and Heidi gets to be spared from all the fools out there. I know how to handle them. She doesn't."

People rarely surprised Steven. He must have a sixth sense or a good B.S. detector, or something, but what Shelly had just revealed shocked him. She'd faked him out a second ago. It wasn't hubris at all. Instead, it was a somewhat sweet but completely misguided attempt to protect her sister. Good-Time-Shelly was showing her depth again. But she didn't really use flirtation to filter out the riff raff for her sister, did she?

An uncomfortable thought took shape in his mind. Silently, he tried to sort it all out. On the one hand, misguided as it might be, finding out that Shelly had her sister's best interest at heart when it came to men was sort of touching, but on the other, a question burned: Was that what she had been doing with him all along? Had it all been fake with her? There was no way to know for sure unless he asked.

"What are you saying? You ran a, sort of, interference for Heidi with men?"

She didn't hesitate. "Yes."

Steven wrinkled his nose in distaste. "Don't you think that's a little ... over the top?"

"No," she denied slowly. "I've helped weed out the losers so Heidi doesn't have to waste her time on them."

Steven's nostrils flared. "*Losers*, huh?" He shook his head. "Nice. So, that's what you thought I was? A loser?"

Shelly's mouth fell open, and she took a step toward him. "Steven, no! I—"

"Oh, come on! You have to admit—you were laying it on pretty thick. Were you just testing me and having yourself a little fun while you were at it?"

Shelly's eyes were wide as she stared back at him. At least she had the grace to look sheepish. "It's not—Steven, I think I misspoke. It wasn't—"

"Shelly," Steven interrupted again. He couldn't stand here for another minute with her. He was cooked. Felt too much all at once. Wounded pride, disappointment, regret, annoyance, anger ... and a whole bunch of other emotions he couldn't name.

It was time for Shelly to go. He didn't trust himself at that moment not to say some very choice words he wouldn't be able to take back later.

"I need to ask you to leave."

"Steven!" she protested in bewilderment. "You've misunderstood. It was never ..."

But something in his expression must have gotten through to her because she put up a hand and nodded her head. "Okay," she agreed with suspiciously shiny eyes. She moved towards the door and mumbled something that sounded like *twice in one day.*

"What?" he snapped.

She turned back and gave him a sweet, sad smile, making him feel about an inch tall. "Nothing. I'm sorry, Steven. I'll go now. But this isn't done. We're talking about this tomorrow."

"Sure, fine," Steven replied. Anything to get her to leave.

"Heidi has to work, but I'm off. You're not working tomorrow, right? It's Saturday."

"I'm not working," Steven answered stiffly, although now he wished he was. He still hadn't moved from his spot behind the counter. Gran would have told him to see her out. He didn't budge.

"Okay. Tomorrow then."

She gave him one last regretful glance before she let herself out of the apartment.

Chapter 16

It had been a truly awful day, Shelly reflected as she walked slowly back to the main house from Steven's apartment. She was short on sleep from the night before, and she'd felt sick to her stomach from the moment Heidi kicked her out of her room that morning. Now, after having just been kicked out of Steven's apartment too, she was well and truly nauseated. Of course, it didn't help that her churning belly was now filled up with pork and coleslaw. She'd pretended to have an appetite throughout dinner, and she'd smiled and laughed with her family as though she were just fine with Heidi leaving. But she wasn't. Not by a long shot.

※

All she'd wanted to do after dinner was hide away in her bedroom, but instead she'd sat with Heidi on the couch and faked a happiness and excitement for her sister she definitely didn't feel. The two of them were back on track, at least.

"I'm sorry I flew off the handle at you this morning," Heidi had apologized.

"It's okay. I deserved it."

"No. You didn't deserve it. You were trying to do something nice for me. I was upset, and I took it out on you. You can't help how you felt. I know that."

Shelly worked at a smile.

"And I know," Heidi went on, "that even though you're trying hard not to show it, you're not cool with this. With me leaving. You can't change how you feel, and you know, I wouldn't want you to try."

A big part of Shelly wanted to admit just how *not cool* with this she was and throw herself into her sister's arms and cry. But she'd been doing that her entire life. It was time for her to stand on her own. Heidi's arms would be in Minnesota from here on out, along with the rest of her. The other half of herself was moving two states away, and all Shelly wanted to do was howl her sadness at the moon. Instead, she swallowed and admitted, "Yes, I'm sad. But I really am happy for you too. I can be both things at once."

"I know that. And I feel both things too. I want to take you with me. If I thought you'd come, I'd ask."

Shelly reached down and squeezed Heidi's hand. Heidi glanced down at their interlocked fingers. "Do you think you ever would?" Heidi asked tentatively.

"Ever would what?"

Heidi slanted her head. "C'mon, Shelly. Would you ever consider going with me? You'd have to finish up school first, I know, but after that. We could be roommates. You could find a job there. Probably a pretty good one too. Rochester is three or four times the size of this place."

Shelly bounced their hands a few times before answering. "Heidi, you know I can't leave here. I'd shrivel up and die in a landlocked city."

Heidi nodded, not answering right away. "I know," she said finally. "I guess I hoped you'd consider giving it a try. For me."

"You know I love you more than anyone, and that won't ever, ever change, but this place is *it* for me. I belong here. I've gotta say, though, it makes me feel better that you want me to go. At least I know I'm not the only one of us who's sad."

Heidi nodded again. "My stomach's all in knots over it, to be honest. Even though I definitely want to go. It's all I've ever wanted, but leaving you is . . . it hurts."

"I know." Shelly knew her sister had already known the answer before she asked Shelly to go. This had been one last-ditch effort for Heidi to have her cake and eat it too.

As if on cue, Heidi said, "You know, I haven't thanked you for the donuts. They were really good."

"So you had some, then?"

"No. I had them all."

Shelly stared at her incredulously. "You ate all those donuts?"

"Mm hmm. Every last crumb."

Shelly grinned widely. "My sister the glutton! How fun!"

"It *was* fun, but I won't be able to look at an apple fritter for a long time."

"I didn't think you even liked apple fritters."

"I don't. And now I *really* don't."

Shelly let out a few short pig snorts, and the two of them dissolved into laughter. But even laughing, Shelly was fighting tears. She'd taken moments like these for granted all her life.

Looking up at movement in the doorway from the kitchen, Shelly saw Maggie and Sepi peering in at them. Both smiled and shook their heads before turning back to the kitchen table, where they were playing a game of scrabble.

The next hour and a half was spent on the couch together. Shelly listened as Heidi went on and on about all her plans and how she'd have to leave soon for orientation. There was so much for her to do to get ready. She needed to find a place to stay. She needed to give her notice at the club. She needed to make an appointment at the bank with their parents so they could co-sign on her loan.

Shelly had done her best to appear excited about it all, but the forced cheerfulness quickly zapped her of her energy. Before she could follow her sister off to bed, however, Shelly had needed to check on Steven.

Heidi had avoided any talk of him, but Shelly knew he must be on her sister's mind, just as he was on hers. Shelly had seen the stricken look on his face when he heard the news, and she thought it might help them both if they could commiserate about it together.

Well, she'd completely botched that plan, and it was with a heaviness that she descended the steps from Steven's apartment. Instead of helping Steven and feeling better herself, she'd upset him, gotten kicked out of his apartment, and made herself even sicker. Good intentions were blowing up in her face today.

It didn't help that she'd had another bad day at work, or more accurately, she'd had a bad moment at work—a frightening one that left her feeling unsettled. Thinking of it now, alone in the dark driveway, it made her shiver, and she quickened her steps towards her lit-up house as she shoved the memory out of her mind.

Chapter 17

Heidi sat in front of the huge windows that spanned, floor to ceiling, the entire front side of the clubhouse. She occupied a chair at one of the many empty tables in the restaurant and watched the rain come down in sheets. It was so heavy, she couldn't even make out the men's tee on the first hole.

It had been like this, without letting up, since she'd awoken that morning, and the club was dead. Dot, the clubhouse manager, had jumped at the chance to head home and chain-smoke with her newly retired husband. Talking to Shelly, Heidi knew Dot ditched work often when Shelly was scheduled in the clubhouse, but this was the first time she'd pulled this on Heidi. Probably because she knew Heidi would call her out on it, and normally Heidi would have made a stink, but she was still flying high from yesterday's news. Nothing could upset her today. Plus, it was dead at the golf course because of the weather, and Dot only lived three miles down the road. She'd promised to come back straight away at the first sign of blue sky.

Heidi glanced at her watch. That had been hours ago. It was three o'clock. Five hours to go until the end of her shift. At this rate, the server Dot had called off and put on standby might not need to come in at all. Heidi sighed and looked around her. What else could she do to kill the time? She'd already picked up the women's locker room, run the vacuum through the restaurant, rolled the silverware, refilled all the ketchups, and wiped down all the tables and chairs. She supposed she could tackle the wait station next.

Or she could sit here and wonder about Steven some more. She'd called last night, pretty late actually, to see if he still wanted to run this morning before she had to go to work. He told her he was a little sore from the Mt. Joliet run and was going to take it easy for a few days.

A few *days*? That seemed fishy to her. He hadn't gotten hurt. Hadn't pulled or sprained anything. Why did he need a few days to rest? She was pretty sure she knew the reason. He just didn't want to run with her. Things had gotten awkward in a hurry, and she'd signed off by wishing him a good weekend. Expecting him to say something about seeing one another Saturday or Sunday, she'd been surprised when he'd answered, "Yeah, you too."

It would be a lie to pretend she didn't know what this was all about. Heidi had read it all on his face yesterday. He liked her. She knew that now without a doubt, just like she knew he didn't want her to go to Mayo.

How ironic that the two things she'd wanted most had presented themselves to her at almost the exact same time. Both the Mayo Clinic and Steven wanted her, and it felt great to be chosen by each of them. The trouble was that she could only have one, and really, it was no contest. It wasn't even a choice because there was nothing she wanted more than medical school. Nothing.

But that didn't mean it was easy to let Steven go. Standing there in front of him on the deck, the two of them all alone, she could have said something. She could have at least acknowledged what had been growing between them all these weeks. She could have expressed regret about the timing. But she hadn't, and she was glad she hadn't. Some things were better left unsaid. She'd assumed by avoiding any awkward declarations, they'd be able to continue their runs together, just like always, but now, it didn't look like that would be happening.

Heidi pushed her chair out. These were dead end thoughts. It was time to get busy doing something productive, but before she'd fully stood up, the door at the front entrance jangled.

Who could that be? Maybe some old timer looking for a BLT and somewhere to pass the afternoon. Lenny, the slightly scary, two-hundred-fifty-pound Hell's Angels biker-turned-chef, would probably be happy if he had something to do. Last she'd checked, he was back in the kitchen playing a grumpy game of solitaire—looking bored enough to take up golf himself.

Heidi craned her neck and broke out in a surprised smile when she saw the mystery patron round the corner and enter the restaurant portion of the clubhouse.

"Dad!"

"Hey, Heidi-ho!"

After rushing to greet him, she gave him a tight hug. "What are you doing here?" she asked, stepping back.

He still held her by the shoulders. "I came for a nice game of golf, of course."

Heidi raised her eyebrows and placed a hand on her hip.

"Okay, okay. Even if it weren't raining like Esther's fanny, you know I can't golf."

"That is the weirdest expression." She shook her head with a smile. Her father claimed this was a cleaned-up version of a common Finnish idiom about heavy rainfall. It made no sense to Heidi, but then neither did "raining cats and dogs," she supposed.

"Are you hungry?" she asked, wiping raindrops from his coat. "I can get us an order of fries to share."

Sepi looked surprised. "Fries, eh? You feeling a bit splurgy?"

"Sometimes an occasion calls for that. Right?"

He inclined his head. "As you say, daughter. Though, I don't wait for occasions. Just do not tell your mother."

"Oh, that's right!" What had she been thinking? Her dad really shouldn't be eating fries, not with a heart like his, but it was too late to reverse course now.

He was wagging his finger at her. "Don't you dare suggest carrots and ranch instead. I now have my heart set on fries. You cannot take that away."

She gave a long-suffering sigh. "Dad . . ."

"If she asks, you have my permission to tell your mother. But if she does not . . ." He mimed zipping closed his lips. "Mum's the word."

A small laugh escaped between Heidi's pursed lips. "Whatever you say." She shot him a smile before heading back towards the kitchen. "Pick any table you want. I'll be right back," she called over her shoulder.

After putting in their order with Lenny, who didn't appear in the least bit thrilled to be put to work after all, Heidi grabbed a ketchup and two bottles of coke from the back fridge and got out of there as quickly as possible. How Shelly liked this guy, Heidi would never understand. She herself had disliked him immediately. Shelly accused her of being "judgy," but Heidi knew it wasn't that at all. Shelly was far too trusting, while Heidi saw people for what they were, and Lenny was bad news. All those tattoos! He was probably tattooed from head to toe.

As Heidi returned to the dining area, she spotted her dad seated in the chair she'd occupied not a few minutes before. Her stride faltered, and she stood and observed him for several seconds without his knowing. His tweed flat cap, as familiar to her as her own shadow, now rested on the table and had left his hair in a slightly disheveled state. Perhaps because of that, or maybe because of his slumped posture, he looked older to Heidi than he ever had before, and she had to fight a sudden urge to weep. It was just like at his birthday party. She loved her father dearly, and she didn't like to think of him aging. And now . . . she was leaving him.

How could she do it? How could she go away and leave her entire family? If she stayed here, she could make the most of each and every day with them. If she left, how often would she see them each year? Five times? Ten? Whatever it would amount to wouldn't be nearly enough.

Even though he hadn't fully retired until the age of sixty-five from the bank he managed, Sepi had been an extremely involved and dedicated father. He hadn't ever been impatient with Heidi, not even when it had taken the entire summer after kindergarten to teach her to ride a bike. Unlike Shelly, who had taken off her own training wheels exactly one day after school let out and had never looked back, Heidi took forever to learn to ride her two-wheeler. She was fearful where Shelly was fearless. But Sepi never compared them, and he never pushed Heidi too hard.

Once he'd gotten her to agree to taking off the training wheels, he'd run alongside her, holding a long, leather belt he'd cinch up under her armpits. If she lost control, he'd simply lift her off the bike by the belt and pull her to safety.

It worked like a charm. Gradually, over days and weeks, he released tension on the belt until she was balancing and riding all on her own, and when she wobbled, he tightened his hold to keep her from falling. Sometimes the bike would crash, but Heidi never did. He kept her safe with that belt all summer until, one day, at the end of August, she no longer needed it.

As long ago as that day was, Heidi could still remember her father running alongside her down their long driveway, yelling words of encouragement and praise and grinning from ear to ear. The memory brought an ache to her throat, and Heidi tried to clear it away.

At the sound, her dad glanced in her direction, and seeing her just standing there, he tipped his head in question. She must look silly, suspended like a statue with a bottle of ketchup in one hand and two bottles of pop in the other.

"I don't think I smell bad," Sepi joked from across the restaurant. "Come on over here and join me, Dr. Lakanen."

Heidi smiled and headed his way. *Dr. Lakanen.* She liked how that sounded. "Sorry. I just got to thinking." She set the bottles down on the table and sat across from Sepi. "You don't mind drinking out of the bottle, do you?" she asked. "If I make any more work for Lenny today, he'll give me attitude for a week."

Sepi shook his head, and he pulled his brows down. "That biker?"

"Yeah, that one. Do you want a glass?"

"No, this is fine," Sepi answered, lifting his bottle and taking a swig. He watched her over the top of the bottle as he drank. Giving a satisfied *ah* before setting it down, he asked, "You said you'd gotten to thinking. What were you thinking about?"

"Learning how to ride a bike," she answered. "Remember the belt?"

Sepi looked up at the ceiling and grinned. "Ah, I remember." He continued to stare at the ceiling, lost in thought.

"Dad?"

He met her gaze. "I was just thinking it is a good analogy for what is to come."

"What do you mean?"

"You've been riding with that belt around you, Shelly too, all these years. Independent to a degree, but relying on us to keep you safe. Secure." He put his hands up. "Don't get me wrong, you will always have that as long as I live, but now it is time for you to go, to ride off without me there running beside you and holding you up. If you take a fall and get a little banged up," he bobbed his head from side to side, "you can still come to me and your mother if you need us. But I imagine you will know how to take care of your own scrapes before too long." He laughed. "Soon enough you will know a lot more medicine than that."

Heidi smiled wistfully. She felt the last vestiges of her childhood slipping away. It really was all in the past now. Being a student, living at home ... she'd been lulled into a middle state somewhere between childhood and adulthood. Why did it feel so painful to now be crossing to the other side?

Sepi read her mind. "It is the natural way of things. It is what all parents want for their children, but it will take some getting used to, for all of us. But, daughter, know this. This is the *right* thing. You are on the *right* path. It is what we want for you, no matter what happens. Please go without a heavy heart." He reached a hand across the table.

It appeared blurry to her, as she blinked back her tears, but Heidi took it and held on tightly. *No matter what happens?* What did he mean by that? "I love you, Dad."

"I love you too, Heidi-ho." He squeezed her hand. "All will be well. You will see."

※

It was Sunday morning, and Steven ran the path up Mt. Joliet alone. The four Lakanens would now be in their pew at church, singing some unsingable hymn or another, but Steven had left on his run well before they would have departed for the service. This was the first Sunday in weeks he hadn't gone with them, and he'd set his alarm to make sure he was out of the driveway long before they would leave themselves. It was an avoidance tactic, plain and simple, and Steven had made a deal with himself that it would be his last one. It was time to man up and stop moping.

The path began its gradual climb up the side of the mountain, and Steven made a conscious effort to stand tall, not leaning too far forward, and flexing his hips to drive his knees up.

He filled his lungs with the fresh, warm air. Running was therapy, at least for him. He'd never be able to go days without it, and he felt guilty for lying to Heidi about needing a break. Growing up, he'd been taught never to lie, not even a little white lie, like telling a telemarketer that Gran wasn't at home when she was. His grandmother had always told him that if a person was willing to lie about the small things, nothing would stop them from lying about the big things. Steven wondered what she'd think of the man he'd become. He knew she never expected perfection, which was good because he was far from perfect. But despite his mistakes, he hoped she'd be proud.

He beat out a nice, even cadence with his stride and replayed the conversation with Shelly from the day before. In the end, he'd had to apologize to her. He hadn't allowed her to explain herself Friday night before kicking her out of his apartment. He'd jumped to conclusions because his pride was pricked by what he'd thought she was saying. It probably hadn't helped that he wasn't in the right frame of mind to begin with that night. He'd been a complete ass, and he was grateful Shelly had forgiven him so easily.

Yesterday, Saturday, had been a miserable day. It had rained nonstop, and Steven spent the entire morning and much of the afternoon stuck in his apartment, so when the phone rang with an invitation from Shelly to come to the main house for a cup of coffee and a homemade blueberry scone Maggie had made that morning, he'd agreed—in part because he had a need to get out of his apartment, but he also knew, even before Shelly's explanation, that he owed her an apology. He'd known it within a minute of her leaving on Friday night.

Steven had no idea if anyone else did this, but he always replayed his conversations with people after the fact—dissecting his words and, often, second-guessing himself. He would worry that something he'd said had come out wrong or maybe been misunderstood. He could almost always find something to berate himself over. It was another character flaw to add to his growing list of shortcomings. It came in just below a new one he hadn't even known existed: He was selfish. How else could he explain his reaction to Heidi's wonderful news on Friday? He was unhappy about her success because of what it meant for *him*. His gran would have called him *solipsistic*, but in her sweet, gentle voice, of course.

He heard her voice again now, reminding him that he had a right to his feelings but cautioning him not to wallow in them. After a breakup or some other letdown in life, Gran used to advise him to feel as sad or as angry as he needed to feel. He could pick the duration: an hour, a day, a week, whatever was appropriate for the circumstance. But when that time was up, it was up. Over and done.

Did it always work? Not always. Feelings couldn't just be turned on and off at will. Gran must have known that, but she must also have known that it wasn't an exercise in futility.

Frequently, Steven felt his feelings long past the set time when he was supposed to be "over it," but whenever that designated time came, he always noticed a change in his frame of mind—a positive one—even if it was subtle, and that was what really made all the difference. She was wise, his gran.

Today was Steven's last day to feel what he wanted to feel, guilt-free. To wallow in whatever that was—self pity, maybe. But after today, that was it. He would no longer indulge his disappointment about Heidi. About her leaving.

For today, he could freely explore the "what might have beens" and feel the loss of them, but not tomorrow. And really, he reasoned with himself, it shouldn't take too long to get over once he set his mind to it. It wasn't as if he loved her or anything. That would be pretty crazy. They'd only known each other a few short weeks. There'd been no relationship beyond some chats while they jogged, and when it came right down to it—he worked to convince himself—all he'd really lost was a running partner.

A beautiful running partner. A sweet running partner. A running partner who "got" him.

An irreplaceable one, actually. And that was saying something, considering she had an identical twin. A twin, who it turned out, hadn't been playing with him after all.

Shelly had explained everything yesterday over scones and coffee as the rain fell outside on the deck behind her in fat, steady droplets. Heidi was at work, and Sepi and Maggie had gone for a morning drive. He and Shelly had the house to themselves, and with no one there to overhear them talking, Shelly spoke plainly.

"At the very beginning, I behaved with you like I always do with a new guy who comes around," she admitted. "I could tell you'd caught Heidi's attention. That doesn't happen all that often, by the way, and I did want to 'test' you, as you put it the other night. But it didn't take long to see you weren't at all like the others. I knew it as early as the night of the party. I guess Heidi knew it too."

"What do you mean?"

"What we both know—that Heidi likes you. She liked you from the start. She denied it, of course. She even gave me the green light to move in on you myself the night of my dad's birthday." She smiled unabashedly. "Can't say I didn't try the last few weeks. But you weren't biting, which . . . I mean, that's fine." Shelly shrugged as if to say, "No big deal," but Steven took notice of her heightened color. "Anyway," she continued, "if she hadn't gotten in to Mayo last minute . . . well, who knows what might've happened between you two. But now . . ."

"Yeah," he said, nodding absently, enjoying the small rush he'd felt at having his suspicions confirmed. Heidi did have feelings for him.

The sliver of hope he felt must have shown through, because Shelly looked at him for a long moment and asked cautiously, "You aren't hoping things could still work out for the two of you?"

Steven shrugged. At that moment, he actually was.

Shelly cleared her throat. "Steven, has Heidi talked to you about what kind of doctor she wants to be?"

"She's mentioned radiology a couple times."

Shelly nodded. "And do you know how many years that will take?"

He pursed his lips. "No."

"*Nine* years. When she told me that's what she wanted to do, I looked it up."

Steven's heart sank. "That's . . . a long time."

Shelly sighed. "Don't I know it."

Steven immediately felt guilty. He'd known Heidi for a few weeks. Shelly had known her forever. Which of them was hurting more in this moment? The answer was obvious, and it was time to shift the focus where it should be. "How are *you* doing?"

Shelly chuckled softly. "Not great, actually. But I'm not going to let her see that. I want her to be completely happy."

"That's sweet, but you know this will be hard for her even if you wear a perma-smile between now and the time she leaves this fall."

Shelly laughed. "A perma-smile. Funny."

Steven smiled. "I can be funny, occasionally."

"You sell yourself short, Steven. Everyone at my dad's party was in stitches because of you. You're plenty funny."

He shrugged, pleased as he was on the inside.

"But back to the perma-smile," Shelly said, growing serious. "I know Heidi will be sad to leave us, no matter what we say or do. But I'm going to make it as easy on her as I can. I owe her that. She's the best sister I could have ever hoped for."

"You girls have a special bond."

Shelly exhaled slowly. "We do. I'm going to miss her like I'd miss one of my own limbs if it were suddenly cut off." She fiddled with her empty coffee cup. "Anyway, enough about that. I—listen, what I really wanted to make sure you know . . . the reason I invited you over today, is to make sure you know I wasn't playing with you, Steven. It wasn't a game." She looked up at him and held his eyes. "Okay? You're different. I went about trying to catch your attention in the wrong way, I think."

Steven reached up to scratch a non-existent itch on the back of his head. "Yeah, sure. Okay." Another one popped up on his neck as she continued to stare at him. Maybe she was waiting for him to say something more. "Thanks," he finished lamely.

Shelly's lips curled up in a slow, flirtatious smile. "I've made you uncomfortable."

Steven thought about denying it. Instead, he treated her to a genuine smile back. "Only a little, and honestly, I think you're enjoying it." She threw her head back and laughed, and Steven joined her. It felt good to laugh.

"And listen," he'd said, once they'd grown serious again. "I'm sorry again for how I treated you last night. I was a jerk."

"Yeah, you were," she agreed with a twinkle in her eye, "but I get it, considering how badly I botched what I was trying to tell you."

He knew she wanted him to ask. She wanted to tell him again, to make it perfectly clear what she felt. But Steven already knew.

Monday and Tuesday passed without seeing the Lakanen twins at all. Between his work schedule and theirs, without having made a deliberate attempt to see one another, it hadn't happened. During dinner with Maggie and Sepi Tuesday night, Sepi told Steven, a little too casually, that Heidi would only be working until four o'clock the following day.

"The girls have been working overtime these last two days. Tomorrow, Dot has them staggered so their shifts overlap." He held up a finger like he'd just remembered something. "That reminds me, Maggie. Shelly asked if she could use one of our cars so she can drive herself home. She will have to stay until close with that great, big biker man."

"Oh, Sepi," Maggie admonished. "Be kind."

"Be kind," he repeated under his breath. "I *am* being kind. He's been sniffing around our daughter all summer by the sounds of it. I don't like it. I do not like the looks of him," he said.

Maggie put her fork down. "Why?" she demanded. "Because he has tattoos?"

"Maggie girl, give me some credit. It is not the tattoos, although you know well enough how I feel about *those*."

"What then? I know! Must be all those muscles," she challenged. "I hear they're legendary." She winked at Steven when Sepi didn't answer right away.

After staring off out the window behind Maggie's chair another few seconds, Sepi finally replied, "I don't know. But I don't like it. He is too persistent with Shelly by far, and Heidi doesn't trust him."

"Well, that's Heidi for you. She takes after *you* that way."

Sepi waved her comment off with one hand.

This was the first time Steven had ever heard of the muscled, tattooed Lenny from work, and he looked back and forth between Maggie and Sepi. He had to agree with Sepi on this one. He didn't want this guy sniffing around Shelly either.

He wanted more information, but Sepi turned to him once again and brought the topic back around to where he'd started. "Have you seen the girls recently? You haven't been coming by much since Heidi got her news."

Maggie directed a warning look at her husband, which he pointedly ignored, adding, "We're used to seeing more of you, that's all. We like having you here, Steven."

Steven finished twirling a forkful of spaghetti before answering. "Thanks, Sepi. I like being here."

"I thought so." He studied Steven, and Steven wondered just how much Sepi had thought about the subject.

"You won't have heard the latest news then, I imagine?" Sepi asked, still watching Steven as he chewed that last forkful. Steven shook his head before washing it down with a sip of milk.

"Heidi and I will travel to Rochester on Friday for a weekend of orientation. While we are there, she will find housing and get the lay of the land."

Steven sat back against his chair. "So soon?"

Sepi shot him an understanding smile. "It seems that way, I am sure, but it is really not soon at all. She begins her courses the first Monday of August."

Steven swallowed again to keep his food where it belonged. "That's less than four weeks away," he said.

Maggie smiled gently. "Right around the corner. It'll be here before we know it." She waited for Steven to say something.

"Time flies." It was trite, but true.

"It does," Maggie agreed.

"Listen, Steven," Sepi began, "At the risk of saying too much, I know Heidi would like to see you before we go this weekend. Perhaps some time together might be arranged?"

Maggie's eyes grew wide. "Sepi!"

Sepi threw his hands up. "Well, *someone* needs to open the lines of communication," he said matter-of-factly.

"Well, it doesn't always have to be *you*, you know." She shook her head, wearing a long-suffering smile, and looked apologetically at Steven.

Steven chuckled. "It's fine," he reassured them both. He was actually grateful to Sepi. He hadn't seen Shelly since their talk on Sunday, which definitely was a break from their normal pattern, but he hadn't seen Heidi since Friday, and that was a massive departure for them.

He hadn't called, and she hadn't either. At this point, it would have felt awkward to call her or suggest getting together. Too much time had gone by to just play it cool, and—for him at least—a type of tension had built. Steven imagined the next time they saw each other, they would each feel a little uncomfortable—at least at first. Even so, he was eager to see her again. Sepi seemed to know it.

"It's going to be beautiful tomorrow," Sepi informed him. "Heidi mentioned wanting to spend some time at Sable Rocks. She hasn't been there yet this summer."

"Oh," Steven said in some surprise. "I didn't know she liked it there. I've been there a bunch of times with Shelly, but never with Heidi."

"She likes it there. But not for the same reasons as her sister. Shelly goes for the thrill; Heidi goes for the view."

"It is a pretty great spot," Steven agreed.

"Alright then, it's a date," Sepi proclaimed with a self-satisfied smile.

Maggie rolled her eyes. "You're shameless, Sepi."

He waggled his brows. "It's what makes me so charming."

Maggie fought the grin that threatened to break out on her face. She lost the battle. So did Steven.

"Can I get you some more spaghetti, boys?" Maggie asked, scooting back her chair and standing.

"Maggie girl, you know I can't say no to another helping of your homemade spaghetti." He turned to Steven. "She makes it from scratch, you know."

"The pasta and everything?" Steven asked, impressed.

Instead of answering, Maggie lurched forward, grabbing on to the countertop near the stove. "Sepi!" she called in a panicked voice.

Sepi popped up so quickly, he knocked his chair over. Steven hopped up too and made it to Maggie a second before Sepi was able to hobble over.

"What's wrong? Are you okay, Maggie?" Her face was ashen, and when Steven reached for one of her hands, it was cold and clammy.

"Steven, help me get her down to the floor." Together, the two men carefully lowered Maggie to the tiled floor in front of the stove.

"Another episode, Maggie girl?"

"I'm sorry," she said weakly.

Sepi sat down on the floor, which took some effort, but when he was settled, he lifted Maggie's head, cradling it in his lap before stroking her hair. "And why should you be sorry? Just relax now. You're okay."

Steven crouched down beside them. "Should I call an ambulance?" he asked.

"No. I thank you, Steven. She will be okay in just a minute. Why don't you grab a cold, wet washcloth from the drawer next to the sink."

As Steven went to work getting the tap as cold as possible before wetting the washcloth, he looked back at the couple on the floor. Sepi massaged Maggie's temples. She had her eyes squeezed tightly shut, but Steven was relieved to see some color coming back into her face. After handing the washcloth to Sepi, who folded it and laid it across Maggie's forehead, Steven crouched down once more beside them. "I take it this has happened before?" he asked.

Sepi hesitated. "Well . . ."

Maggie opened her eyes. "It's okay." Sepi looked questioningly at Maggie, raising his eyebrows in surprise. "He's practically family, anyway," she reasoned before closing her eyes once more.

Sepi nodded slowly and addressed Steven. "Maggie is not well."

That much was clear. The question was, how unwell was she, and with what? Steven spoke slowly. "You mean, generally speaking or at the moment?"

"Both, I suppose. We do not have any answers yet, we are waiting on some tests, but it is looking like it might be serious. We spent some time at the hospital the other day. Maggie was having some dizziness and trouble with her vision. They ran a few tests, and then yesterday they reviewed some results with us. In the neurology department."

Steven felt his heart sink. Neurology. That wasn't good. "How serious is it?" he asked softly.

"I do not know. The doctor has his suspicions, but we'll not know for sure until other test results, like the MRI, come back. It has been a lot to take in, and I am not sure I understand it all yet. We should know more by next Thursday. The doctor believes all the test results will be in by then, and he scheduled us for an appointment."

At that, Maggie began to cry softly. Sepi lifted her head slightly, and lifting the washcloth, leaned down to kiss her forehead.

"Maggie, Sepi. I'm so sorry." Steven searched for something more to say. He wished he had some kind of magic words that would bring true comfort, or better yet, fix their situation completely. But he was helpless to make things better for this amazing couple. A couple that, when he really thought it through, he could say he loved, in the truest sense of the word.

"Thank you, Steven my boy."

"Is there anything I can do? Anything at all—big or small?"

Sepi brought a hand to his chin. "There is, actually. Maggie insists I go with Heidi this weekend. I do not want to leave her. I even put my foot down, not that it did any good. You know by now, I am sure, that even though she's a quiet one, my Maggie rules the roost around here."

He chuckled, and Steven smiled.

"We have arranged for her to go and stay with our pastor and his wife for the weekend. They are good friends of ours. You met them at church, of course. The Ruuspakas."

Steven nodded.

"At any rate, they know what is going on, and they know what to watch for. They will keep a close eye on things. Shelly and Heidi think Maggie is going on a little women's retreat. We hate to lie to our girls. This is a first for us. But we do not want them to know yet, Steven. Not until we know more ourselves. They will just worry themselves sick over it. Even once we do know, we may want to wait until Heidi gets settled in Rochester before telling her. If she finds out beforehand, she may not leave here at all. Somehow, she has always felt duty bound to take care of us."

Maggie, eyes open again, reached for Steven's hand and squeezed it. She looked at him beseechingly. "That can't happen, Steven. This needs to stay a secret."

Steven didn't hesitate. "It will. I promise."

Sepi reached over and pressed a hand against the nape of Steven's neck. "Good boy. But if something should happen this weekend—"

"Which it won't," Maggie insisted.

"But if it does," Sepi insisted, "you take care of my girls."

"I will. You have my word."

Chapter 18

"Dad! Why did you do that? I'm twenty-one years old and completely capable of planning my own dates." It was early morning, and Heidi was having a leisurely coffee with her parents before eating breakfast and getting ready for work. Shelly was still snoring away in her bedroom when Heidi had checked on her ten minutes ago. She'd sleep until noon today without Heidi there to get her lazy bones out of bed. While she wouldn't have minded a little quality family time over coffee and breakfast, Heidi had to admit, sometimes it was nice having their parents all to herself. Even if her father was completely exasperating.

"Is that so?" Sepi said with a small, amused smile. He took a slow sip of coffee. "So, daughter, tell me. When was the last time you even laid eyes on Steven?"

Heidi's face grew warm. Her father might have a point, not that she'd give him the satisfaction of admitting it. "He's going to think I put you up to it."

"No. Steven will not think that."

"Yes, he will," Heidi insisted, putting a hand up to her forehead. This was beyond embarrassing.

"Your father's right," Maggie chimed in from her place in front of the stove. She was scrambling up eggs for breakfast. Oddly, her parents had argued about who should make the breakfast, with Sepi insisting Maggie sit and sip her coffee while he scrambled the eggs. To Heidi's recollection, her father had never manned the stove. Not once in two decades. The grill, now that was a different story. Sepi reigned as king over the grill.

In the end, Maggie had smacked him on the butt with the spatula and told him with a wink to get out of her kitchen. She'd sent him on his way into the living room with the mug of steaming coffee he now held. It was his favorite mug. Shelly had given it to him for Father's Day many years ago, and it had *Sisu* written on it in blue cursive.

"Steven knows you weren't behind this," Maggie continued. "He realizes your father is just a meddlesome old man who can't help himself."

"That's right," Sepi agreed with a shameless grin. "And there is no changing my ways at this late date, so you will both just have to come to terms with that."

"Did he seem okay with the idea?" Heidi directed the question to her mother. She was more likely to get a truthful answer from her at this point.

"You know," Maggie said, turning off the stove before walking closer to the living room, where Sepi and Heidi were drinking their coffee. "I thought he seemed relieved. As much as I hate to admit it, your father was on to something. Steven just needed a little nudge."

Heidi nodded, running a hand through her hair. Finding a small knot, she worked to loosen it with her fingers. "Why did you do that, Dad? I mean, I guess I'm glad you did, but what were you hoping to accomplish?"

"I want whatever you want, Heidi-ho."

"But I don't know what I want."

"And you might never know if you don't face it head on and talk to him." Sepi got up with his empty coffee mug and gave her hair a small tousle as he walked past her into the kitchen.

"Hmm," Heidi said in response. She wasn't so sure. Shouldn't she know what she wanted, what she would say, before talking to Steven about it? But she wasn't even the tiniest bit sure of what that might be. Over the last several days, her mind had been filled with thoughts of Steven. She couldn't help it. Somewhere along the way, she'd begun playing with the idea of them being together, and she'd been flip-flopping between an optimism that long-distance relationships did sometimes work and a pessimism of knowing that they usually didn't. Not that it mattered anyway because, technically, she didn't even *have* a relationship yet. And honestly, now would probably be the worst possible time to start one.

It was all so complicated. And when Heidi factored in her sister, those complications only grew. Shelly appeared to like Steven too—*really* like him. Days ago, the day of her acceptance to medical school, her sister had gone to Steven's apartment, but when she came back a short time later, she'd been pretty closemouthed about what had been said, which was odd. Normally, Shelly shared everything with her.

All Heidi knew for certain was that Shelly had been upset, and Shelly didn't get upset over men. Not unless they meant something to her. It left Heidi with an icky feeling. The last thing she wanted was some sort of sick love triangle involving herself, Steven, and her twin sister.

"Heidi," her mother said, breaking into her thoughts. "I do think whatever you and Steven decide about a relationship moving forward, you both need to be honest with yourselves. And with each other. Rochester is seven hours away. You'll be there for . . . a long time. And who knows where Steven will end up? Maybe here, maybe someplace even further away. The stars would have to align just right for this to work." She hesitated. "And then, there's your sister to consider."

Heidi's skin tingled. "Has Shelly talked to you?"

Maggie spoke gently. "She hasn't had to. I have eyes."

Heidi picked up her coffee cup and headed into the kitchen to pour a refill, giving herself time to form a response. "So then you know this is nothing new. Steven's just the latest in a long line of men."

Maggie met her at the coffee pot and put her hand over Heidi's. "Heidi. Lying doesn't become you, dear."

Heidi's face went hot for the second time in a matter of minutes.

She didn't want to talk about Shelly right now. Everything always ended up being about Shelly. Instead, she said, "So what you're basically saying is that it would be a mistake to start anything with Steven now," Heidi clarified somewhat defensively, even though she'd literally just been thinking this very thing herself.

"What I'm saying is there are already several obstacles to any kind of happily ever after with him. Not that it can't happen, but I think you need to go into this grounded in reality."

Heidi rolled her eyes. "You know me better than that. I don't dream of romantic happily-ever-afters. That's Shelly—before she flits on to the next Romeo, that is."

Maggie shrugged. "I would have agreed with that assessment a month ago, but . . ." She raised her eyebrows and looked pointedly at Heidi. "Things change." She began to turn back to the stove, but she stopped herself, adding one last thing. "Just be honest with yourself and with your sister and Steven. That's my advice to you."

"Okay." Heidi filled her cheeks with air and blew it out slowly. "It's actually not bad advice," she admitted.

"I have been around a long time," Maggie said solemnly

"A looooong time," Sepi agreed with a grin. He got up and wrapped his arms around Maggie, holding her for a moment until she gave him a second playful slap with the spatula before turning to dish up the eggs.

Heidi watched her mother sway and grab the handle of the oven door to steady herself, and Sepi returned quickly to her side.

Heidi laughed. "Whoops! Are you okay there, Mom?"

Maggie turned back with an overly bright smile. "Just turned a little too quickly. Showing my age again," she joked. Sepi treated Heidi to an easy smile before he rubbed Maggie's upper arms and whispered something in her ear.

※

Heidi's shift took forever to end. She was just too jittery to enjoy the things about it that she usually did—the fun banter with club members and other staff that usually helped make the hours go by quickly. When Shelly arrived at two o'clock, Heidi had hoped they could work the clubhouse together for a few hours. It was always so much fun to work alongside each other, and the patrons loved it too since they still saw them as something of a curiosity, but Dot had moved Heidi out onto the beverage cart instead.

By the time four o'clock rolled around, Heidi's nerves were fried. She really had no idea what, if anything, she would say to Steven. The easy, cowardly way out would be to just not say anything at all. She thought she knew Steven well enough to know he'd follow her lead on this, whatever that might be.

One thing she did know. She missed him. She missed him terribly.

They hadn't seen each other since Friday. Today was Wednesday. They'd both been doing this little avoidance dance very artfully and very successfully. She wondered if he'd gone back to running in the mornings. She hadn't been out herself, in part because she felt unmotivated to go for the first time in her life, but also because she was afraid of bumping into him out on the trails. Then she'd have to explain why she hadn't called him to go with her. Things between them were so weird now. But she craved his company, even as she so carefully avoided it.

Finally, tonight, this strange sidestepping would end. As nervous as she was now, Heidi knew she'd be relieved when it was all said and done. According to Sepi, they'd be going to the rocks. It was such a beautiful place—perfect for a heart-to-heart, if that's what she decided to do. The black, volcanic rocks made such a striking contrast to the deep blue water of Lake Superior, which extended out on three sides.

It truly was gorgeous, but most people didn't go there to relax. They went for the rush. Heidi had never jumped off the cliffs. Not once in her entire life, and not for lack of pressure from Shelly. Heidi knew Steven and Shelly had gone there multiple times together to do just that. Shelly had even gotten him to experiment with flips off the edge—front and back. The last time they'd been there together, Heidi heard from Shelly that the two of them had an audience as they synchronized their flips. Sable Rocks was *their* place.

Steven was used to having a blast out at the rocks with her fun sister. Out there, the differences between herself and Shelly would be amplified and as obvious to Steven as the stars on a clear night in Nicolet. Her boringness would be a stark comparison to Shelly's adventurous spirit.

She was beginning to rethink the location of this little chat.

When Heidi pulled back into her driveway twenty minutes after four o'clock, Steven's Blazer was already parked below his apartment. He must have gone in early again. Heidi drove slowly past his car and up the rest of the driveway. Her Corolla's AC had kept her so cool, she actually had goosebumps, and when she opened the door, the rush of heat from outside was a welcome change.

It took Heidi only five minutes to get out of her work clothes and into a pair of jean cut-offs and a baby blue cap-sleeved shirt. Once she was ready, she perched herself in front of the front window and watched for Steven to emerge from his apartment. Luckily, the house was empty. As much as she loved them, she didn't want anyone in her family to see her right now. She would have had to pretend she wasn't nervous, and they would see right through it. This way, she could sit here, knees bouncing, fingers tapping while she practiced, out loud, all the things she might say—testing out how they would sound. Only Taro was there to hear her, and he lifted his head off the hardwood floor at the sound of her voice.

"Steven, I think you already know that I really like you, and you know I'm leaving soon. I don't know what will hap—" She shook her head and tried again. "Steven, we've had some really good times these last few weeks, but—" No, she needed to avoid that word. *But* was a terrible word in instances like this, and she wasn't even sure she meant *but*. "Steven, I like you. Even though I'm leaving soon, I thought maybe we could try to ... date each other anyway. I don't know how that would work with the entire state of Wisconsin between us, but—" And there it was again.

But.

She gave up and stared silently out the window. Taro stared at her. It turned out, watched pots *did* boil, and Steven emerged from the apartment within seconds of Heidi's unfinished soliloquy. Her heart jumped up into her throat at the sight of him. He wore a plain white tee-shirt and a pair of army-green shorts. He shouldn't have looked nearly as good as he did dressed so casually.

Heidi took a deep breath and stood. "Wish me luck boy." Taro answered with a small whine before laying his head down again.

Chapter 19

It felt like it had been months since Steven had seen her, when in reality it had only been six days. Six *long* days. It felt good to finally lay eyes on her though he did his best not to stare.

"Hi," he said when she reached his car.

"Hey there," she answered, squinting into the sunshine at him. They looked at each other stupidly for a second. Someone needed to be the one to break the ice. He might as well do it by stating the obvious. "It's been awhile."

Heidi nodded. "Too long."

"I know. I'm sorry about that."

"Don't be. We've both been busy."

So that was how she wanted to play it. Good to know. Steven could pretend everything was normal if that's what she wanted.

"Dad mentioned Sable Rocks, but we can go somewhere else."

"No, the rocks are good. I haven't been there in a while." He dipped his head towards his car. "I can drive."

"Great!" she chirped in a voice higher than usual before she rounded the car to the passenger side and got in.

Steven could smell Heidi's shampoo as he put the key in the ignition. He loved that shampoo. Man, he'd missed her.

"So . . . what have you been up to?" she asked once they'd left the driveway.

Oh, not much, he thought. *Just working really hard not to bump into you.* Out loud, he said, "Not much, just work. You?"

"Same."

Silence.

"Have you been running at all?"

He shifted in his seat before answering. "A few times. You?"

"No."

More silence. And then they both spoke at the same time.

"Steven, I—"

"Listen, Heidi—"

He chuckled.

Heidi smiled. "This is awkward."

Steven felt his body relax as he made a left onto Baraga Avenue. Good. They were going to address the elephant in the . . . car. "It is. I'm sorry."

"Why, though? Why is this so awkward? I mean, nothing's changed, right?"

He met her eyes briefly and treated her to a wry smile.

"Well, nothing's changed *yet*," she clarified.

Steven cleared his throat before speaking. "Your dad says you're heading over to Minnesota this weekend for orientation and apartment hunting."

"Yeah. He offered to go with me. It's all happening so fast now." She peered over at him.

"Are you excited?"

"I really am. That doesn't mean it's not hard, though. This is absolutely, without a doubt, what I want, but it means leaving my family . . . and everyone else I care about." She looked away and out her window.

That last bit was meant for him. He smiled. "What kinds of things will you do during orientation? Do you have a set schedule?"

"Yeah. I got an itinerary sent to me. They pack a lot in. Meet and greets, medical equipment sales for stethoscopes and stuff, parking pass distribution, student organization fairs, that kind of thing. And there's also a ton of information on housing. I'm hoping I can find a good roommate. We'll see."

"What will your dad do while you're busy with all of that?"

She was thoughtful. "I really don't know. He insisted on making the trip with me this first time, though. You know Dad. If he's bored, he won't be for long. He'll find somebody to talk to and spend time with. People always love him right out of the gate."

Steven smiled. "You're right about that."

"He's just like Shelly, don't you think?" She stared at him, awaiting a response.

Steven sensed a trap, so he made a noncommittal *hum* in his throat but otherwise remained quiet. It wouldn't be like Heidi to pick a fight, but he couldn't be completely sure.

Silence continued for the next several minutes until he pulled into the gravel parking area below Sable Rocks. It was unlike their past silences. This one was not the least bit comfortable, at least for Steven, and it was all he could do to keep from squirming in his seat. Even their walk out onto the rocks was done in silence.

Heidi led the way, taking him to a spot a little higher up and off to the side of the area where people typically congregated to chat between jumps. Today, they had the place all to themselves—for the moment anyway. There was always a crowd here, and Steven imagined someone would join them on the rocks before too long.

They sat down, side by side, and looked out over the water. Heidi pulled her knees up and rested her arms and chin on them. "This is such an amazing place," she said after a long sigh.

Steven agreed. "I feel the same way." He watched a bald eagle soar out over the water. He used to point them out excitedly to anyone close by when he would see them, but it turned out they were almost commonplace here, although that took nothing away from their majesty. The locals always stopped to look. They didn't take these beautiful creatures for granted, but Steven knew their reactions were different from his. Spotting them was still a thrill for him, while for them it served to validate what they already knew—they were living in paradise.

Heidi saw the eagle too, and asked, "Can you imagine being able to float on the wind currents like that? What a life. Not a care in the world."

"Hmm. Pretty great," Steven agreed again, still watching. They continued to observe the eagle several seconds more when it suddenly changed course, diving to the surface of the water in a streak of white and brown. At the last minute, it leveled out, its body parallel to the water, and it dipped its talons in.

Steven couldn't believe it. In the blink of an eye, that eagle had scooped up a fish. Right out in front of them.

"Whoa," Heidi said, sitting up at attention. "Did you see that?"

"I did!" Steven watched alertly as the eagle flapped its enormous wings, propelling itself towards them.

"It's going to fly right over us!" Heidi exclaimed.

And it did. Wriggling fish and all. It was one of the coolest experiences of Steven's life, and as accustomed to seeing bald eagles as Heidi was, he could tell even she was euphoric over what they'd just witnessed.

They both turned to watch the retreating form of that regal bird, and when they turned back again to look at one another, each of them was smiling widely. Heidi even had tears in her eyes. Steven completely understood. What a moment. What a gift.

"Wow!" Heidi shook her head in amazement. "I can't believe that! What an awesome thing to see." She met his eyes. "I'm so glad we saw that together." Immediately, her cheeks reddened, and she looked away.

That was enough of an invitation for Steven, and he reached for her hand. He said nothing as he stroked her soft skin with the pad of his thumb. He wouldn't think about what he was doing. He wouldn't worry about what might come next, which at some point he hoped might involve some kissing. But for now, in this moment, he just wanted to sit here, holding her hand.

Heidi broke the silence, and the contact of their hands, after only a few seconds, and the glorious moment passed. It was like a dark cloud settled overhead, and he could sense the change in her even before she spoke.

"Steven, we need to talk," she said, using the take-charge voice he sometimes heard her use with Shelly.

He blew out a long exhale. "I know."

"We've been doing this little ... dance these last few weeks. We haven't moved forward. We haven't moved back. We're stuck, and we haven't even defined what this thing is between us. We haven't said or *done* anything that would indicate ..."

Steven waited, feeling embarrassed. Did she think he couldn't close the deal? He would have loved to, but he was being a gentleman. He was waiting for a signal, a steady signal, from her. He'd moved slowly, sure, but that's because he'd been trying to do the right thing. Was she being critical of that?

She went on. "But I still *feel* this thing with you, and I think you must feel it too."

He locked eyes with her. "I do, yes." So, they agreed on that. The question was whether or not she thought it was a good thing. He couldn't tell, and he waited for her to say something more. Something that would give him a hint about what was going on in her head.

"So, where do you see this going then?" She asked the question casually enough, but her trembling hand gave her away as she swirled imaginary circles into the rocks with a small stick she'd picked up.

"I don't know," he admitted honestly. And then, instead of speaking plainly, laying it all out there and telling her exactly what he wanted, he decided to feel her out by playing a devil's advocate of sorts. "As great as this news has been for you, it does throw a monkey wrench into any plans we may have had with each other. Don't you think?"

It wouldn't have taken much from her to give him hope, and if she'd suggested they try things long distance for a while to see how it all went, he would have jumped at the chance. Not that it would have been his ideal scenario.

But she didn't suggest they make a go of it. Instead, after a long silence, she followed his lead saying, "You're right."

Steven could have kicked himself. He'd gambled and lost. But it wasn't too late. He could fix this. He could still tell her he was willing to try if she was. Who knew what would happen? If things worked out between them, he could find a job closer to her—maybe even right there in Rochester. It might not be his dream job, like Chester was, but he could sacrifice that to be with her, couldn't he? And if it all worked out in the long term, they could always come back to Nicolet together once her training was over. Chester Biotechnologies would still be here.

Yes, plan B was still a good plan. Any plan that included Heidi was a good plan. Why hadn't he started with that? He didn't want to play games with her. He wanted to be open and honest.

He would suggest it now, he decided. Even though he hadn't even kissed her yet, which he'd remedy in a hurry, he'd tell her what he wanted. But before he could get the words out, she spoke words of her own, and his hopes came crashing down.

"You're right, Steven," she repeated, as if working to convince herself. He could see the moment she accomplished that. She gave a decisive nod and continued. "It's not just the distance thing. We've talked a lot on our runs. I know what you're looking for. When I thought this doctor thing might not work for me, I figured maybe I could create a new dream for my life. A dream that, you know, paralleled yours."

Steven was hesitant. "What do you mean?"

"Just that I know you're looking to settle down here. Have a family. I might not ever be ready for that—the family part, I mean."

"You don't want kids?" How had this never come up?

"I'm not sure I do." She shrugged. "Maybe someday. All I know is that I want to be a doctor. People don't get it, but it's all I've ever wanted. It's a need I have. I want to get married eventually, sure. But my work will be my baby, at least for a while. Then we'll see."

Steven was confused. "Wait. So you're saying you do want kids, but just not until you finish your program?" Anyone listening would probably wonder why he was fixating on kids with a woman he hadn't even gotten to first base with, but he knew why. It was important for him to know where she stood on children. On family.

"I'm saying I don't know. I need to focus on one thing at a time, I think."

And that one thing was medical school. Not a relationship. Not building a future with him. Steven's ears rang. Talk about putting the cart before the horse! He'd been halfway to having himself married off to Heidi in a few years' time, and he hadn't even known she might not want that at all.

Heidi was single-minded in her focus, and it didn't include him. Sure, she'd toyed with the idea of *paralleling* his dreams, whatever that meant, when she thought her own dream might be dead in the water. And she'd spoken of need just now. Well, Steven could understand that perfectly because he had a need too.

Growing up, he'd always wanted what his best friend had. Ben, the middle of three kids, had a family similar to the Lakanens, and as much as they included him in things, he'd always felt like he was on the outside looking in. And as much as he loved the Lakanens, it was the same with them. He had a need for a family of his very own. Heidi didn't feel that way, probably because she'd never experienced the lack of it.

What an idiot he'd been. He was furious with himself. *Friends.* If he'd stuck to that, he wouldn't be in this extremely uncomfortable, thoroughly painful situation now. He was such a fool.

He pulled back from her—not physically, but emotionally. It wasn't anything that could be observed, but he felt it as sure as he felt the sun on his face. He knew how to shut off emotions. Kids who were abandoned by their parents learned that at a young age. He turned on the autopilot, switching the subject away from their relationship, away from Heidi's plans, talking instead about the work he was doing at Chester. He knew she loved hearing about that, and it would distract them both.

"Why did you tell him all that?" Shelly asked later that night, an incredulous look on her face. "It's weird to be discussing kids and marriage like this when you aren't even dating, and now you've sabotaged any chance of that happening. And for what? I mean, there's no way you could know what you might want in a few years. People's plans change all the time. That's why you date someone in the first place. To see if you're compatible. I just . . . I really don't get this at all."

Heidi buried her head in her hands. She didn't get it either. They were both sitting cross-legged on Shelly's bed. It was ten o'clock, but the sky was still light. Lifting her head to gaze out the window to where the lake met the horizon, she was reminded that Shelly had the best view in the entire house.

Heidi loved how long the days were this time of year. Nicolet was far enough north and far enough west in the Eastern Time Zone to give them hours and hours of daylight during summer months.

"You're not answering me," Shelly pointed out, eyebrows raised.

"Did you ask a question?"

Shelly lifted both brows.

"I'm sorry. I'm not trying to dodge anything. I honestly don't know what happened. The words just started coming out of my mouth. And I really was open to moving forward with him. I even practiced telling him that. He's the best guy I've ever met, but maybe it's best it worked out the way it did."

She picked at a hangnail, and Shelly observed her silently.

"I have to face facts. I'm leaving, and soon. The timing is all wrong. I'm going to be swamped with my classes and studying. It's probably for the best that I don't start anything with Steven now. Mom was right. She said I needed to be honest. I guess that's what I'm doing."

Shelly shook her head. "I don't think you are. I still don't get it. You liked him. I backed off . . . as much as I was capable of"—she looked sheepishly at her sister—"because I knew that."

"I'm sorry. I wasn't trying to play games."

"So you don't have any feelings for him anymore? Romantic ones, I mean?" Shelly asked, studying Heidi carefully.

Heidi felt a rising heat in her face and neck. She knew exactly what Shelly was getting at, and she had to push down a possessiveness of Steven that she had no right to feel. "I still feel things, but it can't go anywhere, so I'll try not to think about it. If I focus on school, on what's coming, I'll hardly think of him at all."

"Don't you think he deserves better than that?" Shelly asked.

"Oh, I know he does. He deserves the best," Heidi agreed. Too late, she realized Shelly had her right where she wanted her. She waited for it.

"Heidi, I like Steven too."

And there it was. She wanted permission to move in. Again.

"You like everyone."

Shelly laughed. "Steven's different. I know it's probably weird to ask you this, it's weird to even think it, but I'd like a chance with him if you're not going to take yours."

Heidi pressed her lips together.

"It's not like you guys dated or *did* anything, but if you say no, if it seems too gross, both of us liking the same guy, then that's it. I won't try anything with him."

"If I say no, you'll leave it alone?" Heidi asked. It was her turn to study Shelly's face. She could see her sister meant what she said. There was a determination in her eyes as well as something else. Compassion, maybe.

"I'll leave it alone."

Heidi treated her sister to a tight smile. It was all she could manage. This hurt more than she would have imagined it could. But Steven didn't belong to her. She had no right to make any demands about who he did or didn't date. It would be wrong for her to reject Steven and then tell Shelly she couldn't have him either. She'd be like one of those toddlers who wouldn't let anyone else touch a toy, even though she didn't want to play with it herself.

Heidi knew her emotions were reflected on her face, in plain view of her sister. Shelly could back down at any point and save her from these feelings. But she didn't. "Fine," Heidi heard herself saying. "What reason would I possibly have to say no?"

Shelly looked momentarily surprised, but then she grinned widely and threw her arms around Heidi's neck. "I did *not* expect you to say that. You're the absolute best!"

Wait. Was it too late to go back and give the answer Shelly *had* been expecting? Heidi worked to pry her twin's arms from around her neck, but when her sister looked at her, still smiling and with eyes that sparkled, Heidi smiled back silently. Yes, it was too late.

Chapter 20

Steven's palms were sweating. This might be the moment he'd been waiting for. The moment of truth. If it was, it was happening sooner than he'd expected. If a job offer from Chester were to come, he'd just assumed it would be at the end of his internship in August—not on this first Friday of July. But why else would Kathy Ingram, head of project development, be calling him into her office now, at the end of the work week?

Steven thought hard. He couldn't remember making any errors, but what if he had? He'd been working closely with one of the head engineers, Strom Bradley, on several projects. Strom was no nonsense and a little dry, but Steven had tons of respect for the guy. He was an amazing engineer, and he seemed to have taken Steven under his wing. He was pretty sure if he'd messed up, Strom would have said something. Instead, he'd given Steven great feedback so far, even requesting that he join him in several more O.R. cases.

The last few cases he'd been a part of, Strom had passed him the reins and faded into the background, allowing Steven to run the show. Yesterday, he'd asked Steven to take the lead in a big case coming up next week. He'd be instructing Nicolet's top neurosurgeon in the use of a newly authorized spinal cord stimulator that Chester had developed in conjunction with BioReal, a reputable multinational corporation. While Strom wasn't one for outright compliments, Steven knew he was giving him more and more responsibility, and that spoke louder than any words.

No, Steven determined. His work had been good. More than good. This couldn't be anything other than a positive meeting. Maybe Kathy just wanted to touch base—see how things were going. That must be it. Even so, Steven's hands continued to sweat, and he wiped them on his pants periodically as he watched the second hand on the clock overhead tick by.

Without meaning to, Steven wondered where Heidi might be at that moment. It would be close to four o'clock in Rochester. By his calculation, she and Sepi would have arrived there a few hours earlier. He knew a meet and greet was scheduled for that evening, but he didn't know what time. It was just as well that he didn't know. He needed to continue to separate himself from her, and not just in the physical sense.

He'd been doing well on that front. After their little talk at Sable Rocks, he'd only seen her a few times here and there—once in the driveway, and once out on the Lakanen's deck where he'd been having a beer with Sepi. Each time, they'd greeted each other and smiled. Made a little small talk. It was definitely casual, almost too much so. They had not resumed their morning runs, and Steven had a feeling they wouldn't be spending that time together anymore.

If someone had told him on Wednesday night, there on the rocks and then later in his apartment, that he would feel as detached from her as he now did, he wouldn't have believed them. But when he'd awoken Thursday morning, he'd almost heard Gran's advice to him. *Feel sad as long as you need to, and then be done with it.* Steven had been prepared to give himself the day to be out of sorts about Heidi, but by the time he'd arrived to work, he found himself able to tuck it all away and focus on the tasks laid out for him.

That night, he'd gone for a run after work and felt great during that time too. A few hours later, sitting on the deck with Sepi, he was still okay. He even remained unfazed when Heidi popped her head out of the kitchen to say hello. Somehow, some way, he'd compartmentalized her. He'd closed the lid and sealed it up tight. When Shelly had come out a few minutes later and asked if he wanted to grab a pizza Friday after work, he found that he really did.

Looking up at the clock, Steven saw it was now several minutes after five. Too much longer and he might have to call Shelly to let her know he'd be late. They were supposed to meet at six to drive to 906 Pizza together. This wouldn't be the best night to keep her waiting. He imagined she'd need some good distractions this weekend to keep from missing Heidi too much. Dot was training in her two nieces the next few days, so Shelly had a free weekend. Steven wondered how she planned to keep herself busy. Maybe she'd want to head over to Allouez Harbor for the day tomorrow. He'd been wanting to visit the sand dunes out that way, and this weekend was going to be beautiful. He'd even heard the northern lights were going to be out on Saturday. Experiencing those was a bucket list item for him.

"Steven?"

Kathy's voice broke through his thoughts. He jumped up, smoothing his hands on his trousers once more, and fought to bring his heart back to a normal rhythm. He hoped his nervousness didn't show.

Kathy was an amazon of a woman, and she strode towards him with wide, purposeful steps. She shook his hand the way she did everything else: masterfully and efficiently. "Sorry to keep you waiting, although I think you'll find truth in the expression, *Good things come to those who wait.*" A gleam entered her eye, which did nothing to slow the erratic rhythm of Steven's heart. If anything, it raced faster.

Did that mean what he hoped it did? Instead of asking, he followed Kathy into her office and sat down on the brown leather chair across from her meticulously organized desk. As she seated herself facing him, he noticed a file folder flipped open in front of her.

His file. She picked it up with both hands.

"Well, Steven," she began, "I have your performance review from Strom here, and I'm pleased to tell you, you've impressed him. That's not an easy thing to accomplish. You should know that."

Steven felt a rush of satisfaction color his face. "Strom's a really great guy. I'm learning a lot from him."

Kathy studied him and nodded slowly. She set down the folder. "I'll just cut right to the chase, Steven. Strom says he'd like to see you stay on with us. He believes you would be an invaluable asset to Chester Biotechnologies, and he fears if we wait until the end of summer to offer you a job, you may get scooped up by another company in the interim. I agree with him wholeheartedly, and I've called you in here today to offer you a full-time position with us." She paused, giving him time to react.

Steven sat back in his seat and ran a hand through his hair. "That's . . . honestly, Kathy, that would be a dream come true for me."

She nodded with a knowing smile. "Strom thought so. It gets a little sensitive though, Steven. Just between us, Strom plans to retire at the beginning of the new year. We've known for some time, and he asked to have a say in his replacement. Until you came along, it wasn't looking like anyone was going to fit the bill. He's pretty exacting, as I'm sure you've realized by now. As you also know, a large portion of what he does involves instructing the surgeons on the use of our products in real time. He's chosen *you* as his replacement, Steven."

Steven stuttered, "Th-that'd be great!" This was really happening! Not only was he being offered a job in the company of his choice, but he was also going to get the position he wanted right off the bat. He'd expected to have to work his way up to that.

Kathy shot him a quick smile before she continued, "I know when we met initially, you indicated an interest in working within our product development line, which you would still have a hand in. But I should warn you, we're looking to expand our reach into operating rooms across the Midwest. There might be a fair amount of travel in the future. How would you feel about that?

"I feel fine about that," Steven answered honestly.

"And what about Nicolet?"

"What about Nicolet?" he echoed.

"I mean, how do you like it here?"

"Honestly? I absolutely love it here!"

She held his gaze. "Truly? Because this is important. It takes a special person to want to live here. We don't have a lot of culture or city amenities. The closest thing we have to a city is Green Bay, and that's three hours away."

"That's . . . not a problem at all. I like this place. Small town life suits me."

But Kathy must not have been completely convinced. "Winters are long here," she went on, "and that can be an issue for some, as well. It's not unusual for us to have snow on the ground from November to May. You need to know that up front. It's idyllic in the summer, I'll give you that, but winters can be rough. Do you see that being a problem for you? I'm sorry to ask, but I want to make sure, before you accept this job, that you'll be willing to stick around for the long haul. There will be a fair amount of training you'll need to undergo. We want to invest the time in you, but we want to make sure we get a return on that investment, so we'll be asking you to sign a three-year contract."

Steven spoke slowly. "Kathy, I love it here. This is my dream job in my dream town. I want to stay. This is where I want to build my life. If you're offering me an opportunity to do that, my answer is yes."

Kathy nodded thoughtfully. "That *is* what I'm doing, Steven. I'm offering you an opportunity with us that wouldn't be offered to just anyone, especially a new graduate. We believe you're more than up to the task."

"I appreciate that."

"We're a solid company, but I'm happy to answer any specific questions you might have before you sign any contracts. We'll be offering you a starting salary of 70,000 dollars with twice annual bonuses and other incentives. Medical and dental, too, of course. Between us, I don't believe you'll remain at that base pay for long."

Steven's heart skipped a beat when she'd spoken that figure—a figure Kathy seemed almost apologetic about. To him, it was a small fortune. More than triple the amount of money he and Gran had lived on annually.

"Why don't you take the weekend to think about it, and we'll meet back here in my office Monday morning to continue this discussion. If you'd still like to move forward, we'll work on getting a contract drawn up. You'd be ready to begin before August."

Steven didn't need time to think about it. His answer was yes. Double yes, but instead of sharing that, he nodded in agreement. Maybe waiting out the weekend would look more professional. He needed to clarify something, though. "You're saying I'll start before my internship ends?"

"We like what we see. We want to snag you before anyone else does." Kathy winked at him before she stood up and extended her hand to him.

"Kathy, I can't thank you enough for this opportunity," Steven said, shaking her hand.

She beamed. "I think this will be a win-win for us all, Steven, and I look forward to having you on board with us in an official capacity."

"I'll look forward to it too. Thank you."

Steven hardly remembered the five-minute drive from Chester to the Lakanen's. He was too busy counting his blessings, grinning from ear to ear the entire way. Had that really just happened? He'd impressed them so much they were hiring him even before his internship ended? Steven could hardly believe it.

Driving up the driveway towards the Lakanen house, he saw movement out front. Shelly had Taro on a leash and appeared to be just getting back from a walk with him. Steven checked the clock on his dashboard. It was a quarter to six. He wasn't late, he had a job offer, and he was about to eat the best pizza with one of the two best-looking females he'd ever met. Could life get much better than this?

He gave the horn a quick, light honk to get Shelly's attention. She turned back to look at him and flashed him that smile. As he turned to park, she made her way over to him—Taro looking as tuckered out as if he'd just run the Iditarod. Poor old boy.

Shelly, on the other hand, was as perky as ever, and Steven was enormously gratified over her reaction to his news. He'd wanted to wait and tell her over dinner. They could have toasted to the news then. But Steven couldn't contain his excitement, and he told her the moment he opened his door, right out there in the driveway with Taro looking on in quiet boredom as he laid down with a grunt.

"What? Seriously?" Shelly's bright, smiling face conveyed a surprised delight. "Steven, this is incredible news! So you're going to be living here in Nicolet? Permanently?"

This is home now, Steven thought to himself in disbelief. Out loud he said, "Looks that way."

"This is just the best news! I'm so happy for you," she said, throwing her arms around Steven's neck in a hug. He wrapped his own arms around her waist in return and, although he hadn't intended to, inhaled her scent. Strawberries.

Shelly, still holding Taro's leash, pulled back after a second or two and beamed up at him.

She cocked her head and put a hand on one hip. "I hope you'll stick around here in the apartment for a while. It sure would be a shame not to see each other every day."

He didn't get a chance to respond to that before she added, "I'm really happy for you, Steven. You must be so excited."

"You have no idea. This is what I was hoping for. One of the things, anyway."

"And the other thing is off in Minnesota," she stated matter-of-factly.

He looked down at the black asphalt in embarrassment.

"Well," Shelly said cheerfully, taking him by the hand. "One out of two isn't half bad, and it's definitely enough to go out and celebrate tonight. Dinner and then ... dancing!" She turned towards the house, still holding his hand, but Steven kept his feet planted, and she whipped back around in surprise, a question in her eyes.

"Er, I don't really do dancing," he told her.

She grinned. "What do you mean you don't *do* dancing?"

"I mean, I'm awful at it. I don't really know how."

Shelly shook her head and chuckled softly. "Steven, dancing is just letting your body go and moving to music. So long as you have working limbs, you can dance."

"I'm pretty sure whatever I would do with my limbs would look nothing like dancing."

Giggling, she took a step towards him and entered his personal space. Her face was mere inches from his.

"Wh-what are you doing?"

She took his hands, holding one and placing the other on her hip. "I'm dancing with you, Steven." She tipped her head up and waited for him to look her in the eye. "Anyone can dance, and so can you. You just have to relax a little, stop worrying so much. Just let yourself *be*." She took a step and then another. He did the same. He felt ridiculous, and for cover he joked, "Who's leading who here?"

Shelly continued to gaze at him without answering immediately. The only sound was that of the breeze rustling the leaves of the sugar maples that lined the driveway. Steven looked into her eyes and stopped moving. He'd noticed this before. Whenever she wore yellow, as she did now, golden flecks appeared in her irises. The result was mesmerizing.

"You can take over anytime," she said softly. "I'll follow you whenever you're ready." Steven knew she wasn't only talking about dancing.

S helly chatted happily as they walked up to the main house together. "Dad and Mom are going to be *o* excited to hear this news too," she said. "They already love you like a son, you know. I heard Dad tell her one night after you left the house that if he had a son, he imagined he'd be just like you. Isn't that the sweetest?"

Steven felt his cheeks pink with pleasure. He felt the same about Sepi. Maggie too. He could only hope they'd be okay. He cared so much about them, and Maggie's medical situation had Steven feeling more than a little scared for them both. Honestly, he was afraid for the whole family. In less than a week's time, Maggie and Sepi would have answers, but it seemed like a long time to wait. He'd given his word not to say anything, and he would keep it, but it didn't sit well with him that he knew something this important when their own daughters didn't.

Shelly was still talking. "He was actually bragging you up to Richard Lafayette just the other day. He's our neighbor down the road in the red house with the gable windows. Dad was telling him about your work at Chester, and I'm telling you, he couldn't have been prouder if you were his own son."

Gran used to brag about him to her friends at Bible study, and Steven had to work hard to swallow down the lump that had appeared in his throat at the thought. He replaced it with a different thought. An ironic, comical one. If Sepi saw him as a son, that would mean Shelly would be something akin to a sister, and sisters didn't look at their brothers the way she'd just looked at him a moment earlier. Come to think of it, a brother of Shelly's wouldn't notice things like how good she smelled and how amazing she looked in those short shorts either.

She stopped at the front door. "So, I'll just drop off Taro, and we can get going," she said.

"Sounds good. I'll need to change quick, too, if you don't mind."

She flashed her special smile at him. "I don't mind at all."

---

9 06 Pizza didn't disappoint—though it never did. Shelly was excellent company, which she always was. With her, there were no silences, only an endless flow of conversation that seemed effortless to maintain. Steven loved that about her. Heidi had once said that Shelly could easily carry on a conversation with a houseplant with no trouble at all. Steven smiled as he thought about that.

Shelly noticed and tipped her head. "What is it? What's funny?"

Steven repeated Heidi's words, and Shelly grinned.

"She's said that to me before too. Heidi is always so quick to point out how we're 'complete opposites.'" She used air quotes.

"What? You don't think so?"

Shelly shook her head. "No. Because what that does is it sets up a false dichotomy." She laughed at Steven's expression. "That's right. I know big words too."

Steven grinned and held his hands up. "I never said otherwise."

"Your face did, and you've proven my point," she said matter-of-factly. "If I'm fun, then Heidi's boring. If she's smart, then I'm dumb. If I'm social, then she's reclusive."

She lifted her shoulders in a shrug.

"None of that's true at all. Heidi, as I'm sure you know by now, is plenty fun. And as you can see from my use of big words like *dichotomy* and *reclusive*, I am not completely stupid. And yes, she's more of an introvert than I am, but she's plenty social. She loves spending time with people. Really, she's more of a people watcher than anything else, but still, you should see her out on the course. Everybody loves her, except for maybe Lenny for some reason."

She looked thoughtful.

"Anyway, she shoots the breeze with the members out there all the time. Knows their names, the names of their kids . . . Heidi's great with people. She doesn't think so, but she is. She's reduced herself to being my opposite in almost every way, and it's just not true."

"You're not in the least bit stupid, Shelly."

She waved him off with a hand. "Oh, I know that, but thanks. That doesn't mean it's been easy growing up with a brainiac for a sister, though. She's always known what she wanted to be when she grew up. I'm still wondering and hoping it will come to me in a dream one night." She chuckled. "I've just never cared that much about what I do for work. Obviously, I want to do something to make money, but I'm not sure it matters too much what that is so long as it lets me have the kind of life I want."

"I'm sure you'll find something that's a good fit."

She looked at him from beneath her lashes as she took a sip from her mug of beer. After setting the large mug down, she used a napkin to wipe away the bit of moisture left behind on her upper lip. "I'm not too worried about it. I only worry when I compare myself to Heidi."

"I'm sure it's hard not to do that. I don't have a brother, but even I know something about sibling rivalry."

She played with her napkin, spinning it round and round with her finger. "It's real."

Steven smiled and regarded her silently.

She stopped spinning, and when she looked him in the eye again, he saw a vulnerability there he'd never seen before. "I know I come off as a bit . . . flighty, but I'm not. I guess . . ."

He gave her time to gather her thoughts.

"I don't think many people really know me."

"What do you mean?"

She shrugged. "I like to have fun. I love to flirt with men. But that's not all there is to me."

Steven had already known that, but he was glad she was aware of it herself.

"Anyway, enough about me. Let's talk about you. What are your plans now? I mean, you're taking the job obviously."

Steven sat back against the booth. "Definitely. I'm taking the job. I'm not sure my day-to-day will change all that much. I'll go to work and come home to the apartment. Help Sepi, go for runs, hang out . . ."

"So you'll stay with us awhile longer then? You're not going to run out and buy a house?"

Steven laughed. "Well, not right away."

The napkin was spinning again. "That's good. We wouldn't want to lose you so soon."

Steven didn't want to "lose" them, either. But he did need to expand his network. "I'll need to make some more connections," he said. "I really haven't been trying very hard to meet people since I wasn't sure if I'd be staying, but if this is going to be my home, I need to change that."

"What?" Shelly teased. "The Lakanens and Da Crew aren't enough for you?"

Steven laughed. "You guys are the best, don't get me wrong. I'm just saying I need to join some clubs, maybe a runners' club to start with. Something." He sighed. "Oh man, Shelly. I'm so happy. This is the place I want to put down roots. I knew it the moment I drove in along the lake that first time."

"Do you think about that a lot? Putting down roots, having a family?"

He smiled sardonically. "You don't know the half of it."

"Well, actually, Heidi told me a little bit about your conversation at Sable Rocks, so I did know you thought about it," she admitted. "I just didn't know how much. I think it's cool. That you think about that stuff."

She grew quiet then and stared off to a spot just behind him.

"What are you thinking?"

Her gaze locked with his. "Just that we want the same things." She smiled at him. "I wonder what we should do about that?" As she looked at him with that sweet smile and twinkle in her eye, something inside Steven shifted.

And then a shadow fell over them, and not a metaphorical one. Instead, one of the most enormously muscled men Steven had ever seen in real life stood over them at the end of their booth. He wore a Harley tee-shirt that looked to be at least two sizes too small for him, and tattoos ran up and down both arms, including one of a viper.

"Lenny!" Shelly exclaimed.

The guy smiled and gave Shelly a slow, appreciative scan that made Steven grit his teeth.

"Hey there, fine lady. Couldn't tell at first if it was you or your sister, but then I saw your smile. Don't think your sister knows how to make her mouth do that. Least I never seen one." He looked to Steven, giving him a brief nod before turning his attention back to Shelly. "How you doin' girl?"

"I'm great, but what're you doing here? I thought you were working tonight?"

He shrugged. "Called in sick. Needed a mental health day, or whatever. That place is killin' me."

Shelly shook her head and *tsk-tsked* at him. "That's very naughty, Lenny."

"You know me." Lenny grinned before nodding his head in Steven's direction. "So, who's this lucky guy?"

Shelly made the introduction. "This is my friend, Steven. Steven, this is Lenny. We work together."

"Hey," Steven said. He offered his hand.

Lenny didn't take it right away. He stared at Steven a few seconds longer than was polite.

"Lenny," Shelly warned with a smile, "be nice."

Lenny grabbed Steven's hand and shook it briefly with a grip that was a little too hard.

Leaning down closer, Lenny rested both hands on the table, and when he was eye to eye with Steven, he spoke. "You better treat her right, man, or you'll answer to me. Got it?"

Steven seethed. He'd known from the moment this giant appeared at their table that he didn't like him. Now he actively despised him. He didn't owe this prick any promises or explanations. Who did he think he was anyway? He'd anointed himself Shelly's protector, but that was Steven's job. Not his.

He forced himself to maintain eye contact with the beefy chef from hell. Steven wouldn't give Lenny the satisfaction of looking away. "I got it," he said tightly.

At that, Lenny almost smiled, and he pushed himself away from the table with an air of self-approbation. "Alright you two crazy cats." He pointed both index fingers at them. "Have fun tonight. And Shelly, I'll see you Monday, girl."

Shelly shook her head and laughed. "See you then, Lenny." She reached for her beer, but then she called after Lenny as an afterthought, "And if you're lucky, I won't tell Dot I saw you out tonight." Lenny turned and flashed a grin. Steven was surprised at the transformation. When he smiled, the guy looked almost friendly. Almost.

"Check ya later, babe." He gave Steven one last warning look before pushing through the door out to the parking lot.

Steven watched Lenny's retreating form through the glass door. He cleared his throat and turned back to Shelly. "So . . . that was Lenny."

Shelly chuckled. "That was Lenny. He can be intense sometimes."

Steven raised his eyebrows. "Ya think?"

"He's just a little protective of me. Actually, he's really pretty sweet."

"To you, maybe, and I'm sure you can guess why."

Shelly laughed outright. "I know it could seem that way, but Lenny knows where we stand. He asked me out a few times at the beginning of summer, but he's let it go now."

"Sure he has."

"You're not jealous, are you? Because that would be lovely."

Steven rolled his eyes.

"If you *are* jealous, you can relax. Lenny's not my type."

"That's got to be a relief for Sepi," Steven said, half joking and half serious. He couldn't imagine Lenny hanging out on the back deck with Maggie and Sepi. He couldn't imagine Lenny hanging all over Shelly either. The idea of it did something unpleasant to his stomach. He didn't want this guy talking to Shelly anymore. Not because he was jealous, or anything like that, he just didn't like him. He didn't trust him.

"You need to be careful around him," Steven advised.

Shelly waved a dismissive hand before taking another drink. "Lenny's harmless. Don't worry about him."

"I'm not worried about him. I'm worried about you."

Shelly didn't even bother to hide it. She looked thrilled. "You are?"

Steven stared at her in exasperation. "You're *happy* about that?"

Leaning forward, she batted her eyes. "It's progress."

Chapter 21

So far, this trip had been amazing. Everything had fallen into place. It was Sunday night, the last night of orientation, and Heidi and Sepi would leave early the next morning for home. There was a farewell dinner being held by the Mayo Clinic Alix School of Medicine, but Heidi had spent so much time with her incoming class over the course of the weekend that she was ready for a break. When she'd suggested to her dad that they head out just the two of them for dinner tonight, he'd looked relieved.

Heidi felt guilty at how much time she'd spent apart from him this trip, even though they'd both known her primary purpose was to attend orientation and all the events associated with it. And she really had loved every minute, but she couldn't shake the feeling that her dad had been slightly off all weekend. He seemed distracted and not as upbeat and jokey as he normally was. Heidi wondered if he was as happy for her to be leaving as he claimed to be. She supposed she couldn't fault him if he wasn't. As happy as she was to be there, she felt it too. A little... unsettled.

Although she'd called home three times to talk to Shelly, they hadn't connected, not even once. She'd left long messages filling her sister in on her weekend, but the two messages Shelly had left her in return had been short and bubbly and devoid of any real information. Although she told Heidi she missed her and hoped she was having a wonderful time, she shared nothing about herself or Steven.

Heidi assumed they were spending time together. Even if Shelly did have feelings for him, they were friends first. And friends hung out together. That's what Heidi told herself, anyway, and she did her best to tamp down the jealousy that had set up camp in the pit of her stomach. It wasn't just jealousy aimed at Shelly either. She was jealous of Steven too. He got to be the one spending time with her sister. He was hearing her laugh, listening to her stories, watching her ski or dive or kayak or whatever else she'd be up to on her weekend off. He probably knew exactly what Shelly was up to because he was there beside her, whereas Heidi was so far removed, she had no clue.

She'd have to get used to it, she supposed. She and her sister would lead completely separate lives soon enough. They'd stay in touch by phone, maybe even write some letters. And they'd visit. Of course, they'd visit. But that was all there would ever be for them from here on out. Playing those short messages in her hotel room, Heidi couldn't help but tear up at the sound of her sister's voice each time.

Ready or not, she was moving forward. This was what she wanted, and it was all going according to plan. Heidi found an apartment as well as a roommate she'd liked immediately upon meeting. Her name was Sarah, and she was from Madison, Wisconsin. She was a runner too, and they'd actually snuck away on a run along the Zumbro River yesterday. In the apartment next to theirs would live another classmate, Rita, and her husband. They'd just gotten married in June, and Heidi found herself intrigued by them. She was reminded of Shelly's earlier statement that she could "walk and chew gum." It seemed Rita was doing just that. She was a married medical student, and it turned out Rita wasn't the only one.

Since their dinner reservation wasn't for another half hour, Sepi and Heidi walked along Broadway Avenue, looking at the different buildings as they strolled. Noticing her dad was unusually quiet and observing the notch between his brows, she said, "Penny for your thoughts."

Sepi seemed to startle back into the present. He laughed. "Oh, I'm sorry. Your old man was doing a little daydreaming, that is all."

"About what? You looked worried."

"Worried? No, no. I'm just fine my girl." He looked around them at the tall buildings and street cafés. "Well, Heidi-ho, these will be your stomping grounds for the next several years. What do you think?"

Whatever he'd been thinking, he wasn't saying. Heidi moved on. "I like it, Dad. I really like it here. It feels like a nice mix of big city and small town. A five-minute drive and you're out in farm country, but here in the downtown it almost feels like a bustling metropolis. My professors are amazing and so are my classmates. Sarah's awesome. It's great. Everything."

"Good, good. I think so too. Ah, what's this?" Sepi had stopped in front of a storefront window of a prosthetic company.

Heidi looked at the etching on the glass. "Leeland Prosthetic Technologies," she read aloud. "This is such a medically inclined place, this town."

"It really is," Sepi agreed. "Did you know that every summer the entire royal family of Saudi Arabia comes here for their yearly physicals? They treat royalty here from all over the world."

"I know, I toured the floor where the VIPs stay. It's amazing. Marble everywhere and gold fixtures too. You know," she went on, tapping the glass of the window, "this is the second prosthetic company I've seen in the downtown area since we got here. And yesterday I noticed another company, Rykera I think it was, that makes endograft devices and some kind of fixation technology to treat aortic aneurysms."

Sepi raised his eyebrows in question, as if to say, "And this matters, why?"

Heidi blushed. "Well, I just think it's interesting that, without even looking, I've found two biomedical engineering companies in this town."

"Ah," Sepi said in understanding. "You are thinking of Steven."

Heidi shrugged. "A little," she admitted.

"You think he could find work here, eh? Is that what you hope for?"

She sighed. "I don't know, Dad. It was just a thought."

"Have you and Steven talked about this?"

"Not really. I basically told him that a relationship wasn't going to work. He agreed, I guess. But now, I don't know, maybe I'm rethinking it."

"You are not thinking of asking him to come here, though, right?"

"It crossed my mind."

"Honey, Steven has told me many times that his dream job would be to work for Chester. They have a type of focus there that interests him more than anything else."

"I know," Heidi said stubbornly. "But it's all engineering. I don't see what the big deal would be. Isn't one company as good as another?"

Sepi chuckled. "No, and I would think you, of all people, would understand that best."

"How do you figure?"

"Well, you've mentioned wanting to be a radiologist, eh?"

"Right."

"Because you have a special interest in that area of medicine."

"I do."

"But you do not have that same level of interest in, say, dermatology or proctology. No?"

Heidi stopped walking and turned to her father. She wagged her finger. "You did that on purpose!"

He laughed. "Did what on purpose?"

"Chose two of the most unlikely fields for me to go into—the most boring and the most ... I don't know, *graphic* to use as comparisons. It's not at all the same thing. I'm just saying Steven could work on prosthetics or devices for aneurysms instead of spinal cages or knee joints. There's not really a big difference there. It's not at all comparable to choosing a field of medicine."

Sepi looked unconvinced. "Steven might feel differently, that is all I am saying."

"Hmph." Heidi looked at her watch. "We should probably start walking back towards the restaurant. It's getting close to our reservation time."

"Lead the way, daughter," Sepi said with an amused smile.

They'd chosen an Italian restaurant named Gianni's for dinner that night. It was a quaint little place on Broadway Avenue with a black awning and a retractable pergola to cover their extended sidewalk seating. Heidi looked around.

There were at least a half-dozen other black, powder-coated iron tables surrounding them. All were full. A look through the window into the restaurant showed it was just as busy inside. The many potted ferns and other plantings that dotted this little area of sidewalk created a soft, cozy feel. "Gosh, I feel like we're at a café in Italy."

"This is nice," Sepi agreed.

They put in their orders, parted with their menus, and Heidi was just sitting back to enjoy the sidewalk dining experience when Sepi leaned forward and asked bluntly, "Do you love him?"

It was a good thing their drinks hadn't been delivered yet. Heidi would have choked.

She stared back at her father. There was no trace of his usual jovial nature about him. He was asking in earnest.

A series of responses ran through her head—the first being to play dumb and pretend not to know who he was referring to. But that would be stupid. Her second was to outright deny it. And her third thought was to laugh off his question. That was the one she went with. She worked to effect an ironic tone. "Oh, sure. I just met him last month, but yep, I love him alright."

"I knew I loved your mother after two weeks. I wouldn't ask if I thought it was an impossibility, Heidi-ho. I want to know."

Heidi's smile faded, and she bit down on her lip. Did she love him? She didn't think so. She liked him a whole lot, and she thought she *could* love him, given enough time.

"No. I don't love him."

Sepi sat back against his chair and nodded. She thought he looked relieved.

"But I've never been in love before, Dad. I'm not sure I would even recognize it if I *did* feel it. I care about him, though, and I know I *could* love him. I'm probably in that pre-love place, if there even is such a thing."

She played with her rolled silverware. "I guess I'm saying the potential is there." She thought of an analogy. "This is going to sound totally corny, but it's kind of like one of Mom's perennials before it pops up in the spring. All it takes is a little heat, water and sunshine and it will grow into something lush and beautiful."

Sepi pressed his lips together. He considered her words. "Okay, and following that analogy, which I think is beautiful and not corny at all, if you deny the bulb any of those things, it will not amount to much."

"Are you saying I should deny what I feel?"

"I love you and your sister more than my own life. I hope you know that. I want what is best for you both. I have also come to care a great deal about Steven. He's a good boy. A good man," he corrected.

"I have talked to the three of you. You know me, I cannot help but talk. But I know a few things from those conversations as well as what I have seen with my own eyes. Steven is looking to settle down, Heidi. He wants to live in Nicolet. You know this about him, eh?"

Heidi nodded.

"You, on the other hand, are not looking to settle down. You are ready to venture off—away from Nicolet. You and Steven, you are on two different paths. I think you could be very compatible, but for the timing. It works against you."

Heidi felt her heart sink. She and Steven did want different things. But they had their drive for their careers in common. They shared that, at least. What if he didn't need all the rest?

Shelly had been right. When she focused on the here and now, there was no problem, save the four hundred miles between Nicolet and Rochester, and if they removed those, there was no problem at all. All she wanted right now was for Steven to be her boyfriend. She wasn't in the market for a husband and probably wouldn't be for several years.

She didn't say any of this out loud. To her father, she said, "That might be true, but what about Shelly?"

Sepi raised his eyebrows.

"You said you've talked with Steven, me, and Shelly. So what about Shelly?"

"Heidi-ho, she is your twin. You already know about Shelly."

And she did. She knew all about Shelly. But she also knew Shelly and Steven would be a mismatch. Shelly was too wild for Steven. She'd overwhelm him. He needed someone who was quiet, peaceful. Someone who loved to run like he did. Someone who could match him intellectually. If he tried to talk about his work with any kind of detail, there would be no way her sister could follow along. Shelly would just stare back at him while her eyes glazed over.

Heidi winced. That was mean, and . . . it wasn't really true, either. Shelly was smart. But she didn't have much interest in science or medicine—or Steven's work.

"I know just what you are thinking," Sepi said with a small smile.

Heidi felt her face heat up. "You do?"

"You think if you ask, Steven will follow you here." Relief washed over her. He hadn't known what she'd been thinking. Although, it was true she had thought about Steven coming to Rochester with her more than once on this trip.

"Do you think he would?"

Sepi inclined his head. "He might. But it would not be right of you, and it would be all wrong for him."

Heidi couldn't keep the frustration out of her voice. "Why do you say that?"

"It would be selfish," Sepi said simply.

"Selfish!"

"Yes. And I know it seems a harsh word to use. Especially because you are not, and have never been, a selfish girl. But I happen to know that Steven was offered a job yesterday at Chester."

Heidi stared at him with her mouth agape. "Why didn't you tell me that?"

Sepi ignored the question. "I called home in the morning, while you were away at the school, and spoke with Shelly. She told me Steven is over the moon about it. I am not surprised, of course. It has been all he has spoken of this summer with me. He lights up when he discusses his work. He dreams of a life where he creates a device and then shows a surgeon how to use that creation. He wants the job, Heidi. That job in particular."

Heidi swallowed hard. "Did he accept it then?"

"He should. But no. Not yet. Your sister says he has the weekend to think it over."

Heidi played with her fork. "What have they been doing this weekend?"

Sepi looked her in the eyes long and hard, but when he spoke, his voice was gentle. "What are you asking, daughter?"

She sighed heavily and set down the fork. "You know what I'm asking. Are Shelly and Steven hanging out together this weekend? I've assumed they must be, but . . ."

"I believe your assumptions are correct."

Heidi rested her head in her hands. "Oh, Dad." She looked up. "And I can't even be mad. I told Shelly to go for it with him."

Sepi regarded her with kindness and approval. "Because you know that is what is right. You need to let this go, Heidi. You need to let *him* go."

Heidi heard his words, but she didn't react.

"If not for medical school, perhaps something could have blossomed between you. But as things stand now, you need to withhold that water and sunlight and . . . *heat*, as it were." He winked.

"Ew, okay, Dad." Thankfully, the waiter chose that moment to come with their food. Heidi picked at her fettuccine Alfredo while Sepi attacked his chicken marsala with a gusto. They were careful to steer the conversation to a more comfortable place and keep it there, but Heidi couldn't help but think about her father's words.

She would continue to replay them over and over again the next day on their drive home as well. In her experience, her father was usually right. But maybe this one time it was possible that he could be wrong.

Chapter 22

Steven had an overwhelming sense of well-being, standing at the top of a steep sand dune with Shelly right beside him. They had the place completely to themselves, and while he surveyed the beautiful views around them, he took inventory of his life. Tomorrow, Monday, he would accept the position at Chester and embark on the adult portion of his life's journey. Put that way, today was his last day to be a kid. He was ready for the change and there was no sadness or ambivalence at the closing of this chapter. He was ready to turn the page.

He and Shelly had spent the day exploring the quaint town of Allouez Harbor, its beaches, and the miles of dunes that ridged Lake Superior three hundred feet up. The area they occupied now was known as the Log Slide.

According to the sign at the beginning of the short trail that led to the dune, this particular spot was used by loggers in the late nineteenth century to convey logs down to awaiting ships. From there, the ships would transport them to sawmills. Back then, a large wooden chute ran from the top of the dune down to the water below, and the logs took only ten seconds to descend the three hundred feet to the bottom. Occasionally, the logs created enough friction against the chute to cause them to catch fire on their way down. That would have been something to see.

More information was posted along the path, but Shelly was eager to get to the overlook, so Steven bypassed all the signs but that first one. "Why waste time reading signs when we can experience it ourselves?" she asked in exasperation when it appeared he wanted to read everything. Steven loved reading about things. Once, he'd spent an entire day at the Michigan History Center in Lansing, and he still hadn't seen everything he'd wanted to. He guessed Shelly didn't share his love of history. Oh, well. It would give him an excuse to come back here again.

No wooden chute remained today—just pure white sand. He and Shelly had run down and climbed up the Log Slide twice already, and now they were ready to rest and take in the view. He would be hard pressed to say which view was better, however. The miles and miles of perfect blue water that stretched out to the horizon, or the pair of gorgeous legs being stretched and moved in front of him. Though lean, her legs were softer than her sister's—their muscles slightly less defined—but they were just as sexy, and Steven was having a harder and harder time keeping his eyes directed on the water. He couldn't help it. He was a leg man. He smiled ruefully—and a man in general.

"This weekend has been awesome," Shelly said. "Minus your little accident, of course." She switched from her left leg to her right. "I can't believe I got the entire weekend off, especially with Heidi being gone. Dot's nieces asked for jobs at the perfect time."

"It worked out well for me too. I've had a fun tour guide."

He motioned to a place in the sand up ahead, and she nodded, following him there and sitting down beside him.

She smiled happily. "It's been fun for me too. We've packed a lot in. Celebrating your job on Friday, and yesterday was an amazing day on the water. Plus, you had the added bonus of a near-death experience. An adventure's not complete without one of those, right?" She nudged him with her shoulder. "That might just end up being your favorite part of the entire weekend."

Steven chuckled. "I doubt it, and you're exaggerating."

"It's a good thing I wasn't working, or I wouldn't have been there to rescue you," she teased.

"If you'd been working, I wouldn't have needed any rescuing because I never would have ventured out to Shante Isle by myself in a kayak on such a wavy day."

She smiled sheepishly. "That's probably true. How is this feeling?" she asked, running her hand over his bruised thigh in a feather-light touch. Steven inhaled sharply, and Shelly quickly lifted her hand. "I'm sorry! I didn't realize it would be that sensitive."

"No, no. It's fine. It didn't hurt."

"Oh. Well, you sort of gasped, so I thought . . ."

He didn't try to explain. What would he have said? He couldn't explain it to himself. Every time she touched him this weekend which, being Shelly, was all the time, he had a body-wide reaction. To cover it up, he joked, "I was good and stuck in that kayak, wasn't I?"

"You really were," she responded seriously. "I feel so bad that I was laughing at first. When you flipped, I figured you'd just pop up and see me poking fun. It took me a few seconds to know something was wrong."

Steven had accused her of exaggerating a moment ago, but the truth was that he'd been really panicked. He'd never admit that to her, of course. The waves had kicked up while they'd been out at the remote island, and he'd lost his balance and flipped. Shelly was an expert kayaker, and she'd taught him how to barrel roll before they set out.

Unfortunately for him, he'd been over a shallow sandbar when he flipped, so he couldn't complete the maneuver he'd mastered with her. With his head dragging along the sand, he'd pushed repeatedly against the kayak to try to get out, but he'd been wedged in tight. The rental place had been all out of kayaks his size, so he'd had to settle for one designed for someone of Shelly's stature. As a result, the opening was smaller, as well.

As much as he downplayed it, Steven had been in real trouble, and Shelly, realizing it in time, jumped out to help. She may actually have saved him, truth be told. By holding his kayak, she gave him enough traction to push off and out, but he'd given himself a deep and painful contusion on his thigh in the process.

Looking down in the sand where their hands were resting, side by side, he lifted his and placed it over the top of hers, giving it a small squeeze. "I'm glad you were there to help yesterday. And I'm glad you're here with me today too."

Shelly treated him to that megawatt, and as they held each other's gaze a second longer than two friends should, Steven suddenly found himself imagining what it would be like to kiss her. He wanted to put his hands on her. To touch her smooth skin and feel her soft body underneath him.

Wetting her lips, Shelly looked at him expectantly. He knew she wanted him, and in that moment, she'd give him whatever he asked for. But it wouldn't be right. His feelings for her sister, though faded now, were too fresh. He couldn't do that to Shelly—*wouldn't* do that to her—and he looked away as he removed his hand from hers. He didn't miss the disappointment that flashed across her face. He felt it too, but he pushed it aside.

"So, what do you think? Do you want to catch the northern lights out here or back home?" he asked to distract them both.

"What time is it?" she asked.

Steven glanced at his watch. "Almost seven."

"Hmm. It won't be dark for hours yet. Let's grab a bite at that little diner and then head home. We'll have plenty of time to change into something warmer and head to McCreaty's Cove with some blankets. Maybe I'll even bring some coffee with us. Ooh! Better yet, I'll make a thermos of hot toddy for us."

Steven hesitated. "Shelly, I don't think . . ."

She stood up and brushed the sand from her legs. "What?" she asked innocently.

He let his gaze linger a little too long on her dainty ankles before moving up to her smiling face. He tried to explain, "It's just, I don't want you to get the wrong idea here. This is starting to sound a little . . ."

"A little what?"

"I don't know," Steven felt his ears burn. "Romantic, I guess. I just don't think—"

"Steven?" she interrupted, holding a hand down to him. "You think too much."

He sighed as he grabbed hold and stood. "Yeah. I know I do. That's always been my problem."

He was still thinking as he changed into jeans and a sweatshirt back at his apartment. He should call her to cancel. If he didn't, he was taking a chance that something might happen between them tonight. He could feel it.

Glancing at the phone on the kitchen counter, he found his feet didn't want to walk him over there to make the call. Instead, he turned his back on the kitchen altogether and stared out the window on the far wall behind the sofa. Daylight had nearly finished its transformation into dusk, and the leaves, fluttering in the breeze on the branches outside the window, mirrored the fluttering in his stomach.

He felt like he was standing on the precipice of something. If he took one more step, there would be no turning back. But he wanted to experience the northern lights, and he wanted to experience them with Shelly. Surely, he could control any impulses that might pop up in the moment. His Gran had raised him to be "a man of integrity."

He always did the right thing.

Chapter 23

By the time they arrived in the parking lot overlooking McCreaty's Cove, it was well and truly dark. Shelly took one last look at the clock on the dash before Steven killed the engine. Ten minutes until eleven. A quick look at the sky showed nothing was happening just yet, but the night was young. Of course, there was no guarantee they'd see the aurora borealis, the northern lights, at all tonight. Predicting them wasn't a perfect science, but conditions were supposed to be just right for them tonight, so who knew? Maybe they'd get lucky. Shelly had only ever seen them twice before herself.

Knowing he had a lifetime to see them now that he'd be living up here, Steven said he wouldn't sweat it if they didn't make an appearance tonight. He had endless Nicolet nights ahead of him. The thought made Shelly smile. She could only hope she'd be the lucky girl spending those nights alongside him, or underneath him. Perhaps sensing her eyes on him, Steven turned towards her in the darkened car.

"I've noticed something about you this weekend," she said.

His voice seemed deeper, huskier than it was in the light of day. "Oh yeah? What's that?"

"You're really happy."

Steven shrugged. "I'm always happy."

"Yeah, but you were holding something back before." She was silent a minute, remembering Heidi's initial analysis of him. "You know, when we first met you, Heidi said you had sad eyes. I remember she compared them to Taro's."

Steven scoffed. "Well, that's hardly flattering!"

"Don't you dare diss poor Taro," Shelly warned with a giggle. "He's a sweet boy."

"Sweet, sure. Just not the most attractive. Not to mention, and I'm just pointing out the obvious here, he's a dog."

Shelly laughed outright. "Well, not to worry. You're definitely much cuter than any dog. You're cuter than any man for that matter." She waited a moment, giving him time to take in the compliment. Not surprisingly, he remained silent. "But seriously, Heidi was right. There was something about you that *was* a little sad. I haven't seen that at all this weekend."

When Steven spoke, there was an edge to his voice. "I'm not sure what you're talking about. I wasn't sad before, and of course I'm happy this weekend. I just scored my dream job."

"You're right," Shelly placated. "I'm sure that's what it must be."

They walked down the steps to the beach in silence. The water quietly lapped at the shore, and their feet made scratching noises in the sand as they made their way a hundred or so yards from the parking area.

So much for a romantic night at the beach. How was she going to salvage their evening now that she'd just insulted Steven? She'd basically compared him to a pathetic looking dog—Shelly silently apologized to Taro—and then accused him of being a mopey person. That was the problem with the type of personality she had. Whatever she was thinking about in her head tended to fly straight out of her mouth, completely unfiltered. It had gotten her into trouble more times than she could count.

Since Shelly was the one holding the blanket, she picked the spot and kicked off her sandals before unfolding it and shaking it out. Wordlessly, Steven put down the bag holding the thermos and mugs and helped straighten out the corners. Shelly stood on the edge of the scratchy, wool blanket she was fairly certain was older than she was before sitting down and pulling her legs up under her. It was definitely cooling off, but she felt snug and cozy in her jeans and sweatshirt. She'd packed a second blanket, one made of a soft fleece, just in case, but for now, she didn't think they needed it.

Steven kicked off his own shoes and sat down beside her with a small grunt. "You know," he said casually, "back to your comment before—"

"I'm *so* sorry about that, Steven. You should know me well enough by now to know the things I say often come out wrong. I didn't mean anything by it. You should just . . . ignore me."

Steven chuckled. "Ignore you? That's not possible. And anyway, you're probably right. A part of me has been a little down, I guess. This weekend has been different, and not just because of the job offer."

She scooted closer to him. This sounded promising. "Yeah? What else then?"

"I've told you I was raised by my grandmother?"

"You've mentioned that, yes."

"Well, I never mentioned *why* I grew up with Gran. Honestly, it's not all that important now, but my parents abandoned me when I was little. They left me with her one day, and they never came back. They never wrote; they never called." He shook his head and looked out at the darkness over the lake. "They're still out there somewhere, at least I think they are, but they don't care to find me, and I definitely don't want anything to do with them."

Shelly's entire body tensed, and she turned fully to face him. There was just enough moonlight to make out his features. "That's awful! How could they do something like that to a child? Their own flesh and blood?"

Steven smiled. "Careful, Shelly. Your feisty is showing."

How could he joke about this? He'd been discarded, cast aside by the very people who were supposed to love him more than anything or anyone else in the world. Shelly couldn't even imagine what it must feel like for Steven to know his parents hadn't wanted him. She, for her part, was pissed on his behalf. "If I ever bumped into them, they'd get a whole lot more than a little feistiness, I can tell you that much. I'd come at them swinging!"

"Aw, come on. They wouldn't be worth that."

"You know what? I hope they can't sleep at night over what they did. They should be so ashamed they can't even look at themselves in the mirror." Shelly's heart was racing, and she was breathing as hard as if she'd just free-climbed Pinnacle Rock.

Steven patted her gently, and slightly awkwardly, on the back. "I'm sorry. I'm not telling you this to get you worked up, although"—he laughed—"it's gratifying you care so much. I just wanted to explain what you and Heidi might have noticed early on. Because, you see, you girls are lucky, really lucky to have the family you do. And honestly, *I'm* lucky too. I had Gran. She was loyal to a fault, and she loved me more than enough to compensate for my lack of parents. But when she died . . . I lost my only family. My only home."

He laughed humorlessly.

"Living in a busy dorm, surrounded by people, you wouldn't think feeling lonely could even be a thing, but it hit me like a ton of bricks, and it totally sucked. I've felt a little like a ship adrift in the sea since Gran passed. But then . . ." Steven trailed off.

Shelly was calm again and listening intently. "But then?" she coaxed.

He turned his body towards her so their knees were nearly touching. "But then I came here to Nicolet, and I met your family. You all made me feel . . . I don't know, like a part of the mix. I've spent so much time at your house this summer, and I've watched. I've noticed things."

Shelly snorted. "Hopefully only the good things."

Steven inhaled deeply and blew out a slow breath the way people sometimes do when they're trying to gain control of their emotions, but when he finally spoke again, his voice sounded like it always did. "Only good things. Like your parents stealing a quick kiss when they think nobody's looking. Like how Maggie teases Sepi about how he'll still somehow manage to be the life of the party at his own funeral. How Sepi can tell the driest, most cringy joke one minute and then give the best advice about life the next. He's an amazing guy, by the way."

Shelly smiled. "He is pretty great."

"I notice you too. And Heidi. I see how you light up the room and make everyone laugh even without trying, and how Heidi constantly maneuvers to keep peace and make sure everyone has what they need. Even Taro, the most depressing-looking dog in the world, knows something special when he sees it. He's always underfoot—wanting to be where his family is."

Shelly silently reached for his hand, and when she did, the air between them all but crackled with electricity. Steven must have felt it too because he began caressing her hand with his thumb. It was such a small movement with such huge implications. He sent shivers up her arm and down her spine. They were about to step over the line. She could feel it, and she wet her lips in anticipation.

Steven spoke slowly. "Ever since that first day, the day of Sepi's party, this place has felt like the closest thing to home I've had in a while. I haven't felt quite so alone. But I knew it might not last. I knew it was about as solid as this sand," he said, scooping up a handful with his other hand. He let it fall through his fingers. "Like it might just slip away no matter how hard I tried to hold on to it, and I'd lose it all—your family, this place, the job. But now that I have the offer from Chester, it feels solid. It feels real, like something I can count on. Maybe that's what you're picking up on this weekend when you say I seem happy."

Steven's thumb continued to stroke her skin well after he'd finished speaking, and Shelly had just worked out what to say next when he abruptly dropped her hand and began to fidget with the blanket. "Anyway, enough of that," he said brusquely. "How about a drink?" He moved to grab the thermos and mugs.

Shelly felt off center. She'd been so sure they were having a moment together, and now Steven was back to being all business. Either he was really, really bad at this, or he wasn't interested. Or, she thought to herself, remembering the caressing touch of his thumb, he was waiting for her to make the next move. She could do that. When the time was right. "Absolutely. Bring it on," Shelly said about the drink. She crisscrossed her legs and added, "One last thing, and then we can move on, but I just want you to know that we've all loved having you around this summer. You can count on us, and you've been good for us too."

"Yeah?" She could hear the pleasure in his voice.

"Definitely."

"Well, thanks."

"I mean, someone's got to mow the lawn. Better you than one of us," she teased. "And you've been great eye candy. I'm always watching to see if you'll take your shirt off."

He chuckled. "Nice, Shelly."

Steven handed Shelly her drink, and she promptly lost track of time as they chatted and looked out over the water. After a few refills, they laid down on the blanket and gazed at the stars, the conversation waxing and waning, steering itself wherever it wanted. It lulled her, with the assistance of the alcohol, into a carefree, languorous state.

"I don't know if it's going to happen tonight, Steven," Shelly remarked at one point.

"It's okay. It's been nice to stargaze. In Lansing, you can't see the night sky like this. With all the street lights, it's too bright."

"Hmm. I guess I take that for granted. I look out at the stars all the time. I sleep with the curtain open on the window and stare at the sky as I fall asleep. I do that almost every night."

"Heidi said you have the best view in the house."

"It's true. Heidi and I used to switch rooms all the time when we were little, just for fun. Somehow, I ended up staying put in my room. I'm sure I must have done it on purpose, but I don't remember specifics. I've been in that room since the sixth grade. I get to look out over the lake, and Heidi gets a view of the driveway."

Steven laughed. "That sounds about right."

"Hey!" Shelly swatted at him. "Be nice."

"I am. I'm just stating the obvious here."

Shelly sighed. "I know. But I've turned over a new leaf. I'm the new and improved and not-so-selfish Shelly."

"You're not selfish."

"Yeah right."

"You're not. You just know what you want, and you've got the confidence to take it."

She was quiet so long that Steven must have thought he'd offended her. "Sorry. I didn't mean anything bad by that."

Shelly shifted, stretching out onto her right side, and looked at him. "No. It's fine. And you're right. I do usually take what I want."

Steven responded by stretching himself out on his left side. Somehow, Shelly knew he understood what she was getting at. He'd become very still and seemed to be watching her from his side of the blanket.

Just in case, she thought she should spell it out for him. "What I want is you, Steven," she said. "I've wanted you all summer, from that first day. But it got a little complicated, didn't it?"

He spoke slowly. "You mean Heidi?"

"I mean Heidi."

"I told myself you were both off limits."

She snorted. "How'd that work out for you?"

She saw the shadow of a smile. "Not great."

"Look, I know she was your first choice. And believe it or not, that makes me like you even more. You see my sister how she deserves to be seen. Not everyone does. In fact, most men miss it completely."

She moved a little closer.

"I need you to know something, though. If Heidi had asked me to stay away, I would have. I love my sister. But she didn't. She's told me, twice, that you're fair game. So I don't have a problem moving this thing between us forward. But I need to know how you feel about it. I need to know if you're still hung up on my sister."

Steven rested his head on his hand. "I'm not sure what to say. Obviously, I'm not good at this. I'm sure it's obvious, and that's why I've always gravitated toward women with loads of confidence. Women who are kind of uninhibited. Like you. 'Cause I don't put myself out there real well. Heidi and I are the same that way, I guess. That's probably why nothing happened between us. Neither one of us could jump in feet first. I suppose I should be grateful for that now."

"But you're not?"

"I haven't sorted it all out yet. I just know nothing can happen with Heidi now. It sucked to first realize it, but I'm over it. What I can tell you is, as much fun as you and I have had this summer, and this weekend especially, it feels really, really wrong to even think about . . . being with you. You're her sister. Her twin sister, and I feel like a total scum bag every time I imagine us, you know. . . together."

Shelly shifted even closer, and she thought she could feel his body heat radiating off of him. She wanted him to touch her. She wanted to wrap herself around him, to feel the heat of his skin pressed directly against her own skin. "Do you imagine us like that? Together?" she asked.

Steven waited a few beats before answering. "Every other second."

She wiggled closer. Less than an inch remained between them, and she was close enough to hear the small catch in his breathing. His scent was woody, spicy, divine. "I think about being with you too, Steven," she told him. "I wonder what it would feel like to have you kiss me. To have your hands on me. To feel the weight of you on top of me."

She reached out then and touched his lips with her fingertips. She used a feather touch and was satisfied to find that his mouth was exactly as soft as she'd imagined it would be. She ran her fingers lightly over both his top and bottom lip, parting them slightly, gently exploring the contours. A small shiver ran through her at the intimacy of the moment.

And the next thing Shelly knew, she was pinned, deliciously, beneath him. And then it was all heat and wetness as Steven's soft mouth worked over hers. When she opened for him, he groaned before delving inside and tasting her. She buried her hands in his hair, holding him in place. His five o'clock shadow abraded the sensitive skin on her jaw as the kiss took on a life of its own, but Shelly didn't care. The sensation helped remind her that this was real. This was finally happening.

But when he moved his mouth to her neck, lightly nibbling his way to her earlobe, an unbidden and unwanted thought popped into her head. What if Steven wasn't thinking about her at all? What if he was thinking about Heidi? The question had the effect of a bucket of ice cold water being poured over her, and Steven must have sensed it because he stopped in his tracks. "What is it?" With an arm resting on the blanket on either side of her, he suspended himself above her, removing some of his weight. They were still nose to nose.

"I'm okay. I'm sorry, it's just—Steven, I have to know something." Shelly almost didn't recognize her own voice. It wasn't bold, it wasn't flirtatious. It was shaky and vulnerable, and she hated it.

Steven ran a slow hand through her hair. "You can ask me anything."

"Who are you thinking of when you kiss me?"

His hand stopped momentarily, and her breath caught. She held it until she felt the soft caress of his thumb over her temple. And then he closed the space between them and kissed her. It wasn't hot and needy like before. It was gentle and tender and spoke to her heart.

But in case she had any lingering doubts, Steven spoke the words, and they settled the matter once and for all. "Shelly, you are *all* I'm thinking about right now. Only you. This is about you and me—the two of us. But if you want, we can dial this back. I'd be happy just to hold you here in my arms under this blanket all night."

And that's when she knew. She reached out to brush back a lock of hair that had fallen over his forehead. Shelly had never said the words to any man but her father, and she wouldn't say them out loud to Steven now—she wasn't sure he was ready—but she recited them to herself over and over again, like the refrain of a song, as she lifted her head off the wool blanket and touched her lips to Steven's once more.

She loved him.

If the Northern Lights made an appearance that night, neither Steven nor Shelly would have noticed. It wasn't until the sun began to brighten the horizon that they finally stood and packed up, retracing their steps back to the car through the cold sand, arm in arm.

※

While Steven worked the key in the door of his apartment, which seemed to take longer than it should, Shelly tipped her head back and closed her eyes, reveling in a sort of weightless euphoria. She was in love with Steven—mind, body, and soul. Nothing she'd ever done before could compare to what she'd experienced with him down on the beach. It had been a total rush, a thrill like nothing else. She'd never experienced anything like it. Not when she'd bungee jumped down in Florida, not when she'd paraglided in Colorado, not even that amazing night three years ago with Brandon Corey, a guy everybody knew was the Casanova of Nicolet. No one from her past could compare to him, and there could never be anyone else in her future. Steven was *it* for her.

To prove to herself that she hadn't imagined what they'd shared together on the beach, she grabbed him by the shoulders just as he got the door open and turned him towards her. Before he could ask her what she was up to, she stood on her tip toes and kissed him soundly. His response thrilled her. Dropping his keys, he cradled her head with his hands. Shelly loved when guys did that.

Scratch that.

She loved when *Steven* did that. If she could erase her past history with men, she would do it in a heartbeat. What had she been thinking? Looking back from this vantage point, it had all been so hollow. From here on out, she wanted only thoughts of Steven in her head.

His lips were soft and warm, and she sighed in contentment against his mouth. She felt his lips turn up into a smile, even as she continued to plant small kisses there.

"You're something else," he said before tilting his head and nibbling her neck.

"Hmm. I could do this all day."

"I think we should," Steven said between nibbles.

Shelly laughed. "Well, let's at least move inside."

"Good idea. I need to get sand out of . . . some places."

Giggling, Shelly grabbed the fallen keys and turned and pulled him through the door. "Me too. First, though, I need some water. May I?" she asked, inclining her head towards the kitchen sink.

"Sure. Glasses are in the top right cabinet, but maybe you already know that." Steven set the bag holding the thermos and blankets down on the counter and moved to the corner of the room where the phone and answering machine sat side by side on a small end table. "I've got a message," he said.

"Hmm. Go ahead and listen if you want."

Heidi's voice filled the small space, and Shelly froze in the process of grabbing a glass.

> *Steven, hi. It's me . . . Heidi. Um, so, I know things have been really off with us this last week, and I said some things out on the rocks that night that . . . well, that I didn't really mean. Well, some I did, and some I didn't. Anyway, I wasn't being honest with either one of us, and—Ugh! I'm sorry. I shouldn't be telling you this in a message. It's just . . . I really wish you were home now so we could talk. There's a lot I need to say. Maybe tomorrow? I should be home around dinnertime. Hopefully, we can connect then. Um . . . okay, bye.*

Shelly had turned in horror to look at Steven as Heidi's message played out, and she saw that he'd squeezed his eyes shut as he listened. His expression was pained.

This was not good. Not good at all.

Chapter 24

"This is such a long drive," Heidi said six hours into the trip back home. She stretched as much as she could in the passenger seat of her dad's Lincoln.

Sepi nodded. "Four hundred miles almost exactly."

"It gives me anxiety to think about making this long trip by myself all the time. I almost wonder if I should fly home from Minneapolis when I visit."

"I imagine you will do a bit of both. Of course, we will come to visit you also. I am not sure we will fly. You know I like driving. I find it relaxing."

Heidi smiled. There was nothing relaxing about the way her father drove. Driving brought out a part of his personality that must lie dormant at all other times. He was impatient and hurried, weaving in and out of traffic even if he had nowhere to be. Shelly had inherited his lead foot. She hated driving behind anyone too, and rushed everywhere she went.

It was so bad that Maggie avoided driving with either one of them, and when it couldn't be helped, she'd grip the passenger door and close her eyes every time Sepi or Shelly accelerated to get around somebody. Heidi made a mental note to encourage her mother to fly when she came to visit. Four hundred miles of holding on to the door, and her mother's fingers might just fall off.

Heidi and Sepi had spent much of the trip home engaged in light conversation, but there'd been plenty of time for Heidi to get lost in her thoughts, and although she wouldn't tell her father, she'd made a decision. She had to come clean with Steven. She'd left him a message late last night that she needed to talk to him. That feeling had only grown in its intensity. If she didn't tell him how she felt, she'd always regret it. Always wonder. She didn't want to live her life asking, "What if?"

There was a big part of her that had the sense she was about to completely humiliate herself. This wasn't her. She didn't do this kind of thing, but she knew if she didn't talk to him right away, meaning today, she just might lose her nerve forever.

Shelly was working tonight, so Heidi wouldn't be able to get a read on what, if anything, had happened over the weekend. And as much as she'd prefer going into a talk with Steven knowing that information, she just couldn't wait. It had to happen tonight. By then, he may have already accepted the job at Chester, but that didn't mean he couldn't change his mind. She knew he wanted that job, but he might just want her more—unlikely, maybe, but not impossible.

Pulling into the driveway an hour later, Heidi's stomach did a little dip the way it always did when Shelly drove too fast over the steep hill out on Langley Road. It was only four o'clock, which meant that Heidi had at least an hour to unpack and fret over how to address Steven. Thankfully, her mom kept her distracted with conversation and questions about her weekend, although she was pretty tight lipped about her own weekend.

Usually after a retreat, Maggie was fired up. But this time, after asking a few questions and getting one- or two-word answers back, Heidi gave up. It seemed her mother wanted to focus on the Rochester trip instead, and that was fine with Heidi. Maggie set her up with cookies and milk at the counter, and for the moment, Heidi felt thrown back in time to her high school years.

If her mom sensed Heidi's jitters, she didn't say anything about it directly. Instead, she worked to soothe her oldest daughter's nerves just by being her sweet self, and before Heidi knew it, the clock in the dining room struck five.

"You know, Mom, I was thinking I might try to catch Steven tonight. Maybe head out to Sable Rocks. Is it okay if I miss dinner?"

Maggie, who had been happily moving about the kitchen getting pots and pans ready, abruptly stopped digging around in a cupboard and looked up at Heidi with an odd look on her face.

"What is it? Why are you looking at me like that?" Heidi asked.

Slowly, Maggie turned from the cupboard. She moved closer to Heidi and rested her forearms on the counter. "Have you spoken to your sister recently?"

An awful feeling crept over her. "No. We played phone tag all weekend. It's been really weird. I don't think we've ever gone this long without actually talking. Why? Does . . . does she have something to tell me?"

"She just might," Maggie answered. "I don't know anything for certain, and it certainly wouldn't be my place to say anything if I did, but I think you two need to talk before you see Steven."

"Mom. I know what you're worried about. But it's fine. Okay? Shelly and I will work it all out."

"I don't want to pry. I really don't. But . . . honey, why do you want to see Steven?"

"I have to tell him, Mom. I just have to. I haven't been honest with him about my feelings. And even if it's too late, I have to tell him. Please try to understand."

"Oh, honey. This is a mistake."

That was not what Heidi wanted to hear. She dug in her heels. "Well, it's one I have to make then."

Maggie shook her head. "You're a grown woman now, and you can make your own decisions, but . . . I don't think this is a good idea. For a lot of reasons."

"Give me one."

"Other than the obvious?"

Heidi set her jaw. "I'm going to tell him. It'll be okay."

Maggie smiled weakly. "If you say so."

Another half hour went by before Steven pulled into the driveway. Heidi had been standing at the front window, and when she saw his Blazer make the turn, she bolted out of the house, reaching the side of the car before he'd finished parking. She knew she might appear overly eager. She didn't care.

"Heidi, hi," Steven said with a look of surprise as he opened his door. He didn't quite meet her eyes. "You're back. How was orientation?"

"Really great, but it's good to be back too." Normally, Heidi had a hyperactive filter. She didn't say nearly all the things that popped into her mind. Not by half. This time, she killed the filter. "I missed you. You know what they say, *Distance makes the heart grow fonder.*"

Maybe it shouldn't have, but it pleased her to see Steven's reaction to that. He turned pink from the neck up and he actually stuttered in his response. That had to be a good sign.

"Th-that's right. They do say that." He cleared his throat. "Uh, so, what's up?"

"I have a favor to ask of you. Please don't say no."

"Why would I say no?"

Heidi shrugged.

Steven rubbed the nape of his neck. "Okay. Ask away."

"I need you to go to the rocks with me."

"Sable Rocks? Now?"

"Yes, now. Right now."

"Um . . . can I change first?" he asked, but she was already walking around the car to get in.

Under his breath, he muttered, "I guess not," but Heidi pretended not to hear. She was on auto pilot. She needed to stay the course or she'd lose her nerve.

Steven attempted conversation as they began the short drive over to Sable Rocks. He talked of the weather, how cool it was today and how warm it had been over the weekend. Heidi didn't want to talk about anything having to do with his weekend. They needed to steer clear of it altogether because she didn't want her sister's name to come up.

She didn't want the job offer to come up either. In a sort of preemptive strike, Heidi interrupted with talk all about her weekend, in great detail, and she was still talking when they pulled into the parking lot. She was only through Saturday's events. She talked about Sunday's breakfast with her cohort and was on to the dinner she'd had with Sepi by the time they sat down in the same spot where they'd sat before. It was only then that she allowed herself to stop talking.

If Steven thought her incessant chatter was odd, he didn't remark on it, but he did look at her with a question in his eyes once she grew silent. All of a sudden, she was tongue-tied, and she stared at him helplessly. Steven seemed to know she needed help. "I got your voicemail," he said.

Heidi found her voice. "There were things I should have said to you when we were here last time. I wish now that I had. I guess, I don't know, maybe I was scared. Maybe distance really does make the heart grow fonder, I really don't know. All I know is that I don't want things to end with you. I mean, things haven't really gotten started yet—I know that—but I want to change that. I want us to be together, and I think we could make it work."

Steven exhaled heavily. "Heidi—"

"No, wait a minute. I need to get this out. Tons of people in my program are in relationships. I guess I didn't think that could work for us at first. But why not? Do you know there are companies in Rochester you could apply to? Lots of them. I wasn't even looking, and I found three."

Steven squeezed the bridge of his nose and asked, "Heidi, what are you saying here?"

She bit down on her lip. "I'm saying you could come with me. We could see where this thing goes. I just . . . I don't want to lose you, Steven. I think we could have a really good thing if we let ourselves try."

She reached for his hand and found in dismay that he dodged her grasp. She shook her head in confusion. "What is it? What's wr—" she began as he hopped to his feet.

Steven stood there, scrubbing a hand over his face and looking as though he wanted to take a running jump and fling himself off the edge of the cliff. "Heidi, there's something—" He stopped himself and brought his hand down to his side. "Okay, look," he tried again, "I have to tell you something."

It was her turn to sigh heavily. His behavior, as well as something in his expression—the way his eyes bored into hers—told her she was about to hear something she didn't want to hear, and she was pretty sure she could guess what it was. Still seated, she tipped her head up and met his eyes. "Don't, okay? Please."

Steven looked at her pleadingly, his chest rising and falling rapidly. "Heidi, I'm so sorry, but—"

"It's okay." She quickly cut him off. She didn't want details. In fact, the less she knew, the better. "I forgive you. It was bound to happen. I gave Shelly the green light, idiot that I am. I figured you guys spent the weekend together, and if she kissed you or something, it's fine." She shrugged. "I mean, obviously, I don't like it, but I'll get over it."

Steven went very still as he stared at her, and then he took one step closer. "No, Heidi. Listen to me. It's gone further than that. It's gone . . . too far."

Heidi stood, her eyes never leaving his. "What do you mean?"

He shook his head helplessly. "Please, don't make me say it."

Heidi's hands flew to her face, covering her eyes. "Oh, Steven! You didn't," she whispered.

She felt him come closer, and when he next spoke, his voice was soothing and gentle, the way he might talk to a spooked horse. "Heidi, I'm so sorry. I didn't mean for any of this to happen, but . . ."

Slowly, she dropped her hands, but she couldn't look at him. Instead, she looked down at the tiny blades of grass growing up from a crack in the rock under her feet. Her stomach roiled, and she felt like she might be sick, but when she spoke, her voice was deceptively calm. "But you choose Shelly," she finished for him. She gave a small, hollow laugh. "Why am I not even surprised?"

"Heidi, please—"

Forcing herself to meet his gaze, she put up a hand. "No, it's . . . it's how it's always been. My whole life. Why did I think this would be any different?"

"It's not like that, okay? I *did* choose you."

She snorted. "For all of two seconds. I must not have been all that memorable if you could forget all about me in a weekend." She turned and took a few steps away. Looking out over the water with her arms wrapped tightly around herself, she said tonelessly, "I want to go home now."

Heidi sensed Steven draw up behind her, and when he touched her shoulder, she shrugged him off though she did turn to face him. The expression he wore was one of deep remorse, but she refused to let that affect her. "We need to talk about this, Heidi. I need to explain. See, I realized some things over the weekend."

She braced herself. "Yeah? Like what?"

"Well, like we're too much the same, you and me. You'd think that'd be a strength, but it's not. Don't get me wrong, it works great for friendship, and I hope we still have that because I'd hate to lose you, but for anything more . . ." He shrugged. "We're both so career driven right now, I'm not sure there would be a whole lot of room for anything else."

Heidi narrowed her eyes. "Wait a minute," she said. "So you choose Shelly because she has no career goals?" Heidi could hear her voice becoming shrill as she continued on, but she didn't care. "How perfect for you! That way she can just dote on you and meet all of *your* needs? That's disgusting!"

Steven's face registered such genuine surprise that Heidi knew immediately she'd missed the mark. It didn't matter. She'd never admit to being wrong.

His voice shook. "Is that what you think of me?"

Heidi doubled down. "That's what you just said, isn't it? You don't want a career woman. So you chose the unambitious sister."

Steven's mouth pressed into a grim line. "If you think your sister has no ambition, then you don't know her at all."

Heidi felt something inside her come unglued. Advancing forward a step, she poked a finger in Steven's chest, and she yelled so loudly her voice echoed. "Don't talk to me about my sister! I know her better than anyone else in the world."

Steven tipped his head back briefly and looked up at the sky, and after a deep breath, he met her eyes again. "All I'm saying is she has plans for her future too. And her plans and my plans aren't in direct opposition to each other. That's all I'm trying to say."

"Oh, you're saying a lot more than that. Basically, Shelly and I are interchangeable in your mind. We look almost exactly the same, right? How lucky for you to be able to just swap out one sister for the other. How convenient."

"Come on, Heidi."

She went on as though he hadn't spoken. "You know, Steven, I never took you for a *love the one you're with* kind of guy."

"Heidi, what are you doing? Why are you twisting my words?"

"Why are *you* still talking? You have nothing to say in your defense. Last week it was me, and then as soon as I leave, suddenly it's Shelly? I had no idea you were so shallow."

Steven shook his head sadly. "You don't get it, and I didn't want to have to spell it out for you like this. I don't want to hurt you, Heidi. But . . . no, you're not interchangeable. Not in the least. And yes, I was late in seeing it, but I see it clearly now. Shelly is one of a kind. She lights me up, makes me feel things I haven't felt for a long time. She's like the missing piece of myself that makes me whole. I want to be that for her too, if that's something she needs, although I imagine that the two of you . . . you have each other for that, and that's wonderful."

He shot her a small, genuine smile that Heidi could not return. If she moved even a muscle in her face, it would crack.

"The bottom line is Shelly's *good* for me, Heidi. She helps me not take myself too seriously. And I think, I hope, I'm good for her too. So you see, me being with Shelly has nothing at all to do with you, but it has everything to do with her. I wasn't just scooping up the leftovers the way you make it sound. She's a hell of a lot more special to me than that."

Heidi swallowed. Her throat was too tight to manage more than a one-word reply. "Fine," she said, and she was relieved her voice sounded somewhat normal. Her eyes were another story, and if she wasn't careful, they'd give her away. Dammed up tears burned and threatened to overflow, but she wouldn't let Steven see that. What she wanted was for him to say those words about her. Hadn't they had a special connection? Didn't she complete, or at least complement him in some small way? Wasn't she special too?

They were both quiet as they studied each other. In Steven's face, she could see regret mixed with compassion, and when he spoke again, he took a step toward her. "Look, can we please just—"

"No, we can't. Okay? We can't. This is done." And with that, she stormed off. Her eyes continued to burn, but she didn't allow a single tear to fall as she ran back towards the parking area, leaving Steven to catch up with her. It took him some time since he was wearing dress slacks and dress shoes, but when he did, she was grateful he didn't say anything more. Heidi didn't know if she was more angry or more hurt at that moment, but it didn't really matter anyway. Nothing mattered anymore but medical school. She would focus on that.

Chapter 25

Steven felt physically ill as he drove Heidi back home. The silence in the car was thick enough to choke on. What could he say to make this better? There wasn't anything, and he feared he'd already said too much as it was. In his effort to make it clear that he didn't view Shelly as a substitute Heidi, he feared he'd diminished Heidi's own amazing qualities, and there were many. He worried he'd made her feel like second best, and she wasn't. Not at all. She was special too, and now he'd lost her.

Life, especially when it came to relationships, romantic or otherwise, was a lot like a crowded maze, he decided, with everyone making their own way. Sometimes you journeyed along with another person for a time, often happily, until you hit a dead end or the two of you were pulled away in separate directions. Often, the separation was permanent, but occasionally you might just find each other again down the line.

Other times, your path crossed with someone else's for a brief moment in time. Some of those people pointed you in the right direction, while others tripped you up, and still others provided a nice little rest and distraction. A quick encounter. A hello and goodbye, for better or worse.

Most people in the maze, you never encountered at all because it was simply too vast a space, which when Steven thought about it seemed like such a tragedy. All those beautiful souls you'd never get to meet.

And then, rarely, you found someone headed in the very same direction as you, someone willing to take the twists and turns right alongside you, wherever they led.

Whether it was fate or chance that determined who you paired up with in the maze of life, Steven wasn't sure. Maybe it was both. But maze or not, he'd made a mess of his little corner of it, and there was nothing he could do to change that. There was no going back to the way things used to be with Heidi. Not now.

Heidi was right. It really was done.

What he felt the most terrible about was knowing that he might come between these two sisters. If that happened, he wasn't sure he'd be able to forgive himself. He didn't want to be responsible for a fracture of the family he'd grown to love. Briefly, Steven tried to think of a way he could fix things, but the more he thought, the more he realized he would only do more damage by getting involved beyond what he already had. Not that he'd leave Shelly to face Heidi on her own. He'd support her however she needed him to.

He just wished he could go back and do things differently, but honestly, where would he even begin? If he'd made missteps, and he was certain he had, they'd already left their mark. They were permanent footprints.

It was too late now to go back and redo anything. And even if he could, he was fairly certain he'd been meant to end up with Shelly in the end anyway. Maybe it had taken all those missteps to make it to this point. He just wished they hadn't hurt anyone, but they had, and he was powerless to heal things between the twin sisters. It was out of his hands, and it sucked to realize it. All he could do was be there for Shelly and be open to a friendship with Heidi if she ever wanted one again. That appeared to be a big *if*.

After pulling into the driveway and parking, Heidi was out of the car quick as a flash. He got out himself, leaving the keys in the ignition, and stood helplessly between the open door and the body of the car. He wanted to call out to her, but he knew there wasn't anything more to say tonight. Steven rested his chin on the top of his door as he watched her disappear into the house.

The Corolla was parked out front, which meant Shelly was home from work. What would happen between the girls tonight? And what would Sepi and Maggie think? What if they ended up hating him for this? To them, it might look like he'd played their daughters against each other.

Steven let out a long and heavy breath and retrieved his keys, and as he walked up the steps to his apartment, he stared down at his feet. He didn't want to admire the view of the harbor. He didn't deserve to see anything beautiful. Instead, he was convinced he needed to pay some kind of penance for how he'd handled things. Not bothering to eat, he forced himself out of his work clothes and into a cold shower. He was still shivering an hour later when a soft knock came at his door.

"This is so bad, Steven," Shelly said as soon as he invited her in. "She knows everything, doesn't she?"

Steven gave a small nod. He shouldn't have told Heidi and then just left Shelly to deal with the fallout all on her own. It was another mistake in a whole series of them, and he studied her face to see if she was upset with him. She had every right to be. He deserved a verbal lashing, at least.

Instead, she closed the distance between them and wrapped her arms around him. She rested her head on his chest, and as he held her small, trembling form, he felt an overwhelming need to protect her from the world and all the pain it might toss her way. Gently, he patted her back, but instead of soothing her, it seemed to do the opposite, and she wept. Her body heaved and shook on each sob, and Steven rocked her slowly as he held her tighter.

He didn't know how long they stood there like that at the front door, but after a time, Shelly calmed enough to step back and look up at him with watery eyes and a trembling mouth.

"I've really blown it this time," she whispered.

Steven rubbed a hand over the stubble on his chin that must have grown during his cold shower. He always wondered how it could do that. "Let's sit down."

Nodding, Shelly followed him to the sofa in the living room and sat as close to him as she could without actually sitting on his lap. She let her hand rest on his knee before launching into the story.

"When Heidi came in after you guys got back from Sable Rocks, I had just gotten home from work and was in the kitchen pouring myself an iced tea. The door slammed, which surprised me, and when I looked up, she was standing there with this ... with this look on her face. It was like she *hated* me, Steven. She's never looked at me that way before."

Shelly paused.

"What did she say?"

"Nothing at first. She just glared at me and then turned and walked up the stairs to her room. I went after her, of course, and I asked her what was wrong. She tried to shut the door on me. And then when I stuck my foot into the doorjamb, she totally lost it on me. She accused me of—" Shelly pinched the bridge of her nose with her fingers and closed her eyes, and while Steven waited for her to regain control, he placed his hand on top of hers.

"Honestly, she just told the truth. She just said what we all know. She gives and I take." Shelly shrugged helplessly. "I'm just a big fat taker. She gave you to me, and I took you, even though I knew she wanted you for herself."

Steven ignored the implication that giving and taking reduced him to a mere object. The last thing he wanted to be right now was annoyed. "What did you say?" he asked, instead.

"What could I say? She's right. It's always been that way. But as much as I want to change. As much as I want to be a better sister to her. I can't give you up, Steven. I just can't."

Steven cleared his throat. On second thought ... "You know, I'm not an object, Shelly. You don't get to give me, and she doesn't get to take me."

Shelly was silent for a moment. "Sorry. I do know that." Hesitantly, she asked, "Do you ... want to ... be with her, Steven?"

His response was immediate and genuine. "No." He shook his head and repeated it when she looked up at him doubtfully. "No. I don't."

"But do you have any regrets about last night?" she asked with bright eyes.

What could he say in response? He had plenty of regrets. He felt he'd taken advantage of her. They had all the time in the world, and he'd rushed it with her. He'd known how she felt about him. Known she'd give him anything, and he was ashamed he hadn't exercised that self-control Gran had always gone on about.

So yeah, he regretted his lack of restraint. He regretted the timing. He regretted hurting Heidi and causing trouble between the girls. But he couldn't regret the outcome of last night when it came to him and Shelly. He'd told her he'd been adrift since Gran died, but now, because of her, he felt moored and secure for the first time in a long time. She felt like home to him, this beautiful, vibrant woman.

She eyed him anxiously, and he squeezed her hand. "No. I don't."

Relief passed over her features, and before she threw her arms around his neck, he witnessed a small smile play on her lips. "I'm so glad. I've been a little freaked about it all day, and then when I came home and you and Heidi were gone together, I didn't know what to think."

"I'm sorry you were worried. You don't need to worry about me ever, okay?"

She nodded, and he felt her hair tickle his neck.

"Steven, what are we going to do?" she asked in a muffled voice against his chest.

"I don't know," he said honestly. "But I'm wondering if maybe I should talk to Sepi."

Shelly pulled back and looked at him doubtfully. "You think you should?"

"I think so. I owe it to him, for one thing. I've made a mess of things with his daughters, and I'd like to apologize, you know? Admit my mistakes. I respect your dad, and I think he'll have good advice."

"You won't tell him about—"

Steven gave a small jerk of his head. "No. That's between us."

Shelly nodded, thinking it over for several seconds. "Okay." She smiled at him, but it was weak and fleeting and her lips trembled.

"Hey," he said, caressing her jaw, "It's all going to be okay."

"I know." She didn't sound convinced, so he planted small kisses on those trembling lips, and did his best to convince her.

***

After considering logistics, they decided the best thing would be for Shelly to head back home and ask Sepi to come up to the apartment. As Steven waited, he took inventory of the situation. What had begun as one of the best days of his life as he signed on the dotted line at Chester—making his employment there official—was ending as one of the worst. But it wasn't about him, he reminded himself. And he couldn't make this about him. This was about two twin sisters who were so close and so important to each other that they were able to physically experience each other's pain. It was vital that whatever rift he'd caused between them was healed before Heidi left for school. If anyone could accomplish that, it was Sepi.

Three quick knocks, followed by the opening of the door, brought Steven around.

"Hey, Steven. You decent?" Sepi joked through the cracked opening.

Wasn't that a question with double meaning! Was he decent? He feared he wasn't.

"Come on in, Sepi," he answered, hopping up from the sofa.

"Well, my boy," he began after he'd closed the door and set his cap down on the counter, "you've turned the house into a bit of a war zone, eh?"

Steven was stricken. "Sepi, I'm so sorry."

Sepi waved his hand and walked to the couch. Steven followed. "Oh, it will all blow over in time."

Steven was skeptical. "You think so?"

"Oh, sure. I had two brothers. Both have passed now, but I remember plenty of times vowing never to speak to one or the other of them again. It didn't stick."

This was such a relief for Steven who, as an only child, was unfamiliar with sibling dynamics for the most part. Still, he needed to express his remorse in no uncertain terms. "I never meant for any of this to happen."

"Hmm. I knew it would," Sepi revealed as matter-of-factly as if he were talking about having predicted a rain shower. "I know my girls, and I had you pegged from the beginning."

"You had me pegged?"

"Steven, you're what Finnish women would call *vastustamaton*."

"What's that?"

Sepi grinned. "Irresistible."

Steven laughed humorlessly. "No. I'm really not."

"See. That's part of your charm, I am sure. You don't even know it. Listen. I do not need to know the specifics of what happened; I believe I can guess at enough. I love my Heidi-ho, and maybe you do, too, but she has got ambitions that aren't quite compatible with yours. Quite honestly, I wondered if a man would ever catch her eye and hold it. It speaks well of you that you managed to do that. Under different circumstances . . . who knows what could have happened?"

Steven tried not to wince. Why did that feel painful? He knew why. He had a feeling he'd always wonder about what might have been with Heidi. And then he felt consumed by guilt for even having had the thought.

Sepi continued, "As for Shelly, well, she could use a little taming. I would say she's ready for that now. As much as she loves her adrenaline rushes and living life large when it comes to the day to day, for the bigger picture, she wants a quiet life here in this map-dot town. She will never leave this place. She needs its peace and tranquility as a counterbalance to the hubbub that exists on the inside." Sepi chuckled.

Steven nodded. That made a strange kind of sense.

"You would be good for her for the same reason. You know, I have seen my Shelly look at you, Steven. She has brought plenty of young men by over the years, believe me." He shook his head ruefully. "A whole gaggle of them. All knuckleheads down to the very last one. Her mother and I were well down the road of despair before you came around, eh?" Sepi laughed again. "We are thrilled she has now finally developed some taste."

Steven supposed he should feel flattered.

"It is different with you. Maggie and I knew it from the beginning. Shelly never looked at any of those Romeos the way she looks at you. And, yes, it is true that Heidi lit up every time she saw you, also, but nothing, and I mean *nothing* compares to how her eyes sparkled as she laid out her new medical equipment for me to see this last weekend. You would think that stethoscope was made of gold the way she beheld it. If Maggie ever looked at me that way, oh, I would be a goner for sure."

He winked.

"So, I think it boils down to this. Heidi belongs there, and you belong here. Whether you choose to build a relationship with Shelly, well, that is between the two of you. Selfishly, I would love to see it happen. I like having you around, and I cannot imagine a better man for my Shelly. But, time will tell, eh?"

"That means I would have your blessing then," Steven clarified.

"Yes, Steven. You have my blessing, and Maggie's too."

Relief washed over him at that. Sepi and Maggie didn't hate him, and he even had their blessing with Shelly. It wasn't a free pass to roll around in the sand with her in the dark, of course, but still, it meant more to him than they could know.

"How is she?" Steven asked. He'd thought about Maggie off and on all day.

"She's a bit fretful at the moment. She did not like having me away. She told me to go, but perhaps I should have stayed. She had a few episodes over the weekend. They scared her. It's hard not knowing. It is hard for us both. And now with the girls on the outs . . ."

"When will you tell the girls?"

"After Thursday's appointment. Friday, maybe. They will both be off work that day. In fact, I believe Heidi's last day of work is Thursday."

"What can I do, Sepi? How can I help?"

"Keep coming 'round. It will be awkward for you and for the girls, I am sure. But keep coming, as you always have done. Soon, things will go back to normal with you and my daughters, and I know Maggie would like to see you. You will make a pleasant distraction from her worries, I think. She always spends a little extra time on dinner when she knows you will join us.

"Cooking and baking is her therapy, you know. She hates the grocery shopping, so I do that part. She never did learn to iron properly, so I do that too. Just so long as she does not ask me to do the laundry, I will take on whatever she needs." He leaned towards Steven. "You know, I messed that chore up on purpose once to make sure I would never be asked again. There's a tip, eh?"

Steven chuckled. "I'll remember that. The two of you, you make a good team."

"We do." Sepi smiled wistfully. "We surely do."

Chapter 26

Shelly glanced surreptitiously at Heidi. The entire ten-minute ride to work was a freeze out. Heidi didn't say a word to Shelly. She didn't even grunt when Shelly asked if she wanted the radio on. At least Shelly was the one driving this morning. That way, they got to River Run as quickly as possible.

Her sister continued the freeze out, more or less, the rest of the day, which was a tremendous feat because the two of them were working the clubhouse together. Shelly had been bummed out to discover Dot's niece, Marjorie, was scheduled on the beverage cart all day. It was too gorgeous to be stuck in the restaurant the entire shift, but at least the tips would be good. Nicolet General Hospital was running its annual fundraiser and golf outing today, and all the high rollers would be there.

It came as no surprise to Shelly that she and Heidi were attracting quite a bit of attention from the patrons. The regulars at the course were mostly used to being served by identical twins and, by this point, many could even tell them apart at first glance. But most of the people inside the clubhouse today weren't regulars, and they were downright giddy to be waited on by twin sisters. Shelly really didn't see what the big deal was, but she was bombarded with all the usual questions and comments. People were so predictable—like the women at the table she was currently waiting on. "What's it like to be a twin?" a woman with long, bottle-red hair asked.

"It's pretty great," Shelly answered with her standard reply as she filled their water glasses and waited for the next question, which would be, *Have you ever traded places?*

She was right. "Um, you know, I think maybe once or twice when we were younger."

The pretty blond sighed. "I always wished I had a twin sister."

If Shelly had a dollar for every time she heard that sentiment expressed, she'd have had enough money to buy her own car and drive here alone—without her pissy twin sister. People thought being a twin would be the greatest thing ever and, most of the time, Shelly would agree. It *was* special, and she'd never wish it away. But sometimes it really blew.

"Can you get your sister to come over here so we can look at you two next to each other?" asked the absolute hairiest woman she had ever seen. Shelly nearly flinched when she noticed her sitting at the far end of the table. The poor lady had an actual mustache, and she raised her thick unibrow in question as she waited for Shelly to answer. Just in time, Shelly filtered out her knee-jerk response. Something along the lines of: *Sure! We'll perform like circus animals for you and your friends just as soon as you shave off that mustache.*

Instead, she smiled and said something noncommittal before taking their orders.

It went like that most of the day, minus the female facial hair, thank goodness, and she heard a couple of new ones too: *Do you ever look in the mirror and think you're your sister? How do you know you're really you?* And her new favorite, *Can you use your twin as a mirror?* People could be such morons.

By the time seven o'clock rolled around, the place had mostly cleared out and Shelly was dead on her feet. One look at her sister from across the room, and she could see Heidi was in the same boat. It had been a brutal ten-hour shift without a whole lot of downtime, but judging from the weight of her apron, she'd scored big on tips today, so at least there was that.

"Good work today, girls. You can go now, thanks," Dot said in her deep, raspy voice. She really should give up those cigarettes. They were desiccating her from the inside out. Whatever dewiness had existed in her skin had been sucked away long ago, leaving deep fissures in her face that reminded Shelly of the cracks that appeared in the soil around her mother's plants last summer when Heidi had forgotten to water them for several weeks.

Even Dot's hair, what was left of it, had been reduced to brittle straw. The woman needed to retire. Not only did she look scary, but she seemed to do less and less on the job. She'd sneak off to her house for hours during shifts, and she regularly left Shelly to close up by herself at night, even though Shelly knew for a fact she was required by contract to do that herself or, at the very least, oversee it. She never pulled that crap with Heidi, but with Shelly it had become routine. She wondered if the board knew Dot had given her a key.

During their shift, the twins had worked together well enough, letting each other know that table five was ready for the bill or that the order for table nine was up, but now, as they changed in the women's locker room, they were back to not talking. Shelly was sick of it. Standing there in her bra and underwear, she turned with her hands on her hips to face her sister. "That's it. I've had enough."

Heidi didn't turn around. She didn't even flinch. She didn't do much of anything other than continue changing out of her uniform and into her street clothes.

"Is this how it's going to be then?" she asked, speaking to her sister's back. "Us not talking until the day you walk out of here for good? Is that what you want?"

Heidi threw her khaki shorts on the floor and spun around. "What I *want*? What I want is a sister who's loyal. What I want is a good man, like Steven, to choose *me* for a change."

"Heidi, you told me to go for it. I asked you. *Twice!*"

"Do you not know me at all? You're my twin sister. You knew how I felt. I know you did. And you knew I was lying!"

Shelly couldn't argue with that. She had known. But the best things in life were worth fighting for, and Heidi hadn't lifted so much as a finger to fight for Steven.

"You should have spoken up, Heidi. I told you. All you had to do was say the words. You didn't. That's on you."

"Oh, right. That's on me. That's on me that you knew how I felt about Steven, and you took advantage of me being out of town to seal the deal for yourself. You rounded those bases awfully quickly, Shelly. Don't tell me you didn't plan the whole thing before I even left."

"I didn't plan it!" Shelly insisted. "*We* didn't plan it."

"Here we go with the 'it just happened garbage.' Well, I don't buy it."

"I don't care if you buy it or not. It's the truth. I didn't know what would happen. I had hopes for us, but it's not like I—"

"Oh, spare me." Heidi, who had appeared ready to duke it out all night, suddenly sagged, and all the fight left her body on a long exhale. "You know what? I'm so tired of this. I'm so tired of *you*. I can't wait to get away from you, finally. And when I'm in Rochester, nobody will even know I have a twin sister. I can't wait for that."

She might as well have punched Shelly in the gut . . . or pierced her through the heart. Swallowing hard, Shelly answered tightly, "I'm sorry you feel that way."

They finished dressing in silence. Heidi slammed her locker shut and left the room while Shelly was still tying her shoelaces. She could only hope her sister wouldn't drive off without her. Hearing movement from the back, she looked up to see Mrs. Thames sauntering towards her with a wide smile. She didn't stop as she passed Shelly, didn't even slow down, but as she walked by she said, "See, even your twin sister thinks you're a slut."

Chapter 27

Heidi knew her anger was a self-administered poison. She'd never felt worse in all her life. Her stomach was in constant knots, and she couldn't concentrate on anything. She had the day off, and even though Shelly was at the club working, she was all Heidi could think about.

That afternoon, she admitted a hard truth to herself. She was mourning the loss of Steven, but when it came right down to it, she was actually more upset about losing her sister to Steven than she was about losing Steven to her sister.

Heidi didn't have a crystal ball, but she might as well have because she knew, absolutely positively *knew*, that Steven was in Shelly's life for the long haul. She knew it on a bone-deep level, and it hurt. It was bad enough he'd chosen Shelly instead of her, but now she was going to be replaced—twice over. With Steven, her replacement was Shelly, and with Shelly, her replacement was Steven. They probably wouldn't even miss her when she left, now that they had each other. Even though she knew sadness was at the root of what she was feeling, she still couldn't let go of her anger. She was stewing in it.

"You know," Maggie had said earlier in the day after sitting Heidi down, "you're the one with all the power here."

Heidi scoffed. "Me? Yeah, right."

"Think about it. Forgiveness is yours to extend or withhold. You're calling the shots here. And if there's one thing I've learned over the years, honey, it's that life's too short to cling to anger and resentment. You can let yourself feel it, sure, but indulging it is something else entirely. You need to let it go. For your sake as well as theirs."

But Heidi wasn't ready. And when Shelly came in from work that night and approached her with a hopeful light in her eyes, Heidi couldn't deny the satisfaction she felt watching it fade just before she closed her bedroom door in her sister's face. She was doing that a lot lately. She spent the rest of the night in her room, making herself miserable. She didn't even go down for dinner.

Oddly enough, nobody knocked on her door that night. She'd expected one or the other of her parents to come and coax her out of her room. She'd even wondered if Shelly might try. Why did it bother her so much that they'd left her in peace? Maybe because peace was the last thing she felt.

Chapter 28

This had been Steven's final week as an intern. They'd given him tomorrow, Friday, off, which meant today was his last day as an underling. After the weekend, he would be a full-fledged member of the Chester Biotechnologies team. Almost as exciting as that, he'd also be fully paid. Tonight, he was heading over to the main house for dinner with Sepi and Maggie. Their appointment with the doctor, he assumed, had taken place earlier that afternoon. He'd considered calling from work, but then he'd thought better of it.

It might be best to let them tell him on their own timetable. He expected they'd discuss it at dinner. The girls were working, so Steven could breathe a sigh of relief about not having to navigate the mess he'd caused between the twins—at least for now.

Shelly said Heidi still wasn't speaking to her. This worried Steven, but Sepi remained optimistic. "They will sort it all out, Steven," he'd said last night as they sat together in Steven's apartment drinking a couple of beers and playing cards. "If they were brothers, they'd have come to blows days ago, and it would all be over now. But since they are females, they are doing it the female way. I don't pretend to understand it, but I do know, having been married to a female for more years than I can remember at the moment, this storm will pass."

Steven hoped Sepi was right. Shelly had lost some of that spunk he'd become so accustomed to and had grown to really love. She was still affectionate, always angling for ways to touch him or snuggle up against him. Honestly, he hadn't realized just how starved he'd been for physical touch. He'd had more hugs from Shelly in one evening than he'd had in the entire year since Gran passed. With each hug, each touch, he felt an ever-increasing connection to her.

But even pressed against him on the couch last night after Sepi left, she'd been withdrawn. There'd been a sorrowful quality to her all week that bent his heart, and he wanted to fix it all for her. But he couldn't. She needed things with her sister to be set right. And it really was a *need*. She needed her sister the way lungs needed air.

He cared about Heidi, too—of course—and knew she couldn't be faring much better than Shelly. She may never learn to forgive him, but she had to forgive her sister—for both their sakes. Steven grieved the loss of her friendship because he knew that no matter what happened, even if she did come around, things would never be the same between them again. He also knew that, in a million years, he'd never find another friend as true.

Having had some time to think things over, Steven decided to cut himself a little slack over how he'd handled things with the girls—not a lot of slack, but a little. It was still quite possible that he was the biggest creep around, but it was also possible that there was bound to be a certain level of weirdness in dating an identical twin sister under any circumstance. For him, having been attracted to them both when he'd thought they were one and the same person had set him up for a certain level of disaster and a very confusing summer where he didn't even know his own mind.

For one thing, Heidi and Shelly were literal mirror images of each other. The only way he was able to tell them apart was by the location of their dimples and the knowledge that Shelly's hair was a tad longer than Heidi's. Even their voices and speech patterns were the same. So were most of their mannerisms. So really, it was only logical that if he was physically attracted to one, there'd be the propensity to be physically attracted to the other. Especially if he was only testing the waters and hadn't entered into a relationship with either one, which is how it had been for most of the summer. Even the most clear-headed of men would have been confused in a situation like that. At least, that's how he tried to square it. It had only added to the confusion that he'd also been attracted to both of their personalities—vastly different though they were.

Now that he'd made a commitment to Shelly, it was easier to sort through it all. He no longer pined away for Heidi. He was all in with Shelly, without a doubt, but it was strange to realize that if Heidi hadn't been surprised that day with her acceptance to medical school, they probably would have started something together, and he would most likely have been happy in that scenario too. He didn't want to think about that. It was too weird. Maybe it all boiled down to timing, or maybe he was just the biggest creep this side of the Mackinac Bridge.

Something else he'd realized he'd need to come to terms with was the very real possibility that Shelly would always be more strongly connected to Heidi than to him. That was, if they ever spoke to one another again. If he and Shelly stayed together, and he hoped they would, he knew it was likely that their sisterly bond would always be the stronger one. Sepi had said it best. The girls had been *womb mates*. They were connected on a level that most people never experienced. He'd spent some time thinking about it and knew that he could handle it. He loved them both and wanted their relationship to be as strong as possible.

Yes, he loved them. He loved the whole family. Was he *in* love with Shelly? Well, if love made you smile at nothing all day long . . . then, yeah, maybe he was.

Over steak and a barley casserole that was out of this world, Maggie and Sepi kept the conversation light, but they exchanged several looks, so he knew there were things being left unsaid. It gratified Steven to be so familiar with this couple that he knew when something was going on. They were working up to telling him about Maggie's appointment.

It wasn't until they'd finished with the pie Steven had picked up from the Lakanen's favorite bakery that Maggie put down her napkin and looked him straight in the eye. Steven set down his fork and waited.

"Steven, I had my appointment today."

"I remembered. I wanted to call, but . . ."

"You're such a good boy," Maggie said. She reached over the table and grabbed his hand, giving it a small squeeze before moving on to Sepi. His hand she also squeezed and continued to hold. Sepi looked at her adoringly and with bright eyes.

A wave of dread passed through Steven. He was about to hear something not good. He just knew it. "Did they find something?" he asked.

"They did, yes. They found some . . . lesions, I guess they're called, in my brain. They were looking for them, and they found them."

Lesions. That wasn't good.

"The results are consistent with what you'd see with MS. Multiple sclerosis."

Steven had deduced as much, but hearing the words spoken out loud still rocked him. "Oh, Maggie. I'm so sorry."

Maggie blinked rapidly and nodded several times. "Thank you."

Steven looked back and forth between the two of them. They still held one another's hand. "So, what now?"

Maggie looked to Sepi for the answer. "In the next few weeks, she will be getting a care team. She will have many appointments over the coming days and weeks as they put together a treatment plan. She's on steroids for the time being. Those are for the short term to treat her symptoms now. She is in a flare, but it should settle."

Maggie shook her head. "I'm so lucky to have Sepi here to help me. I think I've forgotten half of what the doctor told us. My mind just feels . . . slow and cloudy."

"I wish this wasn't happening to you," Steven said.

"I know, dear. Me too. But I have to say that, in some ways, it's nice to have a name for my symptoms. I've been so tired. For months. And then when I started to get dizzy and see double, that was scary for me. Now that I know what to call it, it doesn't seem so frightening."

"We know there is no cure, as I am sure you know too, but at least we can treat it. At least there is that." Sepi smiled sadly at Steven.

They needed to look at the positives. Steven could do that. "You're right," he agreed. "They've made so many gains in this field over the last few decades. I don't know a lot about MS, but I know new treatments are always emerging, and so many people around the world live with the disease well enough. Plus, Maggie, you have your own live-in nurse."

Maggie looked at Sepi. "I do. A very handsome *male* nurse at that."

They all laughed, and Steven took a sip of his milk. "When will you tell the girls?"

Maggie and Sepi sobered. "Tomorrow," Sepi answered. "We will get takeout from the bakery and tell them in the morning over donuts and coffee."

"Are you still worried about Heidi's reaction?"

"You know, when I thought it was possible this might be a tumor—"

Maggie was all astonishment. "You never told me that!"

"I didn't want to scare you," Sepi explained.

Maggie laughed.

It was Sepi's turn to be astounded. "Why is that funny?"

"Because I thought it might be a tumor also, but I didn't want to worry *you*."

Sepi chuckled, himself. "Well, aren't we two old marrieds? We even think the same now." He and Maggie grinned at each other before Sepi turned to Steven and answered his question. "I thought Heidi might put things on hold for cancer, but MS is something different. I do not mean to minimize it. It is life changing, but that is better than life *ending*."

"Oh, Sepi," Maggie said on a sigh, "I do feel fortunate when I look at it that way."

"Me too, Maggie girl. Me too."

Chapter 29

Looking out her bedroom window through the translucent, white curtain, Heidi sat on her bed and watched Steven mow perfect lines in the front yard. It was just after three o'clock on Friday. Her parents were at the doctor's office, and Shelly had just left for River Run. One of Dot's nieces had come down with something in the middle of her shift, and they were desperate for someone to cover in the clubhouse.

Shelly hadn't wanted to go, and Heidi couldn't blame her. It had only been a few short hours since they'd sat in the downstairs living room with their parents and heard the news of their mother's illness, and even without the distraction of work, Heidi was still having a difficult time wrapping her head around it.

She knew why. She needed Shelly to help her sort through it all.

Over coffee, donuts, and more than a few tears—on Shelly's end—the two of them had asked their questions, listened to their parents' explanations, given hugs all around, except to one another, of course, and then gone their separate ways. She and Shelly hadn't processed their mother's diagnosis together yet. Nothing ever seemed real in Heidi's life until she'd talked it over with her sister, but when Shelly had shown up at her bedroom door after they'd finished breakfast with their parents, Heidi had stubbornly told her to go away.

And then she'd watched out her window. Sure enough, not a minute later, Heidi saw Shelly head down the driveway to Steven's, and long after her sister had disappeared inside, she sat at the window, staring off. She pictured the two of them talking it all over together, and she imagined Steven saying all the right things to make Shelly feel better while Heidi sat there all alone in her room. Even now, hours later, the jealousy still burned in her gut.

It wasn't easy for Heidi to admit that she was capable of playing games like this. She'd hoped Shelly would beg and plead to come in, and if she'd knocked just one more time, Heidi might have let her in. Then they could have talked. They could have comforted each other. They could have reconciled. Heidi felt ready for that now, more or less.

But everything always came so easily for Shelly, and Heidi wanted this to be hard. She wanted Shelly to have to work for her forgiveness, but it was almost like she didn't care. Now that she had Steven, maybe she didn't. Her sister didn't need her anymore.

Maybe it was best she was leaving. Together, Shelly and Steven could take care of Mom and Dad, and they could take care of each other. Heidi was off the hook now. Nobody needed her anymore.

She cried then. Really cried. And the tears came faster as she realized she was more demonstrably sad now, alone in her room having a pity party for herself, than she had been sitting with her family and discussing her mother's incurable disease. She hadn't allowed herself to cry openly then. But now, here she was, a fountain of tears because she was jealous. When had she become so shallow?

The next hour was spent in her room looking through old photos. She could still hear the lawn mower, more distant now, as Steven worked in the backyard. Heidi had gone downstairs to the bookshelves on either side of the fireplace in the living room and pulled down all the photo albums. Arms full, it had taken her two trips to get them all upstairs.

There were literally hundreds of pictures of herself and Shelly. With the exception of their embarrassingly numerous baby pictures, most of them were taken on vacations. Sepi's job had been demanding of his time, and vacation getaways had been their saving grace as a family. Whether they were posing on a beach in their bathing suits in Hawaii or smiling for the camera over roasted hotdogs at a campsite in Wisconsin, the happiness in their faces was obvious. It was the family time that made each one of those vacations special.

It was funny to Heidi to see that the early pictures, from the newborn phase until about the third grade, had her and Shelly dressed identically, even down to the colored bows and headbands they wore in their hair. But the pictures from the fourth grade on weren't like that. That was when they must have begun to seek out their singularity.

Heidi knew Shelly felt the same way she did—they'd talked about it enough times. They both loved being identical twins, and they wouldn't trade it (most days), but there was also a need to be unique from one another. Looking at all these old photos, Heidi had a thought. What if they'd tried too hard to be different from each other? Maybe they'd inadvertently set themselves up to be opposites. Like two magnets repelling their identical poles.

She'd made it all the way through to high school graduation pictures when the phone rang. "Hello," she answered.

"Heidi-ho. It's Dad."

"Oh! Hey, Dad. Is everything okay?"

"Everything is just fine. We had a good appointment. A long one, too, which was nice. The doctor did not rush us, and asked many, many questions."

Heidi glanced at the clock on her nightstand. It was after five.

"Wonderful. That's great, Dad. You'll have to fill me in later."

"Of course. For now, I wanted to make sure you will be okay there alone for dinner. I would like to take your mother out. We haven't had a proper date in months."

"Go! I'll be fine here. I'm sure I can scrounge up something in the fridge."

"Great. And thanks, eh? This will make your mother happy."

"I'm glad. And listen, have fun. Don't rush home. Maybe you can squeeze a movie in. I know she wanted to see that one with Robert Redford in it. You know how much she loves him."

"Hmm. We will see about that. I am not sure I want the competition tonight."

"Stop. You know you're much better looking."

"You're right. All those actors wear makeup anyway. Not very manly if you ask me."

Heidi was still smiling long after she'd hung up. Her parents had one of those marriages that was inspiring. They were lovers, co-parents, and best friends. It made her happy to think of them sitting together over a glass of wine in a nice restaurant, even if it meant she'd be eating alone. She figured she might as well get used to it, and at least she wouldn't have to choke down that tall glass of milk tonight.

After checking the fridge and grazing on some cold leftovers, she decided to lie down on the couch awhile. Heidi couldn't remember the last time she'd cat-napped on the sofa. Pulling the afghan down over herself, she closed her eyes and sighed, and she let her thoughts roam wherever they wanted to as she allowed sleep to overtake her.

Seagulls screamed overhead as Heidi walked through the early morning mist along the path at Nicolet Harbor. Little by little the sun worked to burn off the moisture, and as it did, Heidi could see further out over the water. Gradually, a sailboat came into view, unmoored and bobbing in the harbor. She stopped to watch as the huge, white mainsail was raised high along the mast.

The voices of the four people moving around on the sloop drifted over the surface of the water, and with a start Heidi realized she recognized them. Peering through the remaining mist, she made them out.

That was her family on that boat! And Steven too.

Since when did they sail? Then she remembered. This was Shelly's new sailboat.

"Guys!" she called. "Shelly!" she yelled again when they didn't respond.

Shelly turned, and with a hand shading her eyes, looked to shore. Spotting Heidi, she waved and shouted. "We're going for a sail. Wanna come?"

"Yes!"

"Oh, hey there, Heidi-ho!" Sepi yelled. "We'll swing the boat around and pick you up. Wait there."

Heidi waited, seated at the very edge of the concrete wall that separated the path from the water in the harbor with her legs dangling over the edge. But instead of drawing closer, the boat continued to move further away.

"Wait!" she yelled, jumping up. "Come get me!"

Shelly was scrambling on the boat, shouting instructions to take down the sail, and although everybody moved to follow her orders, the sail wouldn't budge.

"Heidi, we're coming!" Shelly hollered with her hands cupped around her mouth. "We won't leave you. Just give us a minute, okay?"

Sighing with relief, Heidi nodded. For a second, it had looked like they were going to sail away without her. She moved to sit again, but then, without warning, a strong offshore wind suddenly kicked up, blowing her hair over her eyes. *She pushed it out of the way and looked out at the boat. Wind swept into the mainsail, filling it and propelling the sloop forward and out toward the open water at a rapid clip.*

Shelly shrieked. "We need to get Heidi! We can't leave her."

"The sail won't budge! I can't move it!" Heidi heard Steven yell.

The four of them worked frantically to no avail, and they blew further and further away. Heidi saw the moment Shelly gave up. Her sister, turning slowly, stood defeated at the back of the boat. Although she couldn't see them, Heidi could feel Shelly's eyes on her, and she sensed her sister's sorrow. It mirrored her own, and she watched as her sister grew smaller and smaller until she disappeared completely around the lighthouse at the end of the breakwall.

"Wake up," she told herself.

And, thankfully, she did. Heidi was the only person she knew of who could wake herself up from dreams she didn't like. It was a wonderful talent to have. Sitting up, she rubbed at her eyes and thought about the dream. Nightmares weren't always dark and filled with boogeymen. Sometimes they involved sailboats and a disappearing family. It didn't take a rocket scientist—or a dream expert—to know what had triggered this nightmare.

Draping the folded afghan over the back of the sofa, Heidi looked out the window. Steven's Blazer was still parked outside of his apartment. He must be getting cleaned up after finishing the yard work. She wondered if he'd resumed his runs. She hadn't, except for the one run in Rochester. It was probably the worst possible time to take away her number one stress reliever, but she just wasn't motivated right now.

She was, however, motivated to eat some of the Mackinac Island Fudge ice cream she'd seen in the freezer yesterday, the perfect comfort food, and she was standing there in front of the open freezer trying to find it when it happened. A wave of dread so intense that it stole her breath washed over her, and Heidi knew immediately what it meant.

Shelly.

Shelly was in trouble. Or hurt. Or scared. She couldn't pinpoint it exactly, and she didn't try. She didn't think; she acted, and she nearly forgot to pull the front door closed behind her as she ran out of it. She sprinted across the length of driveway between the main house and the detached garage and took Steven's steps two at a time. He answered the door within seconds, and although she was gasping for breath, she managed to communicate clearly enough. Steven grabbed his keys with one hand and her arm with the other. "Let's go!"

They were high-tailing it out of the driveway within another few seconds. "What are you feeling? Tell me." Steven demanded, the urgency and worry in his voice unmistakable.

"Just that she needs me. Something's wrong."

"You're sure?"

"I'm sure. I think she's in danger."

"I knew it. I knew that guy Lenny was no good. I'd bet money he's done something."

Heidi remained silent. She'd had that thought too. Somehow, she knew this involved a man. Whereas in the second grade she'd felt Shelly's hurt in her own arm, this time, she had a skin-crawling sensation. The kind she'd get sometimes when a creepy old guy checked her out or called something obscene out his car window at her. Although this sensation was far more sinister.

Lenny hadn't ever made her feel that way, but he was enormous, rough, and an ex-con. Plus, he'd asked Shelly out a few times, and she'd turned him down. Maybe he didn't like taking no for an answer. Heidi squeezed her eyes shut. If that were the case, she knew where they'd be.

Sometimes servers would have to run down to the basement for supplies. They all hated to do it. It was dark and musty and too quiet down there, and far enough removed from the noisy dining area that it felt isolated. Whenever Heidi had to go down there, she'd grab what she needed in a hurry and run back up the steps like she was being pursued by the Devil himself.

The drive to River Run seemed to take forever, even though Heidi had glanced at the speedometer and saw Steven was doing seventy on the highway. When they finally reached the parking lot outside of the clubhouse, Steven pulled all the way up to the door and threw the car in park. He flung open his door with the car still running, and with the keys still in the ignition, the two of them ran inside.

"Where is she?" Steven turned back to ask.

Heidi pushed past him, bypassing the restaurant and heading down the long hall that led to the back stairs. The door to the stairwell was slightly ajar.

It was never left open.

With the hairs on the back of her neck standing on end, Heidi pushed through the door all the way, Steven right on her heels. "Shelly!" she called. "Shelly, are you down there?"

The light bulb at the top of the stairs was flickering, and the one at the bottom was completely burned out. As a result, it was even darker and more eerie than it normally was in the stairwell.

Stopping at the top to listen, Heidi heard something. It was muffled, but she heard it. She turned to Steven with wide eyes. "She's down there."

That was all the prompting Steven needed. He took over, rushing down the stairs faster than Heidi could keep up, and when he got to the bottom and pushed through the steel door at the base of the steps, he roared. He actually roared. Heidi froze on the last step and clutched the railing. Whatever he'd found wasn't good, and within seconds, there were loud cries, shouts, and sick thudding sounds—the kind that was made when flesh hit flesh. She was gripped by an intense fear, and her entire body trembled, but she followed Steven through the door. Her sister needed her.

It was completely dark in the storage room, but enough flickering light flooded in from the blinking sconce that she could just make out the supply shelves in front of her. Steven was on the ground, straddling a struggling, cursing man who he was pummeling with both fists. Heidi couldn't see who it was, although she recognized the voice. She didn't try to place it.

Instead, she focused on discovering the direction of the small whimper she'd just heard, and her eyes flew to the dark corner to the right of the two brawling men. Her sister was crouched there, visibly shaking, with a fist in her mouth as she watched the men on the ground. Heidi raced to her side and fell to her knees, taking quick inventory before pulling Shelly into a fierce hug. She'd been crying, and for some time by the looks of it. Her bottom lip was bleeding, and her polo shirt was ripped from the collar down to her belly button.

As Shelly returned Heidi's embrace, she cried harder. "Hush now, you're okay," Heidi soothed. "We're here." She spared a glance over her shoulder to see how Steven was faring. It had grown much quieter, and for good reason. The man on the floor looked unconscious. Heidi still couldn't see his face. Steven's own face had taken a few hits during the altercation, and she watched as he wiped his bloodied nose on his sleeve.

Shelly spoke into her hair in a wobbly voice. "Heidi, he f-followed me down here and he t-tried to—"

Steven's voice interrupted. He spoke with a calm that Heidi could scarcely believe. "Heidi, I need you to go upstairs and call the police." He nodded toward the man on the floor. "He's out now, but he won't stay that way forever. See if Lenny's in the kitchen, and ask him to come back here with you, but try not to let anyone else know . . . for Shelly's sake."

Heidi nodded. She looked back at her sister and gave her hands a reassuring squeeze. "I'll be right back. Stay right here, okay? You'll be safe with Steven."

Shelly sniffled and nodded. "Okay." Heidi moved to stand up, but Shelly held on. "Heidi? I love you."

Heidi took in her sister's tear-stained face. Shelly had what looked to be the beginnings of a black eye, and the sight of it pained her. Literally. Her voice cracked when she spoke. "I love you too, Shell-Shell." She wrapped her sister in another hug before standing. "Okay, I'll be right back." As she walked past Steven and the battered guy on the floor, Heidi got a good look at the unconscious man's face.

It was John Thames.

The clubhouse was fairly quiet for a Saturday night. It could have been the heat that kept people away. It was supposed to have topped out at ninety-six degrees today. In Nicolet, that meant people went to the beach. Or they stayed inside in their air conditioning. Yoopers were great with cold. Not so much with heat.

As she hurried up the steps, she felt herself begin to calm down. Shelly was okay. They'd gotten there in time. She wouldn't let herself think about what would have happened if she'd stayed asleep on the couch another few minutes. Dream control was more handy than she'd realized.

Dot was nowhere in sight—big surprise—but Lenny was back in the kitchen loading dishes into the washer. At the sound of the doors opening, he turned around and gave her a funny look.

"Shelly?" he questioned.

She shook her head. "Heidi."

"Ah. I thought so." He grabbed the towel that had been resting over his left shoulder and wiped his hands dry. Underneath where it had rested, his left triceps area, Heidi was surprised to see a tattoo she hadn't ever noticed before. It was a Bible verse. *Jeremiah 29:11*, which she happened to have memorized. It had been her confirmation verse, and it remained her favorite.

If Lenny had gone to the trouble of having it tattooed on his arm, it must mean something to him too. And that meant there might be more to Lenny than she'd realized. She felt her face flush in shame, and Lenny looked at her with a question in his eyes. Later. Later, she'd ask him about it. Later, she'd apologize.

"Lenny, um, we need you downstairs. Shelly was . . . John Thames tried to . . . hurt her."

Within a millisecond, Lenny's expression changed from curious to murderous, and he responded with a thunderous, "He WHAT?" before starting for the kitchen doors.

Heidi put one hand on his arm to stop him. "Shush! Keep it down. She's okay. Our friend, Steven, is downstairs with her right now. We showed up in time, but Steven might need you to help him until the police get here. I'm calling them now."

Heidi watched the muscle in Lenny's jaw flex before he gave a quick nod. "Got it." He pushed the doors to the kitchen open with such force that they both hit the walls behind them with a loud *bang*. Looking at the few patrons who remained at the bar, he shouted, "Everybody out! We're closed." To Alex, the bartender, he said, "Close out the tabs, and quick. I want everybody gone in five."

Alex, wide eyed, nodded vigorously. Clearly, he had a healthy respect for Lenny and didn't dare question him.

Under different circumstances, Heidi might have found that funny, but she was grim as she turned back to the kitchen and used the phone at the far end to call the police.

Over the next several hours, Heidi learned a few things. First, she really had misjudged Lenny. Though it may have annoyed Steven, he was so solicitous and protective of Shelly that, at first, he wouldn't even let Heidi near her. Second, John Thames was more than just a slimy lawyer. He was a sicko who thought he could just take whatever he wanted, even if what he wanted was another person. Once he came to, he blustered on and on about suing Steven if he didn't get off of him until, finally, Lenny told him to shut his mouth if he wanted to keep his teeth. It was gratifying to see John's eyes go wide before pressing his bloodied lips together in a tight, protective line.

Third, Heidi realized her sister was even tougher than she'd ever imagined. Shelly had just endured something Heidi hoped she'd never have to face, but her twin had somehow pulled herself together, and in short order. By the time the police arrived, her tears were dried. She held her shirt together with both hands and answered the officers' questions with a matter-of-factness that stunned Heidi. The things that man had said to her sister! The threats! At one point, he'd even choked her, and Shelly had the bruises and scratches on her neck to prove it.

Lastly, Heidi learned that Steven loved her sister. After his adrenaline surge had faded, he wouldn't let Shelly out of his sight, and the tenderness he showed her was enough to melt any heart. Including hers. Whatever anger, whatever betrayal she'd felt, it all slipped away, and for the first time in a week, Heidi felt peace, and that was saying something considering the situation she was in at that moment.

Despite her protestations, Shelly was taken to the hospital to be checked out further. Reluctantly, Lenny remained behind to close up the clubhouse, but he gave both girls a hug and shook Steven's hand before they left. "You're a good man," he told Steven firmly.

Before Steven could reply, Heidi said, "So are you, Lenny. Thank you."

A slow smile spread across Lenny's face. "Anytime, girl."

"I can't—I can't quite believe that happened tonight," Steven said once they were on their way.

"Me neither."

He glanced at her. "You saved her."

"*You* saved her."

"Alright then. We both did. We were a team."

Heidi nodded. For a full minute, the only sound was that of the tires on the pavement, but it wasn't a loaded silence. It was a soothing one. For Heidi at least.

"Heidi—" Steven began, but she didn't let him finish.

Turning to him, she said, "Steven, it's okay. We don't need to . . . do this."

"Do what?"

"Have this talk. I don't care about you and Shelly anymore. It's fine. Everything's fine."

"For real?"

Heidi grinned. He sounded like a valley girl. "For real."

He glanced at her again. "And you're not just saying that to kind of, I don't know, sweep it all under the rug? Because I don't want to do that. You're Shelly's twin sister. You're always going to be the closest person to her. I need for us to be okay."

"And we are. I promise."

He shot her a doubtful look.

Heidi struck a joking tone. "Look, don't flatter yourself *too* much here, Steven. You're a special guy, but not so special as to come between mirror twins."

Steven didn't laugh. He didn't smile. Instead, he looked at her and said, "I would never, *never* want to do that. Not ever."

She placed a hand on his arm. Curiously, there weren't many butterflies or sparks when she touched him, at least not the way she used to feel them. It was reassuring. She was going to get over Steven completely in time. She was already well on her way. "And you haven't. All will be well. I know it. And you can know it too. Okay?"

He smiled then. "Okay."

"And I promise, we'll always be a team. We're Shelly's team."

Steven chuckled. "Team Shelly, huh? We have our hands full then, I think."

Heidi laughed. "You're right."

"Well," Steven said, "just so you know *you* can always count on me too."

"Thanks."

Steven took a deep breath and let it out slowly. "Your parents don't know any of this has happened, do they?"

Heidi shook her head. "I thought about calling them, but I decided against it. We'll tell them when we get home. There's nothing they can do right now, anyway, and they've already been through it with my mom the last few days."

"I think that's probably smart. I know your dad pretty well, I think, and nice guy that he is, it still wouldn't be a good idea for him to be anywhere near John Thames right now."

"Is he going to the hospital too?" Heidi asked in surprise.

"Yeah. The cops are bringing him. He's got a broken nose."

"You mean, *you* broke his nose."

"Yep."

"Are you worried he'll actually sue you?"

"Honestly, I don't care. He can try. But with all the pictures the police took of your sister, and I'm sure the hospital will document everything really well too, he won't have a case. And with Shelly bringing charges against him, I'm pretty sure he knows he's sunk. Guys like that, they're all bluster, even when they're going down."

Heidi hoped he was right. The last thing she wanted was for Steven to be in trouble over this. "Steven?"

"Hmm?"

"Thank you. Thank you for being there for us tonight. Thank you for helping my sister. Thank you for . . . you know . . . loving her."

Steven looked at her with a surprised smile. "I haven't even told her that yet."

"You should."

"I will. And you're welcome." He was quiet for a few seconds, seeming to think something over. Heidi watched him.

He met her eyes again briefly. "I love you, too, you know," he said quietly. "I love all of you. Your whole family. There's nothing I wouldn't do for you guys."

Whatever tension may have been left in her body disappeared completely. "That's so nice to know, you have no idea. Honestly, it makes me feel better about leaving. I know they're in excellent hands."

"They are. I promise."

Sepi took the news better than Steven expected. Maybe it was the staying hand Maggie placed on his arm as they stood there in the kitchen, recounting Shelly's assault. Or maybe he remained calm because of the way Shelly held herself, strong and impossibly brave. Or maybe it was just Sepi's way. Steven suspected the old man simply didn't have it in him to go flying off the handle for any reason, not that he wasn't plenty upset over what had happened.

After Sepi and Maggie finished properly fawning over Shelly, and once they'd hugged him and Heidi and thanked them for saving her from *that miscreant*, as Maggie called him, Maggie moved them all into the living room. Sepi sat down on the couch next to Shelly and held her hand, and Steven took the seat on the other side of her, needing to be close. Heidi and Maggie sat opposite them in the matching blue wingback chairs.

"My dear girl," Sepi said, "I'm just so sorry. I am *that* sorry you had to go through such an ordeal tonight."

Shelly rested her head on her father's shoulder. "I'm okay, Dad. Really. Steven and Heidi got there in time. I'm just a little bruised, that's all. I'll heal."

Sepi bounced their entwined hands and stared off, deep in thought. When he spoke again, the groove between his brows deepened. "How *dare* he? How dare Johnny Thames!"

"It's over now," Shelly said simply.

"Happily, not for him. It is far from over for him. He cannot make this go away, no matter how he might try. You know, I always knew Johnny would have a reckoning one day. You cannot go through life the way he has without karma whipping around and biting you in the ass."

"Dad!" Heidi said with wide eyes.

He continued on, unfazed. "I'm just sorry it had to involve you, Shelly girl. I wish I had known he was giving you trouble. I could have done something."

"Everyone will know his true colors now, at least," Shelly said.

Sepi nodded slowly. "Finally. It's about time. I hope they throw the book at him."

"Sepi, vindictiveness doesn't become you," Maggie admonished gently.

"Oh, there is a difference between being vindictive and being satisfied with proper justice, eh? That is all I am. Satisfied he will get what's coming. And as a bonus, our Steven got to break that perfect nose. Well done, son."

Maggie shook her head. "Oh, Sepi. What am I going to do with you?" Her eyes twinkled, and she blew him a kiss.

Sepi beamed, and Steven felt his chest tighten. He loved that Sepi had called him *son*. He loved the knowledge that he was going to be a part of this close-knit, loving family. He *knew* it, just as he knew Lake Superior would glimmer and sparkle in the sun tomorrow. It was a given. Shelly must have picked up on his happiness because she surreptitiously reached for his hand with her free one and gave it a squeeze.

Son.

Sitting there beside Shelly, with her family seated all around them, Steven knew without a sliver of a doubt. He was finally home.

Three weeks later, on a sunny Saturday in August, the time came to send Heidi off to Rochester. They stood, the five of them, in the driveway beside her new 1989 black Jeep Cherokee, which was packed full of boxes. Steven stood back while the Lakanens said their goodbyes. If he choked up a bit watching Heidi hug her parents, it was nothing to how he felt when the twins embraced. They cried and hugged so long, he wondered if they'd ever be able to let each other go. Promises were made to call and write and visit, and reluctantly, the girls separated. Their identical red noses and splotchy faces gave Sepi plenty to joke about, and within minutes, they were all laughing as they wiped at their eyes.

Heidi looked at Steven then, and her smile wavered. Approaching him, she reached out a hand. He took it. "You've been a good friend, Steven."

"Likewise."

"Take care of my family for me."

"I will."

She seemed to be at a loss for what to say next, so Steven pulled her into a hug. "Good luck, Heidi."

"Thank you," she whispered.

And then, a minute later, she pulled out of the driveway. "See you all at Thanksgiving!" she hollered out her window. The four of them stood shoulder to shoulder and waved her off until they could no longer see her. Shelly reached down and squeezed his hand. He gave her a squeeze back before turning and pulling her into his arms. Sepi and Maggie retreated a few steps, giving them some privacy. They murmured to one another in hushed tones.

"It hurts," Shelly whispered.

"I know. It won't always be this hard."

"I don't know what I'm going to do without her."

He kissed her forehead. "I'll do my best to distract you and keep you busy."

She laughed and stretched tall to kiss him. He loved the feel of her lips on his. He hadn't told her yet that he loved her. He'd been holding back for weeks, and he wasn't sure why. It definitely wasn't because he doubted it. No, he knew it was the real thing. Likely, he was just afraid, but of what, he didn't know. But now felt like the time to take the leap. He needed her to know.

"I love you, Shelly."

She went rigid in his arms before stepping back to look him in the eye.

"You do?" she asked with a hopeful smile.

Steven nodded. "I love you so—*oof!*"

Shelly launched herself back into his arms with such force, it knocked the wind out of him. And it was like that, hunched over and gasping for breath, that Steven heard the words he'd been longing to hear from her.

"I love you, too, Steven," she said between giggles.

"Best get used to it, son," Sepi called. "It won't be the last time she knocks you silly." They all laughed like a crew of drunken sailors then—Steven too, as much as he was able—and when he'd caught his breath, he drew Shelly in for a proper hug where they repeated their declarations once more.

"Come on, you two lovebirds," Sepi teased. "Let's go out back for a little happy hour. This calls for a toast."

Shelly looked down at her watch. "It's not even one o'clock yet."

"Well, you know what they say. It is five o'clock somewhere."

"But Mom shouldn't drink."

"She and I will have an iced tea then."

"Let's all have some iced tea," Steven suggested.

"Good idea. I'll get a little tray of some fruit and cheese and crackers ready, and we'll have a light lunch. How does that sound?" Maggie asked.

Shelly nodded. "I'll help."

The women headed inside, and the men walked around the house to the backyard. Steven moved at Sepi's pace, glancing periodically at the older man, who appeared deep in thought. He led them to the edge of the yard and looked out over Nicolet Harbor.

"My cup is full, Steven," Sepi said then.

Steven smiled. It would have been easy enough for Sepi to consider his cup half empty. His daughter had just driven away, probably for good. His wife was at the beginning of a journey with a debilitating illness, and his other daughter had recently been assaulted. But here he stood, counting his blessings. If there was ever a man Steven wanted to pattern himself after, Sepi was it. "I'm glad you feel that way," he responded, reaching a hand out and patting Sepi on the shoulder.

"What I feel is joy." Sepi's voice broke on the word *joy*, and he turned to look at Steven. His eyes shone brightly, and Steven firmly gripped his shoulder in a show of support.

"I must have heard my mother say it a hundred times, if not more. *There's only the joy of today and the hope for tomorrow.*" Steven watched as a single, fat tear streaked down Sepi's cheek.

At the moment, Sepi didn't look like a man who was experiencing joy. "You know, Sepi," he began slowly, "it's okay if you're not totally happy right now. There's a lot going on. A lot of changes."

"Oh, I know that. And I am sad. My Heidi-ho has gone away. It would be dishonest to say I am not sad, but joy and happiness are two separate things, eh? I can be sad and still have joy."

This was news to Steven, and his face must have betrayed his skepticism because Sepi chuckled and turned to face him. "Happiness is a cheap emotion. It depends on your circumstance, and so it is influenced by things outside of yourself. But *joy*, Steven, real joy is a gift of the Spirit, and so it is a condition of the soul. And while you can deny yourself that joy, and many people do, nothing can ever steal it away from you."

Steven thought on that, letting it simmer as he looked back out over the harbor. "Sepi," he said finally, "I just have to say . . . I feel lucky to have met you."

Sepi patted Steven on the back. "It has been a blessing for me too, Steven, and that is the truth." They looked at one another, small smiles playing on their lips, until Sepi clapped his hands together and said, "Now, let us go on up there and see to our women."

Steven followed Sepi's gaze to the deck, and he watched as Shelly set a tray down on the table in the center of the seating area. Even with the yellow and green bruising over her neck and eye and the scab on her lower lip, she was more beautiful to him in that moment than she'd ever been. As if sensing his eyes on her, she looked up at him and beamed that megawatt smile he'd dreamed about for two whole weeks after first seeing it. He loved seeing that dimple appear on her cheek, and he wanted to take the steps three at a time and plant a kiss right over the top of it.

The wide grin that stretched across Steven's face elicited a low laugh from Sepi. "You've got it bad, son," he said. "Go on. I will be up shortly."

Steven didn't need further prompting. He did take those stairs three at a time, and when he reached the top, he found her dimple. As he kissed it, he thought maybe he'd even found some of that joy Sepi had talked about.

Next In Series

Have you ever finished a book and wondered where the characters might be in another ten or twenty years? Find out what happens to Heidi, Shelly, and Steven in the next book in the Nicolet Series, *Hope for Tomorrow*, and fall in love with some new characters while you're at it. Available at all the major book retailers.

Acknowledgements

This book would not have made it to publication so seamlessly without the help of some truly wonderful people. Thank you to my amazing beta reader, Shirley. Your encouragement and willingness to listen made all the difference. Thank you to my fabulous ARC team, especially to Emily, a lightning-fast reader, Goodreads expert, and all around lovely person. Thanks to Emilie, my new friend across the northern border, for the extra set of eyes and very honest critiques. Lastly, to Emily Poole with Midnight Owl Editors, I express my sincere appreciation to you for your enormously helpful insights and suggestions. You went the extra mile for me, and I'm so glad you did. I value and appreciate each and every one of you.

About Author

For Charlotte, few things are more relaxing than an escape into a cozy, little story, and that's what she hopes you'll experience within the pages of her books. An author of contemporary women's fiction, Charlotte writes about small-town women and their families, sprinkling in just the right amount of romance for all the feels. She lives on the Lake Superior shore with her husband and three children, and like most of her characters, she can't imagine ever living anywhere else. Visit her website to learn more, and join her monthly newsletter to receive bonus material and other news.

Website: www.charlotteeverhartbooks.com
Facebook: @CharlotteEverhart.Author

Made in the USA
Monee, IL
24 November 2022